THE SHORES
OF BOUNTIFUL

The Shores of Bountiful

by

Loralee Evans

ISBN 13: 978-0615864150
ISBN 10: 0615864155

Loralee Evans, Duchesne, Utah 84021 www.loraleeevans.com

Library of Congress Control Number: 2013915023
Evans, Loralee; Duchesne, Utah

Cover Design by Loralee Evans
Cover Design © 2017 by Loralee Evans

Adobestock.com Image ID: 67239427 by Simon Dannhaur

Shutterstock.com Image ID: 225569209 by paultarasenko

Shutterstock.com Image ID: 526057900 by ArtofPhotos

Shutterstock.com Image ID: 181822697 by soft_light

Dedication

To my parents, Grant and Marilyn Woolston

"Be strong and of a good courage, fear not, nor be afraid of them: for the Lord thy God, he it is that doth go with thee; he will not fail thee, nor forsake thee." KJV Deuteronomy 31:6

Chapter 1

Shemnon gripped his obsidian-edged scimitar in his fist and peered over the bank of earth at the approaching Nephite soldiers. The air hung heavy, thick with the loamy smell of the forest, and sweat trickled down his bare back. The weariness of his years lay upon him like a heavy cloak, his blood pulsing with the memories of many battles. His eyes narrowed as the figures neared, their feet crunching over low undergrowth.

He counted fifteen at the most. The dim light of the forest muted their forms, but from their sheathed blades, their bows resting across their backs, and their relaxed posture as they marched, the routine patrol expected no danger.

Zarahemla lay in the center of Nephite lands, protected. Or so the Nephites believed. At this moment, the thoughts of these men dwelt on their aching feet, their next meal, perhaps their women. They did not know that in moments, they would all be dead, nor that their great city would be utterly crushed the next day. As Shemnon contemplated this, a shadow of pity touched his heart.

As if sensing his faltering resolve, a voice cut through the darkness behind him like the hiss of a snake. "Remember what the Nephites took from you."

Shemnon turned to look behind him. Coriantumr, his overlord, glared over the heads of the other men where they knelt between him and Shemnon. Coriantumr crouched at the back of the group, little more than a shadow as he brandished a Nephite-forged sword that glinted in the dim light. Even the shadows did not hide his Nephitish features or the pale scruff of his beard.

Shemnon tore his eyes away, his blood seething like lava that he should be forced to obey the orders of such a man. No good thing had ever come out of the Nephite lands. Usurpers and whoremongers, the lot of them.

Especially the lighter-skinned sorcerers from years past who had called themselves *missionaries*. Bile rose in Shemnon's throat at the memory. He had never met Aaron, Ammon, or the others, had never listened to their words about their one god. They were Nephites. He had needed to know nothing else. And what they had taken from him…

Shemnon's skin burned with anger as he remembered the day so many years past when a runner came to the land of Tulum scant days after Shemnon had arrived there, bearing the bewildering news that Nephite missionaries had come to his home village. Had they not been content to stay in Lamoni's city? Had taking hold of the minds of once-great kings not been enough for them, and now they had to invade nameless villages with their poisonous words?

Bitterness rose in Shemnon's throat as he remembered the words on the scrap of bark paper the young runner had given him. The last words he had ever received from his mother scarred into his mind.

My son,

I wish you had not gone, for with your great heart, you would have felt the truth as I did when Ammon and his brethren spoke. Shemnon, there is one true god who loves us. Your wife, Keza whose name you need not fear to speak, is with him, as is your son. I have been baptized, and the joy I feel is only tempered by your absence. If you but speak to these Nephites, you will know that they are not as others say. Please come back. Hana needs her father.

We pray for you.

Your loving mother

"Your mother wishes for news of you," the youth had said.

Shemnon had crumpled the letter in his fist. "Delia is no longer my mother. Tell her that I am dead."

The grief that speared Shemnon's heart that day returned now as he knelt in the silent shadows of the forest.

If he had swallowed his pain like a man when Keza and their newborn son had died, he would not have left his mother and his daughter behind while he grieved. He would have been there when those Nephite demons came. He would not have been beguiled by their words. But he had not been there, and his mother had succumbed. And then the Nephites and their followers had vanished away into the Nephite lands. Regret throbbed like a wound in Shemnon's heart.

His mother was surely dead by now, but Hana might live still.

If she had grown to womanhood, she would have found a husband and borne children. Children who would now be grown themselves.

As the chill of the loam seeped into his knees, he thought again of his little Hana, a child whose features echoed those of her beautiful mother. He would never forget her shining eyes, nor would she ever be gone from his heart.

The tramping of feet neared, and Shemnon returned to himself. About him, his men glanced at one another, their bodies tensing. "Remember what the Nephites did," Coriantumr hissed. "And make them pay."

A river of fire poured through Shemnon's veins. "Attack!" he screamed, launching himself over the bank of earth, his men a roaring wave at his back.

Chapter 2
41ˢᵗ Year of Judges, 51 BC, City of Zarahemla

"Now, little brothers…" Elizabeth paused as a stray lock that had loosened from the long rope of her golden-brown hair, brushed her cheek.

Several pairs of expectant eyes lifted, the scratching of quills falling silent.

Sighing, she brushed the errant strand behind her ear.

Her sandals tapped the stone floor as she moved between the rows of wooden desks and then turned to face the class of young men. The military tunics of the youthful squad still had a look of newness to them, not unlike their boyish faces.

"In the Lamanite tongue," Elizabeth continued, "what would be a fitting reply to…" Speaking now in the Lamanite tongue, she asked, "How are your father and mother, Nephi, son of Helaman?"

Nephi, a sandy-haired boy near the front of the class, straightened in his seat and answered in the same tongue. "My mother and father are well, Lady Elizabeth. How is Lord Pacumeni, your… er… husband?"

"He is well. I thank you," she said before she returned to the Nephite tongue. "Though if speaking to a betrothed woman, you would ask about her *intended* husband."

A boy beside Nephi cleared his throat, his eyes twinkling beneath strands of tawny hair. "The intended husband of Lady Elizabeth thinks she is very beautiful," he said, the Lamanite language falling smoothly from his tongue. "I know this because yesterday, Nephi and I saw Lord Pacumeni—"

He faltered. Nephi leaned near, and in the Lamanite tongue, whispered, "*Kissing…*"

"Yes!" the boy laughed, and finished, "kissing her!"

Laughter filled the room.

"Zeram, son of Jacob!" Elizabeth scolded, though she grinned. "And you, Nephi! Come now! What are these words you're teaching Zeram?"

Nephi blushed, but Zeram chortled, gleefully unrepentant. Elizabeth turned toward her guard, Lieutenant Joshua. Etched in the mid-morning light, his sturdy figure stood at one side of the wide doorway that opened onto the central plaza of Zarahemla. His eyes scanned the busy marketplace, hand on the hilt of his sword.

Beyond Joshua's silhouette, colorful awnings billowed and flapped, the air filled with the calls of merchants. Across the wide plaza, the palace rose above the sea of color and life, a jewel gleaming beneath the sun. Far to the south and east, a bank of clouds lay upon the horizon, the only clouds in the otherwise bright sky.

As if sensing her eyes upon him, Joshua turned. His cream-colored uniform swelled as he met her gaze, the sunlight catching in his eyes, which matched the color of the sea. Elizabeth's heart warmed at his grin that followed, reminding her of the moment they had met as children during the last war. She and her mother, Hana, had just passed beneath Bountiful's gate, the last of the refugees from Mulek, when a boy her age had come trotting toward her, the wind in his dark hair, asking if he could lend them assistance. His name had been Joshua. Her first friend in an unfamiliar city.

Coming back to the present, Elizabeth returned his grin and spoke in the language of the Lamanites. "Your young friend Zeram has great command of the Lamanite tongue, Lieutenant Joshua."

"He does indeed," Joshua agreed in the same language. He cocked a brow and shifted his weight. Zeram blushed beneath Joshua's scrutinizing gaze. "And since he and I both hail from Bountiful and I know his kindred, perhaps I should tell his parents…*everything* he is learning."

Zeram's brows lifted in pretended alarm even as his eyes twinkled with mischief.

A breeze swirled into the room, stirred Joshua's dark hair around his broad shoulders, then darted to Elizabeth. It caught the loose lock of hair tucked behind her ear and tossed it before her face.

Elizabeth caught the wayward strand between two fingers. She brushed it back behind her ear again before she turned to the young recruits and spoke in the Lamanite tongue. "Abram, son of Moshen, what greeting could you offer me?"

A young man, leaning heavily on his elbows, straightened at her words and released a deep sigh, speaking in the Nephite tongue. "Lady Elizabeth, when will we need such knowledge as this in battle? While locked in mortal combat, would I need to ask an enemy about his family's health? What he wants to eat for his next meal? What his favorite color is?"

A few youths chuckled, but their laughter subsided as Elizabeth clasped her hands behind her back and straightened her spine. "I see why you ask this, Abram," she said, her tone firm, "but if you knew only enough to issue commands, threats, or demands for surrender, you would lack the skills to speak as men, one to another. And that may one day prove to be the difference between life and death.

"Come." She dipped her head to the side, a slight smile tugging at the corners of her mouth. "Say something. I know you can."

Abram dropped his eyes, and in the Lamanite tongue, he muttered, "The children of Laman are not men. They are savages."

Anger stabbed Elizabeth's heart at Abram's words. How dare he insult her own kin! Abram knew Elizabeth's own mother had been a Lamanite!

From his place in the doorway, Joshua opened his mouth as if to speak, but Elizabeth raised her hand to stay him, offering her friend a quick shake of her head. He nodded. The taut sinews of his jaw eased, and he retreated a step.

Gentling her voice, Elizabeth asked, "Your father died in the last war, didn't he, Abram?"

Without glancing up, Abram nodded.

"So did mine."

Silence followed this, the walls echoing with the creak of cart wheels and the voices of merchants and buyers from the plaza beyond.

"My father, Nathan," she continued, "served as an officer under Captain Antipus, the father of Lieutenant Joshua, whom you know." She nodded toward her guard. "They fell in the same battle, aiding the Ammonite striplings. And not long after this, my mother, Hana, died too, taken by fevers. Like the Ammonite warriors, she was a descendant of Laman. Was my mother a savage, Abram? Did Captain Antipus and my father die defending savages? Am I a savage? I may not look it, but their blood is in my veins."

Abram's shoulders sagged as he clasped his hands upon the wooden table before him. "I meant the godless idol worshippers up in the southlands."

"Perhaps," Elizabeth suggested quietly, "even among them, there are those who simply know no better." Abram furrowed his brow and studied his hands. "Perhaps even among the Lamanites, there are those who know what honor is."

"Well said, Lady Elizabeth." The head instructor, Master Tuloth, appeared, clapping a good-natured hand against Joshua's back before he turned to the room and grinned. "After all, I was once a Lamanite myself and served in Amalickiah's army before my conversion."

The Ammonite physician, clad in gray, smiled over the youths where he stood in the doorway, his teeth gleaming against the warm brown of his skin. A leather string bound his black hair, leaving it to hang in a tail down his neck.

"Master Tuloth!" Nephi greeted. He turned in his seat toward the wide doorway where Tuloth stood. "We all passed your last exam. We're due for a game in the ball pit with you."

Enthusiastic cries of agreement followed his words.

"With high marks, my sons." Tuloth chuckled. "And I was most pleased with you all."

"Master Tuloth," Abram called, "who'll be our language teacher after Lady Elizabeth and His Eminence marry?"

"I'm uncertain," Tuloth said, dropping his hands to his hips. "I fear you may be stuck with me for both your medical training and your language."

"What? No!" Zeram cried.

"Zeram," Elizabeth scolded. "You know Master Tuloth is a fine teacher."

"But you're prettier that he is," Zeram returned, and the other boys laughed in agreement.

Tuloth's lifted hand subdued the chuckles. "With your leave, Lady Elizabeth, the guards along the south wall are sparse today, and the captain of the south gate asked Sergeant Levi for the aid of this squad. It should be good practice."

The announcement elicited another bout of emotion from the boys, who cackled their enthusiasm, clasping each other's hands in excitement.

Elizabeth nodded. "Yes, but only—" She was cut off by a flurry of squeaky wooden benches as the boys rose. "—if our language class can be extended tomorrow to make up for the lost time."

A murmur of grumbles erupted. "Master Tuloth!" one voice protested.

Tuloth shook his head. "Lady Elizabeth's request is reasonable, my sons."

Another voice wailed, "But why—"

"Men," Joshua said.

As if a thunderclap had echoed through the room, silence fell. The boys stiffened, their backs arrow straight.

"While Master Tuloth and Lady Elizabeth are not officers, they are still your superiors. Remember the oaths you took."

"Yes, sir," their voices returned in unison.

"You're to report to the south gate in half an hour," Tuloth told them. "Sergeant Levi will be waiting for you. Don't be late."

"You're dismissed." Elizabeth's words washed over the young soldiers like a wave. Their postures eased, and grins once again claimed their faces.

With calls of farewell, the youths scattered out into the market until only Zeram remained.

More sedate than her pupils, Elizabeth started toward the wide opening where Joshua and Tuloth stood. The wind that played about the space teased the cloth of her tunic and mantle, brushing the rope of hair over Elizabeth's shoulder. She smiled a greeting, which Tuloth returned.

Joshua glanced away at her approach, his brow furrowed. Her heart twitched with pity. What troubled him?

"Ho, Elizabeth,"

Elizabeth turned as Zeram trotted into the sunlight, stopping to face her with a boyish grin.

She reached out, ruffling his fair hair as she often had when he was a little boy in Bountiful. "You're taller every day, Zeram. Your own mother won't recognize you when you go back to Bountiful."

Grinning, Zeram turned to Joshua. "Do you think I'll ever be taller than you are, Josh—I mean, *sir*?"

"Careful, boy." Joshua growled as he lifted his chin, though a teasing light danced in his eyes. "Don't forget I'm still your superior officer."

Zeram threw his hands up as if to ward off an imaginary foe. "Yes, sir! But with that fearsome appearance, I worry you'll never find a wife. Jacob, my uncle, has been married over a year, and he's younger than you. What if I marry before you do? What if Nephi does, or—" A look of horror spread over Zeram's face. "What if Nephi's little brother Lehi—"

"Silence, insubordinate whelp," Joshua ordered, his mouth quivering with a suppressed laugh as he reached to tweak Zeram's ear. "Remember, I could have you flogged."

"But sir," Zeram breathed with exaggerated reverence, "if you bought some flowers to weave into your hair, the girls would surely look at you then. They'd giggle, too, but—"

Zeram's words cut off in a startled squawk as Joshua lunged for him.

"Help!" Zeram wailed. "Master Tuloth!" He scampered behind Tuloth, but the tall Ammonite merely folded his arms and chuckled as Joshua darted around him to get at the boy.

Zeram squealed and leaped aside to avoid Joshua's grasping hand, scampering farther into the bustle of the market and darting around a farmer who led a sour-faced llama. Confused by Zeram, the poor beast stumbled to a stop. Zeram peered at Joshua over the back of the animal, and Joshua rushed around both man and beast uttering a hasty apology to the disgruntled man.

"Elizabeth, save me!" Zeram squawked. He dashed back toward Elizabeth and Tuloth, Joshua mere steps behind him. "He means to murder me!"

As Zeram ducked behind Elizabeth, Joshua pulled to a stop, abandoning his pursuit. His grin faded as he met Elizabeth's eyes, chest heaving from his chase.

"Come, let us have peace." Tuloth clapped a hand on Zeram's shoulder, drawing him out from behind Elizabeth despite the youth's protest. "Now be on your way, Zeram. You know Sergeant Levi is strict."

"Not as strict as Elizabeth," Zeram said. "She thinks that because both my parents speak the language, I should know more."

"And you do, incorrigible pup," Tuloth said in the Lamanite tongue.

"I understood that well enough," Zeram grumbled, but Elizabeth caught his teasing grin before he turned and trotted toward Nephi, who had stopped at a booth near the edge of the plaza. He briefly turned back and offered a final wave.

"Ah, they're good lads," Tuloth said as Nephi grinned at Zeram's coming. "Would that they did not need to learn the skills of war." He heaved a sigh. "Yet it's a blessing that they can defend those they love, should war ever come again."

Tuloth turned his hands upward and studied them, his brow furrowing. Elizabeth pressed her lips together and swallowed a thick knot. Did his memories of war, of fighting for the tyrant Amalickiah, still trouble him sometimes?

"Even men who have promised never to fight again can find ways to stand for what's right without using weapons, Tuloth," she insisted. "Including you."

Tuloth lifted his head and offered Elizabeth a grateful look. "I do what I can," he murmured, then cast a brief glance skyward. "And I must return to them." He offered a grin. "Farewell to you both."

"And you," Elizabeth and Joshua echoed.

Tuloth turned and strode away through the shifting crowds.

Elizabeth met Joshua's eyes, and he managed a gentle smile. Her heart warmed at the sight of it.

"You wish to return to the palace?" he asked.

She nodded. "I'm to tutor Lehi this morning."

Joshua inclined his head in assent, and together they turned and started along the outer edge of the market toward the palace steps rising above the crowded plaza.

"Tuloth is right," Joshua said, their steps unhurried. "Your pupils are good boys. Zeram, too, for all his jokes and banter. He is growing into a fine man, thanks to your teaching."

Elizabeth smiled. "I think it's because he has you to look up to." She reached out and touched his forearm. "Your father, Antipus, would be proud."

Beneath her fingers, the strong sinews of his arm rippled as Joshua met her eyes. Something twisted in her heart, and she drew her hand back. "For you are a fine man *now,* my friend."

At this, his eyes warmed with gratitude. "I'm glad you think so."

"I *know* you are, Joshua," Elizabeth said. "Pacumeni knows it too."

After all, how could Pacumeni not know? He and Joshua had been the best of friends since they were the age of Nephi and Zeram, when Joshua came to Zarahemla for his training and the two had been assigned to the same squad.

"And now, you are to be married to him." His gaze deepened. "I…"

Joshua glanced away, his words unfinished.

Elizabeth guessed now at his melancholy. "You'll find a wife soon, Joshua." She grinned. "You're not discouraged by the words of an impetuous youth, I hope?"

A terse smile touched his lips as he said in the Lamanite tongue, "Perhaps I need flowers to weave into my hair."

A burst of laughter escaped Elizabeth before she could bite it back, attracting startled looks from passersby.

Subduing her emotions, she chuckled. "You don't need flowers to find a wife. You're already wonderful enough as you are."

Strangely, his smile faded at the compliment. "I'm not looking for a wife," he murmured. "Not now, anyway." He looked away. "You *are* happy, aren't you, Elizabeth?"

She smiled at the question and dropped her gaze. "I could not imagine myself happier. My one sorrow is that I wish my parents had lived to see my wedding."

"But they will."

She looked up, meeting his eyes.

"Nathan and Hana *will* see your wedding, Elizabeth." He reached out, resting a hand upon her shoulder. His thumb caressed the fabric of her mantle, his hand warm through the cloth. "With your grandparents and your great-grandmother, Delia, who first heard and believed Ammon's words and set everything in motion for you to have all that you do. Even Keza and Shemnon, your mother's parents."

Joshua studied the crowd about them, his brow furrowed. "For if they were anything like you are now, I'm certain they would have accepted the truth if they had the chance to hear it while they lived, and I have no doubt that they would have been pleased to know they had such a wise and beautiful granddaughter."

Elizabeth's face warmed. "You are kind to say such things, Joshua."

"I say them because they are true."

"Nevertheless, you're a wonderful man, my friend." Elizabeth studied the strong angles of his face and the warmth in his eyes. "And it won't be long before some blessed maiden sees that and loves you for it. You'll find a wife soon. I'm certain of it."

Joshua's chest rose and fell. "Perhaps after returning to Bountiful—"

Elizabeth's lips parted in surprise. "You're returning to Bountiful?"

His eyes grew apologetic at her tone. "I should have told you. I've requested a transfer." His hand fell from her shoulder, and she noticed the loss of the warmth.

"But… why?" Elizabeth tried to speak gently, but still, his face grew pained.

"Bountiful is my home," Joshua said. "And the shores are there."

Elizabeth dropped her gaze and swallowed a lump in her throat. "The shores," she echoed. "There is nothing so peaceful as the sound of the sea against the shores of Bountiful." She drew in a breath, remembering the tang of the salt air in her lungs, the soothing whisper of waves against the sand. "Nor anything so beautiful." She looked up. "When will you leave?"

"I will stay to see your wedding," he promised. "But soon after that."

"That's less than a month, Joshua."

He flinched. "I know. I'm sorry."

The loose strand of hair that had escaped her braid brushed against her cheek again, but Elizabeth did not have time to lift a hand before Joshua reached out, catching the lock between his thumb and forefinger.

Elizabeth turned to him, studying his pensive, sea-blue eyes. A trait he had inherited from his mother, Alana, who had died when Joshua was only a child. She must have been a wonderful woman to have borne such a son.

Joshua rubbed the strand of her hair and studied it as if testing the softness of a measure of silk. As he did, Elizabeth let her gaze move over her friend's familiar features—the smooth skin, the dark, shoulder-length hair, and the chiseled angles of his face that she knew so well.

"I will miss you, Joshua."

"And I will miss you." His voice deepened. "More than I can say."

Despite their strength, Joshua's fingers felt gentle as they smoothed the hair back, his thumb lingering as it brushed the curve of her ear. "But here in Zarahemla, you have Pacumeni. And you love him." He withdrew his hand.

Elizabeth smiled at his words. "With all my heart."

Joshua's chest swelled. "Then it is a fair trade, for I know he loves you. He is a blessed man, my friend." His smile trembled. "I envy him his fortune."

Elizabeth's cheeks warmed, and she smiled.

"Come." Tenderness filled his voice as he drew back from her and cast his gaze about. "I should get you back to the palace."

The late-morning sun beat down on Zeram's head. He shifted his shoulders beneath the weight of the stiff kapok armor he wore and stifled a weary sigh, struggling not to give in to the temptation to lean on his elbows over the stone balustrade and drop his chin in his hands. Instead, he thumped the butt of his javelin against the walkway that spanned the gate below his feet, and rested his weight upon it like a staff as he gazed southward over the wide grassland.

The road from the gate beneath him rolled away, swallowed by the grassy plain that stretched to the line of the distant forest. At the edge of the horizon, pale mountains rose up through a sea of clouds like so many giant pyramids.

The Lamanite lands lay beyond those distant peaks—the lands of his eternal enemies, and the lands where his birth mother dwelt. If she still lived. He had few other memories from his early childhood. He could not remember the infamous Pachus, his grandfather, who had tried to crown himself king. Nor could he remember his father, Nusair, Pachus' captain. But he could remember his mother's fair hair and blue eyes. Her name had been Lylith.

"What's wrong with you, Zeram?" Nephi's javelin thumped the stone at his side as he drew near. "You look like you've seen some unholy phantom."

Zeram rallied at his friend's voice. "I was just thinking."

"No wonder you're Elizabeth's favorite." Nephi chuckled. "You think too much."

"So you would say, son of Helaman, since *you* don't think nearly enough."

Nephi opened his mouth, but his words fell silent. The merriment disappeared from his face as his eyes focused beyond Zeram's shoulder. "What could that—?" He strode to the balustrade, shading his eyes.

Zeram turned, searching the waving grass. "Where?"

"Look." Nephi pointed. "On the plain. There."

Then Zeram saw it—a tiny shape drawing nearer across the grass. It was the figure of a man, running.

Zeram squinted. The man seemed to stagger like a drunkard as he ran. Long thin shafts protruded from his body, wavering like grotesque flags. Zeram's fingers clenched the rough stone.

"Upon my life," Nephi hissed. "He's—"

Zeram finished Nephi's words in a whisper. "He's filled with arrows."

Chapter 3

Sunlight speared down at an angle through the skylight above Elizabeth as she and Joshua stepped through the palace doors. Dust motes swirled in the bright shaft that illuminated a square on the floor. Beyond the entry, the great doors of the throne room stood open, a guard on either side of the opening. The stone throne upon a dais at the far end of the room sat empty.

"Lady Elizabeth, Lieutenant Joshua," one of the guards greeted as he stepped forward, his javelin tapping the stones, "you're back earlier than expected."

"Yes, sir," Joshua said. "Her pupils were called away on duty. So we returned early."

Elizabeth smiled into the furrowed face of Captain Micha, the oldest of the palace guards, and her favorite, after Joshua. Opposite the doorway from Micha stood Oren, another palace guard near Joshua's age with an agreeable, handsome face and a lieutenant's rank on the shoulder of his uniform. A dark shock of hair fell before his brown eyes. He smiled as Elizabeth met his gaze and offered a polite bob of his head.

"His Eminence is in the garden, giving an audience to one of the lower judges." Oren drew forward a step.

"What of Master Lehi and his cousin, Jonas?" she asked.

"They're still with Lady Pazia in the family quarters." Micha nodded down the long hallway toward Elizabeth's left.

"Then I shall find Pacumeni in the gardens, and wait for them with him," she said.

Oren shifted his weight and glanced at Micha. The older guard nodded, and Oren stepped back to his place.

Elizabeth nodded her head in farewell to Micha and Oren, then with Joshua at her side, turned down the corridor to her right.

As she started down the long passage, the soft pat of her sandals echoed off the stone walls, answered by the tread of Joshua's leather boots. She glanced over her shoulder to where he strode a half-pace behind her. Meeting her eyes, he offered her a faint smile.

"Zarahemla sits securely within the center of our lands, Chief Judge Pacumeni!"

Elizabeth halted at the impatient voice many paces down the corridor, where a golden splash of light spilled in through an open archway.

"We need no more troops here!" the same voice continued.

Joshua stopped at her shoulder, his narrowed eyes fixed upon the sunlit portal through which the voice had come.

"I appreciate your years and experience, yet I cannot agree, Judge Gadianton." Pacumeni's voice sounded taut as rope. "Even now," Pacumeni continued, "we scarcely have enough battle-ready soldiers to man the leagues of walls around Zarahemla. The military strength here is far too weak to protect a city this size. I have no wish to leave the outer cities without sufficient troops, but neither do I wish for Zarahemla to have insufficient guards. It is unwise to lessen our vigilance, even in the center of our lands. We never know when—"

"Any fault with the displacement of troops lies with our chief captain, Moronihah, a youth hardly older than you, Your Eminence, if I may be so bold as to point that out," Gadianton countered.

Elizabeth's spine stiffened at Gadianton's cutting words to her betrothed. She shot a glance toward Joshua, noting the sinews of his jaw clenching beneath the skin.

But Pacumeni did not answer. Instead, another voice, deep and even and filled with strength, spoke in calming tones.

"Chief Captain Moronihah is not to blame for our failure to come to any agreement." The ire in her blood eased as the voice of Helaman, the prophet and Pacumeni's brother-in-law, resonated down the hall. "This constant bickering is a disservice to him, my friends. Without a direct order, he must place his armies where he sees fit. His youth is not the cause for this contention, nor is Chief Judge Pacumeni's."

"Zarahemla is too great to be in danger, Master Helaman, and too far north," Gadianton protested. "The Lamanite savages would never dare to attack us here. Do you wish to draw troops away from the more vulnerable outposts when there is no need?"

"There *is* need!" Pacumeni's voice rose up in response to Gadianton's words. "My father knew this—my older brother also. If they were still alive—"

"Yet they are not, are they?" Gadianton said.

Thick silence fell.

Elizabeth's hands squeezed into fists against her skirt. Pahoran the elder had been a good man and a wise leader; his eldest son, the younger Pahoran, no less than his father. How could Gadianton speak of them in such tones?

"Your kinsmen have been dying like flies!" Gadianton continued. "Your father succumbed to his age, and your faithless brother, Paanchi, deserved death for his treachery. Then an unknown hand slew your eldest brother as he sat upon the very seat you claim now. It has not been forgotten, Your Eminence, that you possess the judgment seat only because wiser men are dead. You did not win it by your own right."

Elizabeth drew in a sharp breath, but Joshua's hand touched her shoulder, soothing her wrath.

Helaman murmured, "Come now, Gadianton. Do not—"

"I know it well, Judge Gadianton." Pacumeni's steady voice silenced Helaman. "Yet I am here, and so I will use what wisdom I possess, little though it is, to serve this people as well as I can. As should we all."

A weighted silence fell then, as if Gadianton had been struck dumb by Pacumeni's humble words. After a lengthy moment, Pacumeni spoke again. "Let's take a short reprieve, friends." His voice fell to a tone of weary dismissal. "We will meet again in the throne room with the other lower judges after the noon meal."

No words answered this, but a moment later, a silhouette blocked the light streaming through the archway, followed by another as two men started along the corridor, their features indistinct with the light at their backs. Their footsteps echoed down the hallway. Elizabeth lifted her chin, her spine stiffening as Gadianton approached, clad in rich colors, a scarlet cloak over one shoulder.

Joshua's hand gripped her arm. Following his urging, she stepped to the side as the two figures neared. As their features grew clearer, the first man stopped. His companion at his shoulder did the same.

"Lady Elizabeth, what a pleasure!" His mouth smiled above a firm, clean-shaven jaw.

"Peace to you, Judge Gadianton." She nodded, struggling to repress her indignation.

Gadianton bowed to her. A step behind him stood his companion, a lean man clad in plain garb, a sheathed knife at his hip.

"And peace to you, Lieutenant." Gadianton turned to Joshua. "It is reassuring to see His Eminence's intended in such…" His lips twisted as if some secret thought amused him. "Capable hands."

At this, Joshua's grip fell from Elizabeth's arm, and his jaw tightened.

"It would be a pity if she fell into the clutches of some…ignoble rogue who saw her beauty and wished to steal her away from our chief judge." Gadianton studied Joshua with a thin smile.

"Thank you, Judge Gadianton, but there is no need to fear." Elizabeth touched Joshua's arm. "I am as safe with Lieutenant Joshua as I would be with a legion of soldiers."

Gadianton lifted a brow. "That is pleasing to hear, my lady." He placed a hand on his chest. "Though I am but a lower judge, I too understand the value of knowing whom I can trust." He nodded at the man beside him. "This is my new guard and trusted friend, Kishkumen, son of Gozal, as capable a fighter as any palace guard."

Elizabeth turned her eyes upon Gadianton's guard, who offered a terse nod before his gaze traveled down her body. Joshua stepped forward, blocking the man's view of her.

Gadianton's eyes danced from her to Joshua and back again. "My lady, as always, it has been a pleasure talking with you." He bowed. "May your life with His Eminence be long and happy."

Elizabeth offered a stiff nod, and Gadianton turned away. She watched him with pursed lips as he and Kishkumen traversed the corridor and then disappeared out into the sunlight of the plaza.

"Lady Elizabeth!" A voice warm with cheer turned her head back toward the sunlight spilling in from the garden. "Lieutenant Joshua. Peace to you both!" A new figure came toward them, taller and more solid than Gadianton. Helaman smiled as he drew near, clad in a brown tunic and a light-colored cloak. Sandy hair brushed his brow, and lines crinkled the corners of his eyes as if he smiled more often than he frowned.

"And to you, Master Helaman," Elizabeth said, grateful for the warmth in Helaman's eyes after Gadianton's greeting.

"I trust my eldest son is behaving himself during your instruction?"

"He is indeed." Elizabeth dared not look at Joshua out of the corner of her eye, fearing she would laugh. "And learning quickly."

Helaman smiled and seemed ready to say more, but behind him, through the sunlit archway, the notes of a flute flowed forth as clear and as bright as a bird's song.

Stilling her breath, Elizabeth moved from Joshua's side toward the bright opening. As she went, the pillared portico that encircled the wide garden opened to her view. She paused beneath the archway and touched a hand to the stone lintel. A few steps beyond her feet, the stone-tiled walkway dropped down a gentle step onto an earthen path that wandered away into the lush growth of the garden as if into a vast, untamed forest. The notes of the song, though, pulled her eyes away from the garden and toward a figure leaning against one pillar at the edge of the walkway, his back to her.

Without the fretted brass crown that rested against his brow, Pacumeni could have been mistaken for a palace guard. His youthful form beneath a thin, light-colored shirt and dark gray kilt attested to his capabilities as a competent warrior in his own right. His hair glistened like so many threads of gold and copper, skin gleaming like burnished bronze. While the strong hands of her betrothed looked more used to holding a sword and shield, they seemed content now to hold a small reed flute to his lips. Pacumeni's lean fingers glided over the holes as tranquil notes issued forth, washing over Elizabeth in a sweet melody.

Why must he be the chief judge? she mused. He was too young to be burdened with so many duties. So many dangers and enemies. Worry stirred in her at the thought. The man who had killed his older brother had never been found. Where was he? Was he even now planning to harm her own beloved?

Seeming to sense her presence, Pacumeni turned and met her gaze. Warmth washed through her, the anxiety easing away to the back of her mind. His soft gray eyes reflected a wisdom that belied his twenty-five years, filling with warmth at the sight of her, though his song continued on, unbroken. Behind her, she heard the steps of Joshua and Helaman nearing, but she did not turn.

Beneath the burnished skin of Pacumeni's bare forearms, she could see the sinews ripple as his fingers brought his song to life. The notes warbled like a bird one moment, then laughed like a clattering brook the next. At last, they trilled to an end. Pacumeni drew the instrument back and smiled at her.

With reverent care, he lifted the flap of a leather pouch at his side and placed his flute within it before he started toward her. His stride, graceful as a young jaguar, quickened the already-rapid beating of her heart.

"Elizabeth." He halted an arm's length from her—close enough that he could touch her if he wished, though he held back for now, his eyes seeming to drink her in. "Peace to you."

"And to you, Pacumeni." Her blood tingled at his nearness.

A short cough behind her turned both their heads. Elizabeth drew back a pace to see Helaman grinning beside Joshua.

Joshua's eyes did not meet hers at first, but at last he lifted his gaze.

"Forgive me, Joshua, Helaman," Pacumeni said.

"You needn't apologize, Pacumeni." Helaman chuckled. "With all the duties you have been given, no one blames you for paying a few moments of attention to your fair betrothed."

Pacumeni's hand cupped Elizabeth's shoulder, warming her skin through the cloth of her mantle.

Elizabeth felt herself coloring and dropped her gaze.

"I should tell you," Helaman continued, "that I have other duties to attend to. I may be late returning for your council with the lower judges."

Pacumeni nodded. "I know how busy you are, Helaman. I'm grateful for any help you're able to give."

"Anything for my wife's little brother." Helaman chuckled again. He stepped forward, clapping Pacumeni's arm. Still grinning, Helaman turned, the tapping of his sandals echoing down the corridor.

As his footsteps faded, Pacumeni's warm grip upon her shoulder squeezed, and warmth pulsed through Elizabeth's body.

She lifted a hand to cover his, running her thumb over his fingers.

"Have you two been here long?" He glanced from her to Joshua. His hand loosened and fell from her shoulder.

Elizabeth shot a glance toward Joshua, though his gaze did not meet hers. He stood as any other guard would, motionless but for the movement of his breath. Did something trouble him?

"Not long," she said.

Pacumeni released a breath through rounded lips. "You overheard the debate with Judge Gadianton?"

Elizabeth relished the warmth that stirred in her as she took his hands in her own, studying the gentle depths of his eyes. "Gadianton's words may be more numerous, but yours carry greater wisdom."

Pacumeni's eyes filled with warmth. "I still have much to learn," he murmured, "but I want to do what is best for our people. With God's help, and yours, I will."

Elizabeth smiled as Pacumeni's hands squeezed hers. She lowered her gaze to their fingers, woven together like the reeds of a basket; hers slender and fair—his, lean and bronzed.

Pacumeni turned and started at a slow pace along the portico, leading her by the hand. Only the steady tread of Joshua's leather boots told Elizabeth that he still remained with them.

"How were your students?" Pacumeni asked, releasing her hand and slipping his arm about her waist, drawing her closer to his side.

"They're doing well. Nephi and Zeram are especially quick." She turned to Joshua for confirmation. His eyes, however, gazed out into the garden, a distant look on his face as if he could not hear them.

"Pazia will be pleased by that." Pacumeni grinned. "And their weapons training?" He turned. "Joshua?"

Joshua looked up as if he had been startled from some private thought. He composed himself and cleared his throat. "Their weapons training is progressing well," he said with formality. "They were ordered to help guard the south gate today. Sergeant Levi feels they have learned enough to be entrusted with the task."

Elizabeth's brows furrowed at Joshua's reserved tone. But Pacumeni grinned. "They must be enjoying that." A soft chuckle escaped him. "Do you remember when we were in training, Joshua? Some of the foolish things we did to drive our sergeant mad? Sometimes I think if my father hadn't been the chief judge, we may not have—"

"I fear for you sometimes, Pacumeni." The words escaped Elizabeth of their own accord.

Pacumeni halted and turned to her, surprise on his face. "Oh? Why do you say that?"

Elizabeth paused, hesitant to meet his eyes. "Because *you* are the chief judge now, and there are those who would harm you if they could."

"Oh." Pacumeni's hands reached out and gripped her elbows. "I see." His fingertips brushed up her bare arms, the contact sending warmth through her body. "Don't be afraid for me."

"How can I not be? The man who killed your brother is still—"

"Elizabeth." Pacumeni's firm hands slid from her shoulders to her back. A delicious shiver trailed through her as he drew her close. His warmth soothed her like the gentle touch of sunlight as the distance closed between them. "Nothing will happen to me. Trust Joshua and the other guards." Pacumeni gestured toward Joshua, just a few paces from them, his eyes turned away. "They are skilled and know their duty. The mistakes of the past won't be repeated."

Elizabeth let herself melt against him, resting her face against his chest. She closed her eyes and inhaled, drinking in his warm, musky scent.

"I want to believe that, Pacumeni," she murmured against the soft cloth of his shirt. Beneath his chest, she could feel the muffled throb of his heart and the subtle shift of his muscles as his arms tightened about her. Wisps of longing shivered along her skin as his hand touched her hair. "But so many things in this world are uncertain." Her voice quivered.

"Yet some things *are* certain," Pacumeni whispered. "Love is stronger than evil, Elizabeth. That is certain. And love that is true, that is founded on love for God, can overcome anything, whether it be the work of evil men or merely our own doubts and fears and pain."

Several paces away, Joshua shifted his weight. And though her eyes remained upon Pacumeni, gratitude warmed her heart at Joshua's devotion to his duty. To the oath he had taken as a palace guard and most especial as her protector.

Elizabeth smiled as Pacumeni's thumb caressed her cheek. He drew back a half step, and his eyes grew somber. "You are happy, Elizabeth?"

"I am, Pacumeni," she returned. "And you?"

"Very happy." His thumb trailed along the line of her jaw again. "It is difficult to believe that there was once a time when I thought I never would be again."

"After Lady Keturah died," Elizabeth offered.

"Yes," he agreed. "Keturah."

At the tender tones with which he spoke the name of his first wife, Elizabeth's heart gave a twinge, and she bit her bottom lip. But then, as if sensing her thoughts, his fingers brushed her jaw, tipping her face upward.

"She will always be a part of my memory," Pacumeni confessed, "but you know that you are *everything* to me, Elizabeth, do you not? I love you. With all my heart."

Elizabeth's heart glowed at his words. She would not begrudge Pacumeni his memories. He loved *her* now. Her mouth drew up in a smile. "And I love you."

Pacumeni returned her smile, his gaze drinking her in, and then, though Joshua stood nearby, he dipped his head and claimed her lips with his own.

Elizabeth found herself wishing she could melt into him as his pliant mouth moved over hers, tender, searching, as his kisses always were. She drank in his fragrant, musky scent as she returned his caresses, conscious of his strong arms about her. After a long moment, Pacumeni's strength eased, and he drew back with a reluctant sigh.

His gray eyes sought hers once more before he drew her close, his jaw coming to rest against her hair. Elizabeth nestled her face against his chest, safe in the comfort of his embrace. Here, all was well. Nothing could harm her. She smiled, calmed by the steady throb of Pacumeni's heart, wishing that his embrace would never have to end.

⌐⋈⋈⌐

"You should have killed them all!" Coriantumr's voice, strident with rage, echoed through the still air of the forest.

The woman who knelt beside the skeleton frame of the stripped tent stiffened at the fury in the voice, but did not look up. Her small, work-calloused hands hardly paused as she folded the leather tent away in its pack. Tying the bindings of the pack shut, she brushed back a loose lock of yellow hair from her cheek and straightened. All around her, the Lamanites, warriors and servants both, moved like wraiths in the misty shadows or sat in huddled groups. The warriors, steeling their nerves before their final plunge toward the Nephite capital, tested the sharpness of their obsidian blades or the springs of their bows. The servants packed away food or tents. Beside her, a wind skittered along the ground, fluttering crumpled leaves in its wake like remnants of torn flags.

"We are less than a day from Zarahemla!" Coriantumr barked. "And on the eve of battle, you falter? Shemnon, you old fool! What manner of high captain are you?"

The woman's head turned now, her eyes narrowing.

Coriantumr sat before a dying fire, glaring across the weak flames at the old warrior Shemnon. The younger man's features could have been handsome but for his furious expression, mottled all the more by the fading flames, making him look like a demon.

A jaguar skin wrapped around Coriantumr's taut waist, his torso bare but for the belts of his weapons that crossed his muscled chest. The blueness of his eyes and the pale scruff of his beard mocked his Lamanitish garb.

Despite Coriantumr's fury, Shemnon's face remained calm. "I followed your orders, my lord."

"You did not kill them *all!*"

"The last was badly wounded," Shemnon returned. "It would have been a waste of our strength and our arrows to pursue him."

"*Any* Nephite who breathes is a threat," Coriantumr spat. "And wounded as you claim the wretch was, he still managed to outrun all your men! What if he lives long enough to reach Zarahemla? What will become of our plans to surprise the Nephite fools?"

Shemnon tightened his jaw. "Then the more noble the battle."

Coriantumr frowned before a harsh laugh escaped his lips. "No wonder King Tubaloth made you my second-in-command. Old man that you are, you have the blood of a jaguar in you, Shemnon. What a pity you have no living sons. Why did you never take another wife after your first died and all your kin deserted you?"

The woman's eyes flashed to Shemnon's face in time to see him flinch, but the pain did not carry to his voice as he said, "I never wanted another beside the wife I took in my youth."

"Ha! If you think so well of her, why do you never speak her name?"

"We do not speak the names of our dead. If you knew the ways of my people, you would know this."

Coriantumr snorted in disdain. He straightened his back and turned his eyes to the woman. "Lylith, daughter of Pachus."

She flinched.

"Bring our food."

Lylith struggled not to show the pain his words caused her as she scrambled to her feet and moved to the fire where a wooden tray waited between the two men, laden with roasted meat and flat corn cakes.

Angry words she dared not speak choked her throat as she scooped up a wooden ladle full of meat and wrapped it in one corn cake, keeping her eyes turned from Coriantumr. She did not wish to be called by her old name, yet he continued to do so, and always with malice in his eyes. Coriantumr leaned nearer.

"For a Nephite slave, you have endured the rigors of the journey well," he crooned in her language.

"No better than any of your concubines would have," she said to the ground.

She felt the weight of his anger at this, but a breath that hinted at a muffled chuckle came from Shemnon, and Coriantumr turned, fixing his eyes on the old warrior. She dared a look at Coriantumr now as he snatched the rolled corn cake from her hand, steaming with the meat inside, and tore into the food like a vulture into carrion.

Repressing a shudder, Lylith rolled another cake full of meat and turned to the old warrior. As his eyes met hers, the impassive set of his countenance softened.

"Thank you, Talilia, my daughter," Shemnon murmured as he took the proffered food.

She nodded acceptance of his thanks.

"*Daughter*," Coriantumr scoffed between mouthfuls. He gestured at Lylith. "What real kin have you, Shemnon? All you have is this castoff who betrayed her own people. You should have let her die in the jungle where you found her and let the gods have her. When will you realize she's not the urchin your mother carried off to live with the Nephites?"

Coriantumr sneered, and a cold light sparked in his eyes. "Doubtless, your real daughter found a Nephite to marry. You may slay your own grandsons tomorrow and not know it." He nodded at Shemnon's bloody scimitar. "Perhaps you already have."

Lylith's eyes fell to Shemnon's scimitar, the familiar blades and the wood discolored with new blood in the dying firelight. She swallowed hard.

Coriantumr's eyes traveled down Lylith's form. "And if *I* possessed such a lovely slave, I would not treat her like a daughter. I would—"

"My *daughter*," Shemnon cut in, "is neither castoff nor slave. And why speak to me of the gods? You believe in nothing. Not even the god of the Nephites."

Coriantumr's eyes shot back to Shemnon. "I owe you no answer! The king gave *me* charge of this army."

"I have not forgotten." Shemnon's eyes simmered like coals.

"See that you don't," Coriantumr hissed, then thrust himself to his feet. "We march out within the quarter hour. Prepare the men to depart!"

With this, he turned and strode through the trees, snapping at a group of servants packing dried meat into baskets.

As Coriantumr's form disappeared, Shemnon placed his hands on his knees. He pushed himself to his feet with a soft groan.

"I must see to my duties and rally the men." He turned away, paused, and turned back. "What is wrong, my bright candle?"

Lylith looked up as the old warrior spoke, her vision swimming. She had not even known there were tears in her eyes. "You would have been wiser to let me die where you found me, as he said."

Shemnon frowned. "You usually do not heed that idiot's words. Why now?"

"Because they are true." Her voice grew thick with misery. "My father *did* betray his people." She heaved a breath. "And I—"

"Talilia," Shemnon gently reproved. "You are not the man who sired you."

"But I have done many other foolish things." She dropped her eyes. "I could not count them all."

"That may be, but have I ever condemned you?"

"Never, Father."

"Then will you not tell me what else troubles your heart?" Shemnon's voice grew heavy with concern. "Coriantumr's foolish words do not often cause you such distress."

She dropped her gaze to the scimitar leaning against the log he had risen from. In a small voice, she asked, "The men you...killed. Were any of them young?"

Understanding touched the lines of Shemnon's face. "Ah." He bent and picked up the weapon, studying its discolored blades. "From what I saw, none appeared young enough to be the son you bore."

"Would you spare them if they were young enough to be my little Zeram?"

Shemnon heaved a deep sigh, his eyes sorrowful. "I will not lie, my daughter. Tomorrow's sun will rise on a bloody day. The Nephites' great city will fall. The gods have decreed it. War is not a time for pity or mercy. Even the Nephites, savages that they are, know that one truth."

"Yet you showed me pity and mercy. And *I* am a Nephite."

"You are no warrior, my child," Shemnon murmured. "And you were hurt when my comrades and I found you so many years ago. I could not leave you to die."

Lylith said nothing, her eyes upon the weakening flames.

He rose again, hesitated, and turned back. "On my honor, Talilia, I will spare all I can."

She lifted her gaze, the kindness on his face warming her heart. "Thank you, Father."

Shemnon touched her hair with a gentle hand. "Ready yourself, my daughter. See to your duties. It will soon be time to march out."

With this, he turned and strode away after Coriantumr.

Chapter 4

Sunlight fell over Joshua's face, and the scent of growing things surrounded him as he stepped off the tiles of the portico onto the earthen path of the palace garden.

His sword belt clattered as his foot struck the pathway that wound away into the trees. The sound turned Elizabeth's head from where she walked with her arm looped through Pacumeni's a few steps in front of Joshua. Her jade-green eyes sparkled in the sunlight as she offered him a smile, which Joshua managed to return before he glanced away.

Upon a stone bench just off the path sat Pacumeni's older sister, Lady Pazia, Helaman's wife, stitching with a small bone needle at a mound of white cloth in her lap. A contented smile played at the corners of her mouth. Her mahogany hair, traced with faint strands of gray, twined in graceful plaits against her head. She and her charges must have arrived while he had been on the far side of the portico with Pacumeni and Elizabeth.

Beside Pazia sat her second son, Lehi, a younger copy of his elder brother, Nephi. Lehi studied the folded pages of a book, engrossed by what he read. At their feet, a little boy with honey-brown skin and dark hair sat cross-legged upon the ground, a basket filled with wooden animals beside him. A jaguar in one hand and a peccary in the other seemed to be carrying on a sociable conversation before the little boy looked up, his gray eyes lighting on Pacumeni.

"Abba!" He scrambled to his feet, dropping his toys to the ground.

Lehi looked up, blinking. Beside him, Pazia's face brightened. She set aside her stitching and rose. Her eyes met Joshua's, and her smile warmed him. She reminded him of his own mother, whose features he could faintly remember. And like her husband, she carried an air of wisdom and gentleness as if she could see into Joshua's very heart, yet still judge with kindness what she saw there.

"Jonas!" Pacumeni greeted as Jonas scampered toward him. The little boy squealed as Pacumeni scooped him up and tossed him into the air.

"Elizabeth!" Jonas's arms flung wide as Pacumeni caught him again. "Look at me!"

"You're flying." Elizabeth laughed as Pacumeni set his son down. Jonas scampered toward her, hugging her knees in his excitement before he turned and ran to Joshua, his eyes gleaming.

"Master Joshua, did you see?" He tugged on the hem of Joshua's kilt. "Did you see me? I flew!"

A grin came to Joshua's face, and he reached down, ruffling his hand through the little boy's dark hair. "Like a hawk."

"Your turn, Lehi?" Pacumeni turned toward his nephew, who remained seated, his book folded in his hands.

"Ah! No!" Lehi snorted, laughing, throwing up a hand as if to ward Pacumeni off. "I'm too big for that, Uncle!"

"Me again!" Jonas scrambled back to his father. Pacumeni swung him up as the boy crowed with delight.

Pazia glided toward Elizabeth. She caught the younger woman's hands in her own and squeezed, grinning like a young girl. "You are well, my soon-to-be sister?"

"I am," Elizabeth answered, returning the smile.

Pazia's gaze found Joshua's over Elizabeth's shoulder, and she drew back. Her brow furrowed for a moment as if she sensed something amiss.

"Pazia, my sister," Pacumeni greeted, as he settled Jonas on his shoulder, and hugged her with his free arm.

Pazia laughed and tapped Pacumeni's nose with a playful finger. "Little brother, it seems you have a jaguar cub on your back."

Pacumeni chuckled as Jonas kicked himself off his father's shoulders and swung to the ground, darting back to his toys at his cousin's feet. Lehi had returned to his book.

His arms free, Pacumeni moved behind Elizabeth, resting a hand upon the soft curve of her shoulder as his eyes followed his son.

Pacumeni's thumb strayed to the smooth flesh of her neck just above the embroidered collar of her mantle. Elizabeth blushed and smiled, turning her head to look up at him.

That same wayward lock of honey-brown hair brushed against her cheek.

Joshua's fingers ached to feel its softness again as he had in the marketplace. He shouldn't have, for it made the ache in him all the more difficult to bear.

Joshua tore his eyes away, following the glimmer of a single dew drop that trailed down the spine of a large leaf. The shimmering drop hung suspended at the tip, then fell away through the air, gleaming like a diamond before splashing against the earth and disappearing.

He felt someone's eyes on him and looked up, meeting Pazia's gaze. Sympathy filled her eyes. Did she guess—?

"Abba." Jonas's small voice cut in. The little boy scampered to his father's side, tugging on the hem of his kilt. "Come play with me."

Pacumeni chuckled and let his son pull him to the basket of toys, then down to his knees.

Elizabeth moved to sit on the stone bench beside Lehi as Pacumeni and Jonas played upon the ground at their feet. She studied the text Lehi read and said something, touching a finger to the parchment, to which Lehi offered a reply.

"Lieutenant Joshua," Pazia called. He looked up as she approached, her bearing like a queen even as her eyes filled with motherly gentleness.

He bowed his head. "My lady."

She nodded in return as she reached his side. "I owe you many thanks. It is because of you, after all, that they first met." A smile touched her face. "The day you and Pacumeni both became officers."

The corners of Joshua's mouth curved upward at the memory, and he released a short breath. "She came with a caravan all the way from Bountiful to see me commissioned as a lieutenant. I'd written to her that I hoped she'd come. I wasn't certain she could, and my joy was without bounds when I saw her in the crowd at the ceremony. We'd been apart for two years. She had become so…" He faltered. "And I…"

Pazia's gaze softened. "And you had missed her," she finished gently.

"More than words could say," he murmured.

"You've been friends since you were children." Her hand touched his arm. "I understand, Joshua." She drew in a breath. "There was a time when I feared Pacumeni would never be happy again." She turned and studied her brother, her brows furrowed. "He was inconsolable when he lost Keturah."

"I remember."

Pazia turned to him, her eyes steady. "But after time, and with God's help, his broken heart healed. And then, thanks to you, he met Elizabeth."

Joshua studied Pazia's gaze a long moment. At last, his eyes moved to Elizabeth, where she sat beside Lehi. The boy asked a question, and she answered as a slender finger moved over a line of text upon his page. At her feet, Pacumeni looked up from his son's play to say something. Elizabeth's eyes danced as their gazes met.

"Pacumeni and Elizabeth owe you much," Pazia said.

Joshua shook his head. "They owe me nothing. That they are happy is enough."

"You should be happy too."

Joshua's throat tightened. "I am."

"Are you?" she asked.

Joshua studied the shadows the trees cast across the ground at Elizabeth's feet. With her eyes fixed upon Pacumeni, Elizabeth did not even notice his glance.

"Joshua."

He lifted his eyes, meeting Pazia's gaze. Her eyes like his own mother's, calmed him despite his troubled heart.

"You are a good man, son of Antipus. And if you live as God wishes, all will come to the best for you one day." She spoke in soft tones, yet her words rang in his heart like the voice of a prophetess.

"God is the Father of this world, and knows the end from the beginning. Trust Him."

Joshua swallowed hard. "I always have."

Pazia smiled. "And you will be blessed for it."

"Abba!" Jonas's small voice cut into Joshua's thoughts. "You have to go already?"

Joshua turned to see Pacumeni rise, dusting his hands on his kilt. His son studied him with upturned eyes.

"I wish I could stay with you all day, but I have duties." Pacumeni ruffled Jonas's dark hair. "Be the good boy I know you are," he admonished.

"I will, Abba."

To this, Pacumeni stooped and pressed a kiss to the child's brow. Then he stood and turned to Elizabeth, who came to her feet.

"I must go now." He clasped her hand and brought it to his lips. "Remember I love you."

Elizabeth's smile glowed like the sun. "Always. I love you too." She tilted her face toward his as Pacumeni bent over her.

Joshua pulled his eyes away, catching Pazia's gentle gaze as he did.

"Joshua."

Joshua's eyes jerked up at Pacumeni's voice. The young chief judge's steps quickened as he strode near. "Will you come with me?"

"Of course." Joshua followed as Pacumeni stepped up on the tiles of the portico.

"There's something I wish to discuss with you," Pacumeni said more quietly now that Joshua stood at his side.

Despite the casual tones of his friend's voice, Joshua's heart faltered in his chest. But he nodded and said nothing as the young chief judge started toward the archway into the palace.

Pausing just beneath the arch, Pacumeni turned back and lifted a hand in farewell.

A smile touched Elizabeth's lips where she stood beside Pazia. Jonas came to her side to take her hand. Elizabeth pressed a kiss to the fingers of her free hand, then returned Pacumeni's wave.

Joshua's chest swelled, his eyes moving from Elizabeth to Pazia. The prophet's wife smiled, her eyes filling with sympathy.

His jaw set, Joshua turned and followed Pacumeni into the palace corridor.

Coarse grass slashed like scythes at Zeram's shins as he ran toward the wounded man. Blood streaked the soldier's uniform as he stumbled forward. The markings on his shoulder showed him to be a lieutenant.

"Sir!" Panic rose like bile in Zeram's throat.

The man's head lifted. A gleam of hope mingled with the pain on his face. Sweat and dried blood matted the man's brown hair, and arrows protruded from his arm and side. How was he still alive, let alone able to run?

"Sir," Zeram said, "let me help you into the city—"

"No," the man gasped. "No time." Blood flecked his lips as he spoke, seeping into his beard. The words seemed to drain him, and his legs buckled. Zeram lunged forward, catching the man's full weight as the soldier crumpled.

Zeram staggered, laying the man on the grass, wincing as he jarred the arrows.

"Sir!" Zeram said. "What happened?"

"Listen to me, boy!" The wounded man seized Zeram's arm in a painful grip. "There's no time! They're coming!"

"Wh-who?"

"Run with all the strength in you, and tell the chief judge…" The man's grip on Zeram's arm tightened like a vise. He coughed, and blood splattered Zeram's uniform. Zeram fought the instinct to recoil, fixing his gaze on the wounded man.

"Tell him the demons of the abyss have been set loose!"

Like a candle's flame abruptly extinguished, the man's grip slackened and his head sagged to the ground. An exhaled breath stirred the grass near his mouth.

The grass did not stir again.

"Sir?" Zeram shook the limp arm that had been strong as steel moments before. "Sir, please." The glowing idealism he had felt when he took the soldier's oath, when he had received his uniform, his gleaming blade—it all seemed a foreign thing now.

"Son of Jacob!" His sergeant, Levi, staggered to a stop behind him. "What were you thinking, leaving your post?"

Zeram scrambled to his feet, and Levi's gaze fell to the figure in the grass. He dropped to a knee and fitted his fingers to the man's throat. A soft curse escaped him. "May Laman and all his misbegotten seed rot!" Levi struck a fist against his thigh. Looking up, he barked, "Return to your post, soldier, and put your armor back on. I will see that—"

"He gave me an order," Zeram blurted.

Levi rose to his feet. "What was it?"

"He told me to tell the chief judge that the demons of the abyss have been set loose."

A cold pallor washed over Levi's face, and his gaze slid past Zeram's shoulder to focus in the distance.

Zeram turned to follow Levi's eyes. The line where the forests began far away seemed to have darkened. A creeping shadow appeared, seeping like a bleeding wound from the distant green line of trees. A stony fist clenched in his belly.

A soft curse escaped Levi's lips. "Why have the patrols not..." He did not finish as he turned his eyes upon the dead soldier and uttered a curse. "Then by all the powers, obey him!" Sergeant Levi snapped. "And run as if jaguars were at your heels!"

Zeram spun and sprinted back toward the gate, his heart pounding with the ferocity of a war drum.

Chapter 5

Joshua's heart thundered within him, a fist of nervousness tightening in his chest. Even so, he managed to match Pacumeni's stride along the echoing corridor. The doors of the throne room passed them, then the corridor that turned down toward the living chambers of the chief judge and his kindred. At last they reached the end of the corridor and the door into Pacumeni's private office. Pacumeni lifted the latch, giving a casual gesture of his head for Joshua to join him. Struggling to hide his rising apprehension, Joshua entered the small chamber.

A wooden desk sat in the middle of the room, its surface strewn with sheets of parchment and a clay lamp, unlit. Daylight spilled in through a window that looked out over the market below.

The latch fell with a clatter as Pacumeni shut the door then crossed to his desk. He heaved a relieved breath as he peeled off the brass circlet that marked his station. He tossed his crown casually onto the desk, where it rattled before it lay still. Heaving a sigh, he ran his hand through his damp hair.

"Captain Micha doesn't often bring such matters to my attention," Pacumeni said, lifting his gaze. "But as you and I have been friends for years, he thought I might wish to know."

"You're wondering why I requested a transfer." Joshua's throat tightened.

"It surprised me," Pacumeni said. He drew the chair back with a scrape and sat down. He drew one sheet of parchment close. Joshua recognized his own writing. "I hoped you could explain it."

Joshua's chest constricted. "There is nothing to explain. I filled it out thoroughly. I prefer Bountiful, but I'm willing to go wherever there is need. The request did not require a reason."

"True." Pacumeni's brows quivered. "But as your friend, not as the chief judge, will you not tell me why? Joshua, have I…have I grown arrogant? Is that why—?"

"No." Joshua's heart wrenched at the confusion on his friend's face. "You've done no wrong. I'm the one at fault."

"How?" Pacumeni shook his head. "Joshua, you perform every duty given you with faithfulness and exactness, and Elizabeth has nothing but praise for you. Surely her good opinion counts, even if mine doesn't. I had hoped that you would remain here as a palace guard after she and I are wed. I thought Elizabeth was a dear friend to you."

"She is," Joshua said. "Still, I must go."

The confusion on Pacumeni's face grew more pronounced. "Knowing you, Joshua, you would take an assassin's blade for me. I have no truer friend than you. We trained and studied together. We became as close as brothers. You stood at my side in my deepest grief after Keturah died. Because of you, I met Elizabeth. No man is more loyal to me, to our country than you. I trust you with my life. Will you not trust me and tell me why you wish for this transfer?"

Joshua clenched his jaw as he studied his friend's eyes. "I trust you, Pacumeni. You are my friend. Always. But some things are better left unspoken."

"I won't censure you, no matter what the reason."

"You will censure me for this," Joshua insisted.

"I promise, Joshua, as I live, I won't. Please."

This final plea broke him at last, and the words spilled forth before Joshua could bite them back. "My feelings for Elizabeth go deeper than the caring of a brother for a sister. They have for years."

At once, he felt a rush of relief and a stab of agony. Pacumeni's features stiffened.

The silence that followed felt weighted, as if the air between them had thickened. For several painful seconds their eyes locked, Pacumeni's gaze unreadable before the scrape of his chair upon stone shredded the silence and he rose to his feet.

"I didn't know." Pacumeni glanced away and moved to the window to lean against the ledge. "It never even entered my thoughts—"

"Now you understand why I must go." Joshua began to turn away.

A lift of Pacumeni's hand, however, stopped his retreat. Joshua halted, bracing for Pacumeni's words.

"Do you...?" Pacumeni's words gave Joshua pause, spoken in broken, yet sincere tones. "Do you wish me to withdraw my intentions? To give you a chance—"

"What?" Joshua turned back, aghast. "Never!"

Pacumeni's face betrayed nothing, but his hand clenched the windowsill, fingers digging into the unyielding stone.

"Releasing her from your betrothal would break her heart," Joshua said. "She loves you. You love her. I do not—should not—matter at all!"

Pacumeni turned and faced Joshua. "That cannot be so, for as I have just discovered, you love her also. And have far longer than I."

Joshua's jaw tensed beneath his skin. "And because of that very love, I *want* her to marry you. This bond that you share with Elizabeth is good and right. Do not sever it."

Pacumeni looked up. His eyes met and held Joshua's. At last, he pushed away from the window with a soft groan. "I am sorry, Joshua." He lifted his hands and let them fall against his kilt in a helpless gesture. "If I had not come between you and Elizabeth—"

"Do you wish you had never met her?" Joshua asked.

The sinews of Pacumeni's jaw grew taut. "Of course not."

"Then don't apologize," Joshua returned.

Pacumeni looked away, frustration etching his face as he ran a hand through his hair. "But I've caused you pain." The irritation vanished from his voice. "And for that, I *am* sorry. Your regard for Elizabeth is sincere. You truly care for her. You would die to protect her."

"As would you, Pacumeni."

Pacumeni turned back, defeated. "You will leave Zarahemla, then?"

"It's for the best."

"Then I'll respect your wishes, and recommend you to a suitable post in Bountiful."

"Thank you." Joshua stepped to the doorway. He paused, then looked back.

Pacumeni looked out over the plaza, his face weary.

"Pacumeni," Joshua ventured. His friend lifted his head. Joshua felt foolish for asking the question, but he needed to hear the answer. "We are friends still?"

At this, Pacumeni turned. He regarded Joshua a long moment then strode forward. Pacumeni's hands reached out and clasped Joshua's forearms. "*Brothers*, Joshua. Always."

A tentative grin touched Joshua's face.

"Your Eminence!" A shout echoed through the window from the plaza below.

Pacumeni's eyes filled with alarm. He turned and strode back to the window, gripping the stone as his eyes strained through the bright sunlight.

"Judge Pacumeni!"

Joshua started, recognizing Zeram's voice, filled with tension and fear.

Striding behind Pacumeni, Joshua saw Zeram sprinting across the plaza toward the palace steps. The commerce had fallen to a standstill as all eyes followed him. Zeram leaped like a deer up the steps toward the palace doors, ignoring the guards who tried to hail him, the front of his uniform splattered with what appeared to be blood as the breathless youth cried words that filled Joshua's veins with splinters of fear.

"Lamanites!" Zeram's voice echoed across the plaza. "Coming! To Zarahemla!"

Joshua's heart clenched. Pacumeni's countenance grew rigid. Their eyes met as the weight of the words settled on Joshua's heart.

Pacumeni spun away and flung the door open. Joshua followed him.

Zeram's harsh breathing echoed down the stone corridor as he staggered through the doorway, pushing past Micha and Oren, his legs trembling.

Oren, a scowl on his face, moved to grab Zeram's arm, but Pacumeni held out a hand. "Leave him," he ordered, and Oren stepped back.

Beyond the outer doors, the market had exploded in a flurry of sound. The awnings of shops clapped shut like so many metal traps, and frightened cries filled the air. Joshua's hand slid over the hilt of his sword as he and Pacumeni strode toward Zeram, though the feel of the weapon gave him little comfort.

Pacumeni seemed infused with strength, and his eyes glinted like fire. He reached Zeram, who was bent over in exhaustion, his hands braced against his knees. Pacumeni caught the gasping young man by the shoulder and jerked him erect.

"How far away are they?" Pacumeni asked.

"Coming…steady pace…from…south," Zeram gasped. "Already cut off…pass to Gideon."

"How many?" Pacumeni's grip tightened.

Zeram flinched. "As if…all their lands…set loose."

The sinews of Pacumeni's jaw worked beneath his skin. He did not speak, but his face said enough. The greater strength of their armies lay in the outer cities. They had no time to send for help. Zarahemla could not repel this invasion.

"What will…we do, sir?" Zeram asked.

"We will fight them," Pacumeni said. A fearsome determination took hold of his features. "And they will feel the fury of our blades."

Zeram looked frightened. He hardly seemed suited for the uniform he wore. Micha, Oren, and the other guards shifted their weight. Joshua's own heart echoed their unspoken trepidation.

Yet Pacumeni's expression betrayed no fear.

"Captain Micha," Pacumeni called.

"Your Eminence?"

"Send your two swiftest runners to Melek and Noah. Send two by boat northeast to Bountiful and the cities about her, with the message that they must prepare for war. Then have all men able to bear arms meet at the garrison near the southern gate. All those unable to fight…"

Pacumeni turned to Zeram. "Is there time for the women and children to take the north road to Melek?"

Zeram gulped. "The Lamanites are coming too fast, sir."

"Then we must gather them into the main plaza," Joshua said. He swallowed an acrid taste, wishing he could wake from this bitter dream. "That's the greatest safety they'll find."

Pacumeni's eyes met Joshua's. "Agreed." He turned again to Micha.

"Captain, send the order throughout Zarahemla that the women and children are to gather here in the central plaza. Go."

His face set like flint, Micha clapped his fist against his chest. He disappeared in a moment, the pounding of his feet fading as he leaped down the steps.

"The women and children will need to be watched over," Joshua said. "Many of the young soldiers, including Zeram, could fill that duty."

"Agreed." Turning to Zeram, Pacumeni ordered, "Find Master Tuloth. He'll know what to do. Stay here in the plaza and obey his commands. Take care of—"

"Sir," Zeram pleaded, "Nephi's still out there, and my other friends. I want to stand with them." He glanced toward Joshua. "Joshua!" Zeram grasped Joshua's arm. "Please—"

"Zeram, son of Jacob!" Pacumeni snarled. He seized Zeram's arm and spun the youth to face him. Raw terror filled Zeram's eyes. "I am your supreme commander! You will not counter nor question my orders!"

For a moment, Zeram's jaw trembled as if he would burst into tears before Pacumeni's hard grip on his shoulder eased.

"Stay here, Zeram," Pacumeni commanded, his voice falling back to its normal tone. "Do all in your power to keep Elizabeth and Jonas safe, so long as they need your protection. That is the greatest duty I can entrust to any man. Will you swear it?"

"I swear it, sir." Zeram's voice shook.

"Then go," Pacumeni ordered. "Get yourself suited at the armory, then find my sister and Elizabeth. Tell them what happened and get them to the plaza."

Zeram saluted, his lower lip trembling before he turned away. Joshua watched him leave, a heavy stone settling into his chest.

"Zarahemla will not be taken without giving the Lamanites a taste of Nephite steel," Pacumeni promised as he strode through the doors out onto the wide veranda.

"Yes, sir," Joshua said as his leaden legs followed his friend. The sunlight seemed harsh as he gazed down the steps to the plaza where merchants and buyers scattered, frightened cries echoing through the streets.

"I'll be at the head of the men who will hold the southern gate. If we had more time—" Pacumeni broke off. "Joshua, go find Helaman. Help him—"

"I'm staying with you." Joshua's words came of their own accord.

Pacumeni's head whipped back, his eyes stern. "Joshua—"

"I will not leave your side, Pacumeni."

"No. Joshua, I order you to—"

"Don't force me to disobey you. If you'll be at the south gate, so will I."

Pacumeni's tone became one of controlled fury, and his eyes gleamed with ferocity. "Lieutenant, I have no time for this. I will give no more quarter to your insubordination than I did Zeram. I am the chief judge, and I order you to—"

"Then have me flogged, Your Eminence," Joshua seethed, his eyes boring into Pacumeni's, "stripped of my rank and put in irons. For I will not leave your side."

Pacumeni's jaw grew taut. Joshua met his furious gaze, unflinching.

Finally, Pacumeni growled and spun away. "Then come with me to the armory!"

Chapter 6

Sweet scents wafted around Elizabeth in the center of the palace garden. Trees and thick growth surrounded her and her companions as if they were secluded in a deep forest.

She lifted her gaze from the pages in her hand to the boy sitting across the path from her, his back straight, eyes attentive. "Now, the colors in the tongue of the Lamanites," Elizabeth said. Switching to the Lamanite language, she pointed upward at a thick leaf. "What color is that leaf?"

"Green," Lehi said.

Elizabeth lifted her brows. On the stone bench beside her son, Pazia smiled, focused on the sewing in her lap.

"The leaf is green," Lehi added in the Lamanite tongue, sheepish now.

"And what is that?" Elizabeth pointed to a crimson blossom.

"That is a…" Lehi narrowed his eyes. "A flower." He paused. "It is red."

"Very skillful!" Elizabeth praised, and Lehi grinned.

"Red," echoed a small voice in the Lamanite tongue. Jonas sat on the ground a pace away, with a wooden peccary in one hand. Delight sparkled in the boy's eyes, so much like his father's. "This is red," Jonas said again, touching a scarlet hem on his shirt.

Elizabeth smiled and looked to Pazia and Lehi.

"Jonas is a quick learner," Pazia murmured in the Nephite tongue. "He'll make a fine older brother to your many children."

"Pazia!" Elizabeth laughed, nodding to the small mound of white cloth in Pazia's lap. "The wedding is still a month away, and it will likely be a year at least before a baby comes!"

Pazia smoothed the unfinished folds of the infant's sleeping gown across her lap. "True," she admitted, a smile teasing her lips. She pulled the small bone needle through the fabric. "But still—"

"They must be out here, Master Tuloth," Zeram's youthful voice called from somewhere down the path. Elizabeth's smile fell, and she looked up. "If they're in the center of the garden, they wouldn't have heard the commotion."

"I'll get them," Tuloth's deeper voice replied, steadier, but still strained. "You go back. Watch over the maidservants."

The voices grew silent at this, replaced by the hollow beat of footsteps coming from beyond the trees. Elizabeth traded a confused look with Pazia just as Tuloth appeared around the bend in the path, moving at a near run.

Seeing them, the tall Ammonite pulled to a stop. "Here you are!"

"What's wrong?" Lehi asked.

"Elizabeth, Lady Pazia," Tuloth gasped. "Bring the boys. Come. Quickly!"

Elizabeth set the book down and stood. She cast a worried look at Pazia, who set her sewing aside and rose to her feet, drawing Lehi up with her. Pazia's voice grew terse. "Master Tuloth—"

"I will explain in good time." Tuloth reached down, catching Jonas's weight up in one arm and snatching Elizabeth's hand with the other. He pulled her back the way he had come, and Pazia and Lehi hurried behind them. "The other men are already gone," he said as Elizabeth trotted at his side. "Chief Judge Pacumeni, Joshua, the other guards. The women and children of the city are to gather in the plaza."

"What are you talking about?" Elizabeth demanded, but Tuloth did not look at her as they broke through the trees and continued toward the portico.

Jonas looked at her over Tuloth's shoulder, his eyes wide with confusion.

"At least let me take Jonas," Elizabeth pleaded.

Without protest, Tuloth surrendered the child into her free arm. Her other arm remained clasped in his grip as they scrambled up onto the portico, then hurried through the door into the shadows of the corridor. The hallway, empty of servants or guards, echoed with the sound of their footfalls. Then the outer doors fell behind them as Tuloth guided them into the open air again. Clouds had been in the far south earlier, but now they reached across the sky, fingers of mist muting the sun.

As Elizabeth cast her eyes below her at the plaza, her heart all but stopped.

She hardly recognized the plaza without the carts and colorful awnings, the smoke of cooking fires, and the bleating flocks. Instead, women and children huddled across the wide expanse. More streamed in from the roads all about the plaza, many of them in tears. As Tuloth guided her down the steps, Elizabeth's confusion now mingled with rising fear.

"Lady Pazia!" Martha, one of the maidservants, looked up at them, her eyes wide. She stood in a crowd of other female servants at the base of the steps. A young soldier stood by, and Elizabeth's heart clenched as she recognized Zeram, a helmet concealing his light-colored hair, a stiff chest-covering of quilted kapok over his torso.

As Elizabeth's small group reached the base of the steps, Pazia put a comforting arm around Martha. "What's happening?" Pazia asked.

Elizabeth's heart throbbed, the answer clamoring at the door of her mind. She set Jonas on the ground, pressing a hand to his cheek to reassure him. "Tuloth, tell us what's going on," she pleaded.

The tall Ammonite set his jaw, then opened his mouth.

"Lamanites," Zeram said before Tuloth could speak. Elizabeth's eyes turned to the youth, whose face remained void of emotion. "An army is coming," Zeram continued. "Chief Judge Pacumeni ordered the women and children to gather here." He nodded toward Tuloth. "We'll watch over you."

"Whatever you do," Tuloth said, his dark eyes sharp as chips of obsidian, "when—if they make it this far, do not let them know you are kin to the chief judge. Whether their captains have any honor or not, I cannot say. But do nothing to stand out."

Zeram's careful façade crumbled. His brows pulled together, and his chin trembled. He seemed younger and smaller in the armor he wore, like a little boy playing soldier. But when he spoke, his words did not sound like those of a child. "I won't let anything happen to you, Elizabeth." His eyes glimmered with wetness, but his jaw clenched. "I made an oath to Chief Judge Pacumeni that I would watch over you and Jonas. And as the Lord lives, I *will* keep it."

The words stabbed a shard of cold fear into Elizabeth's heart, and she wavered.

"Father and Nephi and Uncle Pacumeni will beat them back." Lehi's voice bore a confidence his face did not show. "Won't they, Zeram?"

Zeram, barely taller than Lehi, shifted his weight. He glanced at Elizabeth in silence.

"Where is my son Nephi?" Pazia demanded, her voice fierce.

"Nephi and my other friends have been sent to the seventh street from the southern gate."

Elizabeth started as she recalled the eyes of Nephi and her other students, whom she had sent off to the south gate a fleeting hour before. By the heavens, they were only *children!*

"What of my husband?" Pazia demanded. "And my brother?"

"Master Helaman is with Nephi and the others," Zeram said. "His Eminence, Chief Judge Pacumeni has gone to the south gate."

"And Joshua?" Elizabeth asked.

"He is with Pacumeni."

"Where the brunt of the attack will be," she whispered.

Zeram managed a nod.

"*Both* of them?"

"Yes."

Beside Elizabeth, Jonas began to cry. The sound twisted her heart, but she did not look down. Instead, she swung on Tuloth, her eyes boring into his. "Pacumeni is at the gate where the Lamanites will strike first? And Joshua? I have to go to them."

Tuloth began to speak. "It's too dangerous—"

"Then go with me, Tuloth! I must—"

"Elizabeth!" Pazia's thin fingers possessed uncommon strength as they gripped Elizabeth's hands and turned her away from Tuloth. She studied Elizabeth with both compassion and severity. "Don't be foolish," she insisted. "Keep your head, Elizabeth. Be strong. My little brother wouldn't want you to lose yourself to despair." She paused. "Nor would Joshua."

"But—"

"Think of Jonas," Pazia urged. "Pacumeni's son needs your strength!"

Elizabeth swallowed thickly, remembering the little boy beside her. She turned toward the spot where she had set Jonas down, but stopped. He had disappeared. "Jonas?" Her eyes darted wildly about. "Jonas!"

Her frantic gaze locked on Jonas's small figure scampering toward the south edge of the plaza. He had reached the long, flat-roofed buildings that enclosed the wide marketplace. A cluster of frightened women and children dressed in worn clothing emerged from a narrow road between two shops. He ignored them as he darted past, and in their fear, they did not see him.

Seeing the distance Jonas had gone, Zeram darted several steps in that direction. "Jonas, come back here!"

The child did not slow as he reached the narrow road. It was an often overlooked gap, but Elizabeth knew of it well enough. It led into the older quarter of the city, an illogical maze of crumbling buildings, streets, and alleys built by the people of Mulek long before the Nephites had come to the valley. A child as small as Jonas could easily lose his way.

Wild fear gripped Elizabeth as Jonas vanished between the narrow stone walls. She snatched up her skirts and darted after him.

"Elizabeth!" Zeram cried. "Wait!" But Elizabeth only ran faster.

An iron-gray dome hid the sky above the southern gate of Zarahemla where Joshua stood upon the battlement, gazing southward. A chill wind carried the smell of rain. On the plain before Zarahemla forests of spears like rows of stripped cornstalks rose into the air, interspersed with fluttering guidons.

The steady rhythm of marching feet vibrated through the stones beneath him. To his right and left, his comrades gazed at their approaching enemies with somber expressions.

He felt a presence at his side. "Joshua."

He turned at the sound of Pacumeni's voice. Beneath a helmet adorned with golden-green quetzal feathers, Pacumeni's eyes flickered. His armor of quilted kapok lifted and fell as he breathed, and his shield, emblazoned with the crest of the chief judge, glimmered in the gloom.

"Pacumeni."

"What will become of our people?" Pacumeni asked. "Will the Lamanites spare Elizabeth and my son?" He gazed out over the shadowed plains as he spoke, his eyes on the approaching horde.

"Zeram and Tuloth will protect them."

Pacumeni's chest heaved. "If I die in this—"

"You won't die, Pacumeni."

Pacumeni did not turn his head, and continued as if he had not heard. "Know this, Joshua. You have my blessing, if Elizabeth's heart one day—"

"Enough!" Joshua seethed with such quiet fury that Pacumeni fell silent. "As this earth endures, you will live to marry her. I swear it."

Pacumeni turned, his eyes meeting Joshua's at last. "Take care what oaths you make, my friend. For the Father of us all rules this earth you swear by, and you do not know the end from the beginning, as He does."

"I *will* keep you safe," Joshua insisted. "If one of us dies, it will be me. I will not fail you. Or Elizabeth."

"Her mourning would be no less if you were slain, Joshua."

"She would mourn me as she would the loss of a good friend. Nothing more."

"Friend?" Pacumeni chuckled dryly. "You say the word as if you have no understanding of its strength. A friend is a treasure greater than all the wealth in the world. True love for a woman always grows from genuine regard. It cannot come any other way."

Joshua dropped his gaze.

"I would ask you to promise me something," Pacumeni said.

"Anything."

Pacumeni reached out and grasped Joshua's shoulder, turning him so that the two men faced each other fully. "Give me a brother's oath that if you live and I die, you will one day tell Elizabeth your true feelings for her."

Joshua winced at the words and tried to pull away, but Pacumeni's grip tightened, firm as steel.

"Joshua!" Pacumeni begged, his eyes like those of a doomed man pleading for his life. "Please!"

Joshua relented. "There is no need, Pacumeni, but for your sake—" He reached up and grasped Pacumeni's shoulder in return. He heaved a deep sigh. "You have my oath."

A breath escaped Pacumeni's chest, and his eyes filled with gratitude. "Thank you."

Joshua nodded.

Their hands fell, and together they turned to gaze across the balustrade and over the darkening plains as the Lamanites marched ever nearer.

"Jonas!" Elizabeth wailed. A maze of narrow streets surrounded her, hemming her in between rows of decrepit houses. Hollow windows gaped at her like lifeless skulls. The pathways here twined about in maddening disorder, now rising up a set of broken steps, now down a narrow passage where the walls blocked out all but a strip of sky.

Elizabeth found herself alone. The clumps of women and children she had encountered at first had all gone. None had seen Jonas, and only silence filled the air.

Elizabeth's heart leaped in her throat at a choking, gasping sound, and a large woman, clad in a tattered robe, lumbered around a corner. A heavy pack across the woman's back swayed as she clumped along.

"Please." Elizabeth grasped the woman's fleshy arm. "I'm lost, and I—"

"The plaza is this way!" the woman said. "You must come too."

"I'm looking for a small boy of about five years," Elizabeth insisted, her fingers tightening. "Have you seen one?"

"No!" The frightened woman wrenched her arm from Elizabeth's hold. "I've seen no children. I must go!"

"Please! Will you not help me?"

But the woman did not turn back, and disappeared around a jutting stone wall.

Her heart weighted with despair, Elizabeth turned and hurried on. "Jonas!" Her voice echoed off the walls of crumbling stone. Oh, she should not have put him down!

She stumbled to a halt where the corner of a stone building spotted with lichen split the pathway in two. To the right, the narrow walkway ran in a long, straight line before bending again. To the left, the pathway curved around a wall, disappearing from her sight.

"Which way?" She drew in a breath and turned left. Her feet tapped on the worn paving stones as she rounded the curved wall. Around the corner, crumbling steps fell sharply. Elizabeth teetered on the brink, but reached out and steadied herself. Carefully, she clambered down the steep, broken steps to the pathway below, deep fissures and empty spaces where paving stones used to be now filled with grass. Empty windows and looming doorways gaped at her.

"Jonas!" Her breath came in gasps as despair clawed at her.

But then a faint sound met her ears, and her head snapped up. The despair shrank back, and a shard of desperate hope thrust into her heart as a weak cry found its way from a shadowed alcove between two buildings. "Elizabeth?"

She darted toward it, vaulted across a gap where a paving block was missing, and stumbled against the corner of the narrow alley. Her gaze alighted on a small figure huddled against one wall, cradling his ankle.

"Jonas!" The word came out in a relieved sob as she tumbled to her knees and caught him up into her arms, clutching him close and pressing a fierce kiss to his brow. Bloody scrapes covered his knees and the palms of his hands, and a wicked gash scraped across one cheek.

"Elizabeth," he sobbed, his arms tight around her neck.

"Jonas." She gulped, touching fingers to his bleeding cheek. "What happened?"

Jonas winced. "I fell down the steps!"

"But why did you run away?"

Jonas's lower lip trembled. "I want Abba."

Just as quickly, her relief melted into tears. "Oh, Jonas. I know you do. So do I."

A soft sound behind Elizabeth caused her to start. She spun to see Zeram's silhouette, blocking the alley's mouth.

"Here you are!" Zeram's chest heaved beneath his armor as he looked down at them, frustration and anxiety etching his face, his helmet gone.

"Zeram," she gasped, relieved.

"We have to go back!" He strode toward the two of them. His face held a stern expression until his gaze fell to the boy in her arms and traveled over the scrapes, resting on the little boy's discolored ankle.

"What happened?" He dropped to his knees beside Elizabeth and reached out, cupping his fingers under the boy's leg just above the swollen bruising.

"I was running," Jonas's voice jerked, "and I fell down some stairs I did not see."

Zeram palpated the bruised skin. "You're too fast for your own good, Jonas," he joked, to which the little boy managed a smile.

"No bones are broken, but it's a bad sprain," Zeram said, and stood. "He shouldn't put weight on it. He needs it to be wrapped, and he needs herbs for the swelling. I have none, but even if I did, we have no time. We must return to the plaza."

Elizabeth nodded. She grasped Zeram's proffered hand and clambered to her feet, then stooped and lifted Jonas from the ground.

At that moment, a distant roar rolled over them, as if the very clouds were alive and angry. A low rumble trembled through the stones beneath them like a mild earthquake, passing as quickly as it came. Jonas buried his head against her throat.

A desperate fear rose within Elizabeth. "Zeram—"

Another vibration trembled through the earth. "Battering ram," Zeram said. "They're at the south gate now."

"Pacumeni is there." A third vibration trembled up through Elizabeth's legs. "And Joshua." Her heart felt ripped in two.

"Come on!" Zeram pulled her back the way they had come, Jonas's arms clinging about her neck.

Chapter 7

Despair tore into Joshua's heart like sharp claws. But he clenched his teeth, determined to stave off his terror. The crackle of fires near and far filled his senses. He coughed fiercely against the bitter smoke as he turned one way, then the other. Shattering wood and the screams of men echoed in his mind as the memory of Lamanites pouring through the broken gate came back to him.

An indistinct shape, as if called to life by his thoughts, lunged at him through the smoke. Joshua raised his shield a moment before a heavy wooden cudgel smashed into it, sending him stumbling backward. Recovering from the blow, he lunged forward and shoved his shield into his enemy's chest. With a cry of anger and surprise, the man tripped over the body of one of his fallen comrades and tumbled to the street.

Joshua gulped in a breath of burning air and glanced at his comrades on his left and right. The city's east wall rose through the smoke-choked air not far to Joshua's left.

Several steps away, a rope seller's stall had been torn down, the table overturned, various lengths of cord scattered about like crushed snakes. Pacumeni struggled to find his footing amongst the tangled mounds of rope as he traded blows with another foe. Lines of sweat streaked through layers of ash and blood that caked his skin. Cracks and dents covered his battered shield. His helmet, like Joshua's, had been torn away and lost in the confusion.

At a roar of fury, Joshua spun back, meeting the angry eyes of his opponent, who had scrambled to his feet. Joshua blocked the man's blow, and with a fierce thrust, his blade found an unguarded spot. The man's eyes flew open in shock, then dimmed. He crumpled, his unseeing eyes gazing up at the colorless sky.

For a fleeting moment, Joshua studied his face—a man no different than he, as frightened by the thought of death as Joshua, compelled here by whatever promises or threats his overlords had given him.

Joshua had no time to feel sorrow or relief, for an angry howl shattered the air as a new enemy came at him, the man's face twisted with rage, a wicked-looking axe in his fist.

Clenching his teeth, Joshua lifted his shield, battering aside the blow that would have been his death, and thrust his blade forward, feeling it punch through soft flesh. This man, like his comrade before him, groaned and crumpled to the street.

Joshua clenched his sword in his fist, the blade already darkened with the blood of more men than he wished to count. His body burned with exhaustion, and his weary thoughts gave him no strength. As his eyes flashed about, his exhaustion vanished as he saw his friend's danger.

Two Lamanites had come at Pacumeni at once. The young chief judge battered aside the blade of one warrior with his shield and sliced his sword into the man's side. The man fell, but his comrade, all the more enraged, smashed his cudgel into Pacumeni's battered shield. The sweat-drenched limbs of the Lamanite gleamed in the mottled light of distant fire as he swung his club into Pacumeni's shield again and again. Nearly beaten to his knees, Pacumeni still managed to push past the Lamanite's defenses and caught an unguarded spot upon the man's thigh. The man howled and staggered, but did not fall. With a roar of rage, he raised his left arm and slammed his shield into the side of Pacumeni's head.

Reeling, Pacumeni tumbled to the paving stones. Above him, the Lamanite raised his heavy cudgel over his head, unaware of Joshua's nearing footsteps.

Joshua's blade found its mark, and the man's weapon tumbled to the earth. With a soft moan, the Lamanite crumpled to the ground and did not move again.

"Pacumeni!" Joshua dropped to the ground where Pacumeni lay gasping and dazed, a gash on the side of his head dripping blood.

Joshua grinned. "Come, Pacumeni." He reached down a hand.

Pacumeni reached up as if groping in the dark, and Joshua clasped his forearm.

"Thanks," Pacumeni gasped, leaning heavily on Joshua as he staggered to his feet. Once upright, Pacumeni wavered, struggling to balance himself. He touched a hand to his head and drew it away, blinking as he struggled to focus on his bloody fingers.

"Pick up your sword, Pacumeni," Joshua said. "We still have work to do."

As a dark chuckle rolled through the smoky air, Joshua's smile died.

He spun toward the sound as a man clad in the garb of a Lamanite overlord materialized through the wafting smoke like a sinister apparition, stepping over the men who lay dead and dying around him without even looking down.

Joshua clenched his blade with stony determination, realizing with a sinking heart that he and Pacumeni were alone. Their comrades had fled or fallen. Flames lit the man's face as he came to a stop several paces from the two Nephites. He wore a breastplate covered over with a swirl of blood-caked feathers. In one hand, he held a Nephite-forged sword, dark with blood. His damp hair clung against his scalp, his face covered in pale scruff.

Joshua's lips drew back from his teeth in disgust. A dissenter.

"I am Coriantumr," the man said, his eyes burning into Pacumeni, "lord of these bold Lamanites. And I've been searching for you, Chief Judge Pacumeni."

"A pity, Lord Coriantumr." Joshua strode forward to place himself between the dissenter and Pacumeni, "for you have come in vain. You won't harm him while I live."

The man turned upon Joshua, disdain in his cold blue eyes. "Very well." He lifted his blade.

Joshua clenched his jaw as he lifted his shield and took a step forward. But instead of meeting his challenge, Coriantumr fell back a step, nearer to the empty shops. Joshua advanced again only to have Coriantumr fall back several steps more.

Joshua narrowed his eyes. *Why would Coriantumr challenge him, only to retreat?* He shot a fleeting glance at Pacumeni.

Something moved in the corner of his eye. Joshua's attention jerked back as the dissenter snatched up a crumpled coil of rope, flinging it with a grunt.

Like a heavy snake, the coils of rope tumbled over Joshua's head and shoulders, tangling his arms in a heavy, blinding net. He staggered back, desperately trying to fling off the bulky mass, but a moment later, a burning fire lanced into his side, sending shards of agony slicing across his chest. An involuntary wail of pain burst from his lungs. His sword dropped from his hand and clattered to the stones as the thick cording crumpled to the ground.

"Joshua!" Pacumeni's voice pierced the haze of pain enveloping Joshua's thoughts.

Coriantumr jerked his blade free from the gap in Joshua's armor beneath his right arm. Another strangled cry tore from Joshua's lungs. Fresh red blood colored the gleaming metal.

My blood.

Time slowed. Warm wetness spread down Joshua's side. He tried to take a step and stumbled over the crumpled rope at his feet. His legs buckled and he fell to his knees. With weighted effort, he lifted his eyes. Coriantumr raised his blade, grinning like a demon.

The memory of sunlight on Elizabeth's hair danced across Joshua's memory. Her laughter echoed in his thoughts. He wondered how it would have felt to hold her in his arms, to feel her softness against him, to see love in her eyes, to taste the sweetness of her lips—

As the Nephite dissenter's blade began to swing down, a crash and a burst of sparks shattered the air above Joshua's face.

Coriantumr's eyes jerked away as Pacumeni lunged into Joshua's vision, his blade and Coriantumr's throwing sparks as they struck again.

"Leave him!" Pacumeni yelled, thrusting Coriantumr back. "I'm the one you want!"

A furious clatter of weapons followed. Joshua willed himself to rise, to do his duty. His body refused to obey, and even as he struggled to stand, he crumpled to the unforgiving stones.

Darkness pushed against the edges of his thoughts. Across a vast chasm, he heard Pacumeni shout, "He's nothing to you, son of Belial! Come after me!"

The clash of blades ceased. A pair of feet pounding against the stones faded away in the direction of the eastern wall before another set of feet dashed off after the first.

"No!" Joshua groaned. Despair filled his heart. Pacumeni was leading Coriantumr away to protect him! This should not be! Gritting his teeth, Joshua struggled again to push himself up. He did not heed the crimson pool that puddled beneath him, the sticky warmth that soaked his trembling fingers. He had to protect the chief judge. The man Elizabeth loved. His friend. His *brother*!

Against his will, Joshua's elbows buckled. His body struck the ground, his cheek scraping stone. Lights burst before his vision, and all plunged into darkness.

⊏⋈⋈⊐

Elizabeth studied Jonas's ankle, swollen now where his legs dangled over her arm. Tears of pain dampened his eyes, but Jonas did not weep aloud. He had inherited his father's strength.

"You're so brave, Jonas," she praised, a faint smile touching her lips despite the fear in her heart as she followed Zeram along the winding alley lined with crumbling buildings.

Here and there, a torn awning jutted out over the pathway. A stray monkey, confused at the absence of people, screeched at their coming before it darted away. The stone walls rose high above their heads. The gray clouds claimed only a narrow strip of sky, casting the alley into deep shadow.

Faint echoes met her ears as if carried through the very stones beneath their feet, and distant shrieks mingled with the clash of weapons. She glanced behind as they went, her eyes lifting toward the sky and the flicker of red that reflected off the bellies of the clouds. The sharp scent of ash stung her nostrils.

Somewhere in the midst of the battle, Pacumeni and Joshua fought for their lives. A throb of helpless agony smote her heart.

Jonas needed her, and Zeram, as brave as he strove to be, needed her strength also. But what strength had she to give?

Zeram glanced back, his boyish face furrowed with worry.

"We're almost there," he promised. "We'll be safe when we reach the plaza."

Elizabeth nodded, desperately needing to believe his words. Zeram turned forward again as the path bent around the crumbling corner of an ancient building. Ahead of them, the narrow alley opened onto a wider street that seemed empty but for a few overturned baskets.

Zeram turned back to her, tentative hope in his eyes. "I think I remember this way." He turned forward again, but had not taken more than three steps before he sucked in a sharp breath.

"Elizabeth, get down!" He grasped her arm, pushing her to her knees behind a mound of broken baskets piled against the stone wall beside them. His fumbling hand grasped the hilt of his sword and drew it forth with a metallic hiss.

Elizabeth's heart stopped at the sound of voices coming from just beyond the corner where the alley ended. They did not speak in the Nephite tongue.

Elizabeth stiffened. Jonas's arm tensed about her neck. A group of men strode into view, crossing the mouth of the alleyway where the three crouched like frightened tapirs behind the mound of broken baskets.

The columns of Lamanites seemed endless as they crossed the alley's narrow mouth, their hair bound on the tops of their heads and cropped short. Each man carried a bow across his back and a quiver of arrows, as well as a wooden scimitar edged with blades of obsidian.

Elizabeth waited, tense, hoping they would soon be gone, but when they slowed, then stopped, her heart sank like a leaden weight.

She glanced at Zeram, meeting his uncertain gaze.

Several warriors shifted and turned, observing what seemed to be a scuffle behind them. Four soldiers came forward, revealing the cause for their delay—a pair of bound Nephite soldiers who struggled against their captors.

Ropes lashed both Nephites' arms behind their backs, yet they still jerked against their bonds, one Nephite soldier cursing his captors. A Lamanite shoved the soldier in the back, sending him sprawling, unable to catch himself.

"No! Leave him alone!" his companion barked in the Lamanite tongue, but this did not keep the Lamanite from giving the downed soldier a vicious kick in the side.

Elizabeth's heart seemed to stop. She recognized the pair.

"Nephi!" Zeram hissed. A gash slashed down Nephi's cheek, oozing blood. The youth sprawled on the ground was Abram.

"I tire of these foolish pups!" one of the Lamanites barked as he strode forward, jerking a short blade from his belt. He put a foot on Abram's back, the youth still struggling beneath him. "They have slowed us enough. Let me silence them both."

"Hold, Katar," one of the other men said. "You remember the orders. Slay none who do not oppose us, nor any of these helpless children the Nephite savages recklessly sent to battle. Taking their weapons was no more troublesome than taking a stick from an infant."

The man called Katar snorted. "Coriantumr, the pale-skinned fool. I spit on his orders."

"Coriantumr did not give those orders," his comrade said. "They came from—"

The man's words cut short as his eyes fixed upon something beyond Katar's shoulder. In an instant, he straightened his back and grew silent. Katar turned and followed his comrade's gaze, then drew in a hasty breath. Reaching down, he seized Abram's arm and wrenched him up. Elizabeth winced at the gash on Abram's cheek as he staggered, barely able to stand.

"What is the trouble?" a deep voice asked. "The prisoners must be gathered."

A new figure strode into view, his back to Elizabeth. A man of high rank, she guessed, from the deference the other men showed to him.

The corded muscles of his shoulders and back shifted beneath his skin as he lifted his great scimitar and rested the flat of it against his shoulder.

"Yes—yes, sir," Katar stammered, "but this brace of whelps has fought us the whole way. They've been nothing but a burden, and—"

"Then a burden they will be," the captain cut him off.

The Lamanite captain turned to Nephi now. "Your city is taken," he said, his accent thick as he struggled with the Nephite tongue. "You have lost. There is no need to fight against us."

"You are the ones fighting against us!" Nephi spat in the tongue of the Lamanites.

A swell of bitter pride rose in Elizabeth's heart at how fluidly the words fell from his lips.

"We mean only to defend our families and our homes! You have—"

"Listen to me, boy," the Lamanite captain cut in, speaking now in his own tongue as well. He lowered his scimitar so the point touched the ground. "Your elders are either dead or captured. Your city is in our hands. Your struggles will do you no good. I will do what I can to see that you and your comrade are treated justly, but I cannot protect you against your own foolishness!"

Nephi clenched his teeth, his lips bared as he glared up into the eyes of the Lamanite.

For a moment, the Lamanite glowered down upon the angry youth like a brooding shadow before his features eased. "Tell me your name." His words sounded stern, but not harsh.

Elizabeth frowned. Her eyes fell to the weapon the Lamanite clutched in his hand, noting the dulled coloring where blood had dried on the wood. He was her enemy, yet even so, Elizabeth could sense a quiet strength in the man that puzzled her.

"Nephi, son of Helaman," Nephi said. "I am an enlisted soldier. I serve under—"

"I did not ask whom you served under," the Lamanite cut in. He stepped forward as if studying Nephi's face with greater care. "What is your mother's name?"

Nephi's features hardened. "If you mean harm to her, I swear I—"

"On my honor, I will not allow any of your women or children to be mistreated."

Nephi's chest heaved. His glaring eyes moved from the Lamanite captain to the soldiers about him to Abram's bleeding face.

"If you have honor," Nephi spoke through clenched teeth, "you will know why I will never tell you my mother's name."

The Lamanite seemed to contemplate Nephi's words as he drew a deep breath.

He turned and stepped toward Abram. "And you, boy? What is your name and rank?"

Abram spat in the man's face. "Worthless savage."

Katar cursed and slammed his fist into Abram's stomach. The boy doubled and dropped to his knees, gasping. Katar lifted his fist to bring it down on Abram's head.

"Hold!" The captain caught Katar's wrist with one hand. "Do not strike him again!"

Katar pulled his hand back, astonished. "But he just—"

"I said," the captain lifted his hand, wiping away the spittle from his face, "do not strike him."

"My name is Abram, son of Moshen," Abram said, and wheezed. "Same rank and squad as Nephi." He lifted his head, and his eyes burned into the Lamanite's. "If you ask my mother's name, I will tear your throat out!"

"Peace, Abram," Nephi said in his own tongue. "I think their captain wants to show us mercy. But don't aggravate them beyond need,"

"How do you know? Why would he even ask—?"

"I don't know. Just...trust God. It's all we can do now."

At this, the Lamanite narrowed his eyes. "You worship the god of the Nephites, boy?"

Drawing in a deep breath, Nephi met the man's eyes. "Yes."

"Why?" The captain stepped nearer.

"Because He lives." Nephi's voice grew firm. "And your gods are only lifeless stone."

Beside Nephi, Katar snarled, but the captain held out a hand, subduing Katar's anger.

"You speak bold words for a boy bound and weaponless."

"My words are true," Nephi said, unwavering. "I do not fear to speak them."

Fear and pride swelled in Elizabeth's heart at the youth's courageous words.

Against her shoulder, Jonas whimpered. At the faint sound, Nephi's eyes flickered past the Lamanite and into the alley.

Nephi's eyes narrowed as his gaze came to rest upon the small group crouched behind the mound of baskets. Then, comprehending what he saw, his eyes widened. A look of warning flashed in his eyes.

The muscles in the Lamanite captain's back stiffened at the change upon Nephi's face.

The man began to turn, and Zeram snatched Elizabeth's hand yanking her to her feet. She glanced back, and caught a glimpse of half of the man's face before Zeram jerked her around the corner, and the wall hid the man from view.

"Hurry!" Zeram hissed.

Elizabeth obeyed, clutching Jonas tightly as she dashed behind Zeram down the alley, her last image of the Lamanite burned into her thoughts. His face had been lined with age, but still strong. Stern, but not cruel. And something about him seemed strangely familiar. As if she had known him long ago, in a time before memory. But it was impossible. She had never seen the man before in her life.

She pushed the thought from her mind, and continued to run.

Chapter 8

The thrust of Coriantumr's sword shoved Pacumeni backward. The pain in his abdomen ripped through him like a blade of fire. His back struck the hard stone of the city wall behind him, his head snapping back and cracking against the unyielding rock. His sword clattered at his feet, falling from numb fingers.

Pacumeni struggled to gasp in a breath. He tasted blood in his mouth. His blurring vision fell to the sword blade buried halfway to the hilt in his abdomen. He blinked heavily and looked up into the sneering face of his foe. Blood seeped through the armor over Coriantumr's left shoulder. A trickle of blood oozed down the dissenter's leg. Pacumeni smiled.

The traitor snarled and wrenched the blade out of Pacumeni's body with a cruel twist. Pain tore through him again, and a grunt burst past his lips as his legs buckled. The rough stone of the wall grated against Pacumeni's armor as he slid to the ground. He pressed a trembling hand against his side, and warm wetness soaked his fingers.

Pacumeni drew in a short breath and looked away from his looming foe. His thoughts turned to Elizabeth. The feel of her supple form in his arms, the warm stirrings he felt when he held her—longings he once thought had died with his beloved Keturah—all returned now with excruciating clarity. He imagined Elizabeth's unbound hair in his hands once more, and he tasted again the warmth of her fervent mouth as it responded to his own.

For a moment, a wave of despair seized him, and he wanted to weep. She would never truly be his now, would never lie in his arms beneath the stars, would never bear his children... Yet the swell of misery ebbed as another thought entered his mind, cooling his soul like a pleasant breeze.

"Love *is* stronger than evil."

He drew in a broken breath.

"Joshua," he whispered. "Take care of her."

With these words, Pacumeni closed his eyes, and another beloved face took form in his thoughts. Her hair flowed like liquid obsidian about her slender shoulders. Her eyes, pools of quiet wisdom, gleamed in welcome. She moved toward him, growing clearer as she came, clothed in a gown as bright as the sun.

"Pacumeni," she called, her voice sweet, like music. Her hand stretched toward him.

"Keturah," he murmured between cracked lips.

He reached out, and Keturah grasped his hand, drawing him to his feet.

The wall at his back and the burning pain of the sword that had pierced through him faded. The heaviness of his broken body disappeared.

"I've missed you," he said.

Her eyes gleamed. "I've missed you too."

Pacumeni pulled her close, and Keturah melted into his arms.

Coriantumr stared at the body crumpled at the base of the city wall. Serenity rested on the dead Nephite's face, filling Coriantumr with rage as if the corpse at his feet had claimed the victory instead.

What was he muttering before he died? It didn't matter.

With a snort, he kicked the dead man's shoulder, trying to banish the sense of unease. The body crumpled to the side.

He wiped the blood from his blade on the hem of his kilt, then clapped his sword into its sheath.

"Fool," he said as he turned to stagger away.

Coriantumr's voice echoed off the walls about him, and he shuddered at the coldness of the sound. The fires had died; the smoke dissipated. Evening fell and heavy clouds lowered over the city, draping the streets in a thickening silver mist. He could not see beyond a few paces. He shuddered, imagining the eyes of so many tormented ghosts watching him, the spirits of the Nephites he had slain, or his own men he had sent to their deaths. He pushed away the thoughts as he moved on, the mist opening and then closing behind him like a heavy curtain when he passed.

Fallen warriors—most of them Lamanites—materialized like dark shadows, unmoving against the paving stones.

One figure, clad in the armor of a Nephite, lay apart from the others.

He drew near to the man—the guard who had fallen trying to protect the chief judge. A sneer spread across Coriantumr's lips as he stood over the body, wondering if he should stab him again.

He nudged the body with his boot. The limp form did not move.

The man was already dead. "Just as well," he muttered. Coriantumr's bones ached with weariness, and, too tired to draw his blade forth again, he turned to stagger away.

Something moved out of the corner of his eye, and Coriantumr jerked back, his eyes fixing upon the dead Nephite. Had the fallen warrior's hand twitched?

Coriantumr heaved a sigh and relaxed. No, it was nothing but the mist playing tricks on his mind. He turned again, and staggered away.

A heavy weariness pulled at Shemnon as he trudged across the plaza, studying the pattern of stones beneath his feet. The tiles fit precisely, stone against stone, no mortar between them. Such patience and skill it must have taken.

"Captain!"

He looked up to see a small group of his men striding near, a bound prisoner between them. His eyes met those of the prisoner, and he drew in a long breath. But for the man's long hair falling to his shoulders and his Nephite garb, this prisoner could have been one of Shemnon's own comrades.

The man appeared a little older than the youthful soldiers flanking him, but still young; perhaps near Talilia's age. He stood erect, his shoulders thick beneath the tunic he wore. Though no warrior, the man was still used to hard work. His dark eyes fixed upon Shemnon's face.

"This is the *Ammonite.*" Katar spat the word. "You wished to speak to him."

"Indeed," Shemnon said. "I thank you for bringing him."

Katar nodded and stepped back, releasing the prisoner, who remained where he stood.

"Since I first came to this plaza, I have wished to speak with you." Shemnon stepped forward.

The man lifted his chin. "Then speak."

"You are a riddle to me," Shemnon said. "You dress in the manner of these ill-gotten dogs, yet your accent gives you away as one raised to manhood in our lands. And you do not fight. Only the fathers of those who followed the Nephite preachers so many years ago gave up their weapons. You are the age of their sons who made no promise. Why do you bear no arms? Who are you, and who are your kin?"

"I am Tuloth," the young man said, his voice deep and even. "My father was Zadock, son of Jath of Shemlon. My mother was Shala, daughter of Tahir of Shemlon. They have both been dead since my childhood. My mother bore no other children alive, and I have no other kin. I was a Lamanite warrior once, yet I am no longer. I have learned the skills of a healer so I may be of use to this people. I have made an oath to God never to shed the blood of His children again."

"You worship the god of the Nephites?"

"If you call Him that," Tuloth murmured. "But He is not the god of the Nephites alone." He stepped forward, his eyes burning into Shemnon's face, "And these people are not ill-gotten. You have been taught a lie."

Shemnon narrowed his eyes. *The impertinence.* What did this defenseless boy think kept Shemnon from striking him across the face?

Tuloth's eyes did not waver, and Shemnon looked away. He knew what stayed his hand. Foolish or not, this boy had courage.

"That is enough." Shemnon nodded to Katar and his fellows, who stepped forward and took the man's arms again. Shemnon met Tuloth's even gaze.

"I may speak to you again," Shemnon said. "For now, you may treat your wounded—and ours."

Tuloth nodded.

Katar turned him away, and Tuloth obeyed without argument.

"Katar," Shemnon called.

The young Lamanite turned back.

"See that the prisoners are fed. The women and children first."

"Yes, sir." Katar saluted, and with the other guards, he led Tuloth away.

As they marched off, a small voice spoke to Shemnon's left. "Why are you doing this to us?"

He turned toward a group of women and children huddled around one of the many fires he had ordered his men to kindle. A young boy sat upon the ground staring at him. He resembled the youth named Nephi Shemnon had questioned earlier. Shemnon withdrew a step, shame washing over his heart. What answer could he give the child?

"Don't worry, Lehi," a woman said, circling an arm about the boy's shoulder, turning him away from Shemnon's stare. The mother turned now and studied Shemnon, lifting her chin. Though her city had fallen, her husband likely slain, she would not let him frighten her or hurt her child. Shemnon glanced down at his scimitar in his right hand and squeezed the solid, comfortable shaft. The obsidian blade glimmered in the firelight. He looked back at the woman, her glare still unbroken. Her countenance reminded him of a queen, unbending and fearless.

Shemnon turned and strode away, keeping his eyes fixed forward as the glow of fires and the huddled forms of prisoners flickered past him. He could hear the whispers among them. Soft sobs scattered here and there, and he dared not meet their eyes. He kept his gaze fixed on the base of a wide set of steps that led up to a structure that took up one full side of the plaza. Around the fire there, a small group of officers sat with Coriantumr at their head. They all feasted on the meat of a duck. Another duck roasted on a spit.

The savory scent found his nostrils, and Shemnon's stomach grumbled, reminding him that he had not eaten in more than a day. Despite this, he hesitated before moving forward.

"Captain Shemnon!" Coriantumr called. "You have fulfilled your duties?"

"The gates are posted with sufficient guards, my lord," Shemnon answered. "None will enter or leave this city without their say."

"Sir!" One of the younger officers leaped to his feet, swiping at his mouth with the back of his hand. "Take my seat." The young officer gestured to his vacated spot beside another warrior who knelt, spearing the second roasted duck onto a wide, flat leaf. "There is plenty."

Shemnon licked his lips at the crisp, roasted meat, but he felt the presence of the prisoners huddled across the plaza behind him like a cold wind at his back, and a fist of guilt settled in his stomach, pushing away his hunger.

"Thank you, Koreb," he said.

With reluctance, he sat across from Coriantumr and folded his legs. He studied the overlord's eyes as they reflected the flames. Blood smeared Coriantumr's armor, discoloring the bright feathers, matting them together. A wound in his shoulder had caked over with blood, and dried blood trailed down one leg. Whoever his foes had been, they had fought well.

Malevolence shot from Coriantumr's eyes as Shemnon met his gaze. "Their chief judge lies dead against the eastern wall," Coriantumr declared through mouthfuls of meat.

The other warriors murmured approval at the news.

Coriantumr straightened his back. "And now I have but to fetch his head back as my trophy, and set it on a pike."

Shemnon's throat tightened at Coriantumr's words.

Coriantumr's sneer twisted. "You disapprove?"

"It would not be seemly to show him such dishonor."

"Gah!" Coriantumr flung the gnawed bones of a wing into the fire. "You and *honor*! I am sick of that word! Honor is but another word for cowardice! It makes a man weak!"

Shemnon noted the silent faces of the officers, who stopped eating. They looked from Coriantumr to him, awaiting his reply. "It is only a *lack* of honor that weakens a man."

"He's dead, you old bear! He doesn't care what happens to him now!"

"He led his men against impossible odds. He was a worthy foe. For his people to see his severed head displayed so would—"

"You speak like one who has no loyalty for his own people." Coriantumr sneered.

"Do not distort my words," Shemnon spat. "I am loyal to my people."

"Prove it." Coriantumr surveyed each of the faces of the subdued officers. His expression grew sinister. "Fetch the head of their leader for me."

Shemnon's chest clenched. "My lord, do not ask me—"

"I am not asking. King Tubaloth gave *me* command of these armies. Thus, all are beneath me, including you. I have given you an order."

Shemnon rose to his feet, rancor boiling in his heart.

"Do you wish to take refreshment before you do your duty?" Coriantumr asked, his mocking tone scraping across Shemnon's skin like claws.

"No." Turning, Shemnon stalked away into the darkness. Coriantumr's chuckle faded behind him.

Thick haze lingered in the air about Elizabeth where she huddled with Jonas and Zeram in the storeroom of a small pottery shop. Night had fallen while they had hidden here listening to the tramp of Lamanite patrols. They had not been discovered, and only heavy silence hung over them now. Elizabeth could not say which she feared more—the marching feet of the Lamanites, or this unnatural stillness that lingered over the foggy streets. Through a crack in the doorway, Elizabeth could see the massive east wall, a shadow in the darkness, fading into the gray nothingness of the mist.

Jonas's weary head lay against her breast. Though he did not speak, the tension in his little body betrayed his pain. She bit her lip, wishing she could do more for him than she had already done. Frayed threads hung from the bottom of her skirt where she had torn away a strip for Zeram to wrap around the boy's ankle, hoping that the pressure would keep the swelling down. But they could do little else.

A scraping sound beside her seemed amplified in the silence, and Elizabeth jerked before she realized the sound came from Zeram, who scooted toward the doorway and peeked out. He glanced one way and then the other before he drew back again and leaned his back against the wall. His arms circled his drawn-up knees and his head sagged wearily.

"What are we to do, Zeram?" Elizabeth asked.

"I don't know," Zeram returned. Sweat trailed like tears down his cheeks. "But we won't go back, not to the plaza." He lifted his head with a sudden thought. "If we got past the east gate, took the road to Gideon—"

His words ended, and his head drooped. "Lamanites will be guarding the east gate," he said.

Fear shrouded Elizabeth's heart at the thought. They could not get out, yet they could not hide from the Lamanites forever.

"We must do something," she whispered. "We cannot stay here."

"You're right." With a grunt, Zeram staggered to his feet, then offered her his hand.

Taking it, she struggled to her feet, burdened beneath Jonas' weight and the stiffness of her long immobility.

"Come on," Zeram whispered, his sword scraping from its sheath.

With Jonas in her arms, Elizabeth followed behind Zeram as he crept out of the dark and into the open street. Haze enfolded them, and she shivered. Elizabeth glanced about, imagining malignant shadows shifting about, just beyond the reach of her sight.

"Elizabeth, you're tired," Zeram said. "Let me carry Jonas."

"No. You might need to use your sword."

"The eastern wall is not far," Zeram said. "Perhaps there's some way over it. If we found a rope long enough…"

As they pushed their way farther, a shadow materialized, slumped motionless against the base of a low wall. As they neared, Elizabeth shuddered. The Lamanite did not appear young, yet he didn't seem very old, either.

Her foot struck something, and it gave a hollow rattle. The clattering object rolled to a stop in the middle of the lane. The long, hollow piece of wood prickled Elizabeth's memory.

"Wait," she demanded. Zeram stopped as Elizabeth dropped to one knee, shifting Jonas's weight to her hip. She picked up the small object. Her thumb caressed the length of the little flute, scratched as if it had been kicked or stepped on several times.

Elizabeth rose, contemplating the forlorn instrument that lay in her palm. Her heartstrings tightened in painful clarity.

Jonas lifted his head from her shoulder. "That's Abba's."

This *was* Pacumeni's flute. She could not mistake it.

She clutched it in her fist, her breath quickening. Would she find Pacumeni nearby, wounded and in need of her care? Her eyes darted about, straining to see.

"Elizabeth, what is it?" Zeram asked, drawing a step nearer.

She did not answer him as her eyes studied the city wall through the thick fog.

Beyond Zeram's shoulder, the mist parted for a moment, revealing the wall's base and the figure that lay there, his arm beneath his head as if he slept. Elizabeth's heart paused a beat, for though the figure appeared as little more than a shadow now, she knew his form as she knew her own soul.

Her legs trembled, and Zeram grasped her arms as if he feared she would drop Jonas.

"Elizabeth, what's wrong?"

"Look," she said, and Zeram turned his head. His eyes alighted on the figure, and he stiffened.

"Let me take Jonas." He shoved his sword back in its sheath.

This time, Elizabeth did not protest as Zeram took the little boy from her. Jonas shifted in Zeram's arms, but made no sound as Elizabeth scrambled toward the still figure.

The dusty ash that had settled upon Pacumeni's hair could not conceal the sheen of gold beneath it. He seemed only to sleep, as if he would awaken at any moment, his eyes filling with warmth, his hand lifting to touch her cheek.

Numbness spread from her core to her fingertips as she lowered herself to her knees at Pacumeni's side. She caught up his limp hand in hers and cradled it beneath her throat as she bent to press a kiss against his knuckles.

"Pacumeni," she murmured, "I'm here. We found your flute."

As she slipped the instrument into his unresponsive hand, several of her tears fell and struck against his cheek. Elizabeth brushed them away, leaving streaks in the ashy residue that had settled there. "Pacumeni?" She struggled to push away her pain, wishing to deny it forever.

"Elizabeth," Zeram muttered behind her. "I'm so sorry."

"*Abba?*"

Her heart tore at the confusion in Jonas's tone. She ran her thumb over Pacumeni's mouth before she bent over him and pressed her lips against his. They tasted of ash and dust, returning no warmth, no answering kiss, no soft breath. Trembling, she drew back.

Zeram's hand found her shoulder, but his touch did nothing to suppress the wild agony that burst from her like water through a shattered dam. With a wail that tore her soul, Elizabeth collapsed onto Pacumeni's body and sobbed into his chest.

Chapter 9

Chill air clung like spider webs to Shemnon's skin as the mist swirled about him. The outline of the city's eastern wall loomed through the fog as he strode toward it.

The gray clouds surrounding him recalled to his mind stories of demons who haunted the fields of battle, waiting to drag the souls of slain Nephites down into Xibalba, the underworld. Shemnon repressed a shudder.

The bruised face of the boy who called himself Nephi appeared in his mind, his arms weaponless and bound, his eyes void of fear as he defended his god. Then the face of the man Tuloth, who had once been a Lamanite, his arms also bound as he boldly defended the same god. The god Shemnon's mother had given up all she knew to follow after, taking Hana with her. What sort of god inspired such loyalty? Did the followers of such a god deserve to endure eternal punishment?

An eerie sound echoed through the mist. Shemnon stopped, his heart leaping in a spasm of fear and wonder, for the sound that found its way into his ears was not the wailing of demons, but the moan of a living man.

Shemnon turned and started toward the sound. The mist drew back, revealing burnt buildings and the motionless figures of dead warriors. He paused as he came to a cluster of fallen men, all of them Lamanites. He scanned the faces, his heart heavy with sorrow, until his eyes fell upon one figure—a young Nephite who lay apart from the others. Shemnon took a step. Had the Nephite's hand moved, or had the mist played a trick?

His throat dry, Shemnon moved near and dropped to one knee at the Nephite's side. The young man lay on his chest in a pool of clotted blood. Shemnon set his scimitar upon the paving stones next to him, pushed aside a tangle of heavy rope that lay on the ground beside the still form, and touched two fingers to the Nephite's throat.

A weak pulse beat against his fingertips. Shemnon's eyes moved to the man's face. He bore no resemblance to Hana, and he was too old to be the son of Talilia. What did Shemnon owe this Nephite? The gods would not punish him if he left the young warrior to his doom. Yet if he did not aide him, this weak pulse that beat against Shemnon's fingers would soon falter and cease.

Shemnon reached inside his supply pouch and withdrew a roll of thick bandaging.

At that moment, another sound echoed through the mist. Shemnon's head jerked up. He knew the sound too well—the keening of a woman's sobs.

▭⋈⋈▭

"Elizabeth," Zeram pleaded as she bent over Pacumeni, whose motionless chest was wet with her tears. "Someone might hear us. We have to go!"

Jonas clung to Pacumeni's arm, his little body jerking with sobs.

"We cannot just leave him here," Elizabeth pleaded. "And where is Joshua? He would not have left Pacumeni's side!" She gazed into the swathes of mist that shrouded all but the nearest objects from her view. "Zeram, what have they done to *him*?"

"I don't know. But we have to—"

The scuff of a footstep on stone cut off his words, and Zeram whirled toward the sound.

Elizabeth dropped Pacumeni's cold hand and scrambled to her feet, snatching up Jonas, who buried his face in her mantle. Through the mist, a shadow moved.

Zeram drew his sword.

The sound of the scraping blade hissed through the fog, and the blurred form hesitated, then continued to draw nearer.

"Stay back!" Zeram demanded in the Lamanite tongue.

But the figure continued forward, growing more distinct as the mist gave way.

A man grew clearer, his hair bound at the top of his head and cropped short like a sheaf of wheat. He bore a heavy burden in his arms, a slain warrior wrapped to the waist in a ragged cloak as if to shield him from cold. Elizabeth wondered as he came closer why he would be carrying such a burden. One of the Lamanite's own comrades, she thought. Perhaps a kinsman. But as the man materialized before them and studied them with impassive eyes, she realized that the warrior he carried was clad in the kilt and bound leather boots of a Nephite warrior.

Why would a Lamanite trouble himself with the body of a Nephite? Elizabeth's eyes shot to the Lamanite's face.

Her mouth fell open. Here stood the same Lamanite captain they had seen from their hiding place in the alley. The man's face bore the look of long years and unspoken pains, but he carried himself like a younger warrior, the sinews of his arms bulging against the weight of his silent charge.

As the Lamanite studied them, he shifted his burden, and the Nephite's head lolled in Elizabeth's direction.

Her heart stopped.

"*Joshua!*" she wailed, staggering forward a step.

Zeram shoved himself between Elizabeth and the Lamanite, stiff with fury. "You pig-eater!" he barked. "Put him down!"

Zeram's words struck the Lamanite like stones, and the man fell back a pace. Elizabeth's arms tightened around Jonas and she flinched, fearing the Lamanite's backlash, but the man's expression remained stolid as he lowered himself to one knee, laying Joshua's limp form on the paving stones near the base of a low wall.

The Lamanite rose again, his gaze fixed upon Zeram. He spoke in the Nephite tongue. "Put down your sword, boy, and hear my words."

Heedless of the Lamanite's command, Zeram lunged forward, his sword raised, poised to slice like a scythe down on the Lamanite's head.

The Lamanite's hand snatched the young Nephite's wrist and twisted, forcing him to spin around, his sword arm bent behind him.

Zeram released a sharp cry as the Lamanite shoved him, chest first, against a crumbling stone wall, wrenched his sword from his hand, and tossed it aside with a clatter.

"Leave him alone!" Elizabeth cried in the Lamanite's tongue. She stepped forward, clutching Jonas. "Have you not killed enough men?"

The Lamanite's eyes shot to her. His gaze flicked from her to the child in her arms and back again.

"How does a Nephite woman speak...?" He cast the unfinished question aside and continued, "I have no desire to harm this mewling cub. I wish only to speak as men speak, one to another."

"You have nothing to say to me!" Zeram snarled, fighting to get free. "You killed Joshua! Go back to the cesspit that spawned you!"

"Foolish whelp," the Lamanite grunted, his grip tight on Zeram's arm. "He is not dead."

At this declaration, a shard of agonizing hope lanced through Elizabeth. Her eyes shot past the Lamanite toward Joshua. Shifting Jonas in her arms to shield the little boy from the Lamanite's gaze, she scrambled past the man, drawing closer to Joshua.

"Joshua?" Elizabeth collapsed to her knees at his side. She drew back the folds of the worn cloak, fearing what she would see.

His armor and shirt were gone. A thick bandage encircled his torso, leaving his shoulders and upper chest exposed. Elizabeth's eyes moved to his expressionless face.

"*Joshua?*" She touched his cheek. Her breath paused as she felt the warmth of life beneath her fingers. Joshua stirred, turning toward her hand.

His lips moved, forming a single word— *Elizabeth*— though no sound came forth.

The shard of hope that had pierced her, twisted painfully, sending tears of bitter relief onto her cheeks.

"Joshua! I'm here, my friend. I'm here," she whispered, brushing a hand over his face.

Joshua's lips moved once again, and his chest swelled faintly.

"Zeram, this man spoke the truth." Elizabeth looked back. "Joshua is alive."

"What?" Zeram's struggles eased, and the Lamanite's grip relaxed.

"Your name is Zeram?" the Lamanite demanded.

"Zeram, son of Jacob," Zeram spat. "An enlisted soldier. I serve under Sergeant Levi of the tenth squad, eighth battalion of the city of Zarahemla."

"Is it an offense to ask your mother's name?"

Zeram snorted with contempt then growled, "It's Miriam."

"Ah." The Lamanite sounded disappointed.

"But she's far from here," Zeram snarled. "You can't hurt her."

"I have no wish to." The Lamanite released Zeram and stepped back.

Free from the man's hold, Zeram spun to face him, his eyes bright with wrath, his fingers opening and closing as if he wished to do battle with his bare fists. But instead, he turned from the Lamanite and scrambled toward Elizabeth, where he too dropped to his knees at Joshua's side.

"Joshua?" He touched a hand to his friend's throat, seeking his pulse. Then he turned back to the Lamanite, distrust tightening his features. "Why did you bind his wound?" he demanded.

The Lamanite's brow furrowed. "He would have died otherwise."

"Hours ago, you would have tried to kill him if you had met him in battle," Zeram shot back. "Why save him now?"

The Lamanite did not reply, and instead turned to Elizabeth, his gaze moving over both her and Jonas and lingering on the swell of Jonas's bandaged ankle, the purple bruising peeking from beneath the torn cloth.

"Your little one is injured," the Lamanite said, stepping nearer. "He needs the root of the jaguar paw to lessen the swelling, and it should be bound with thicker cloth."

"We have no such medicines, nor bandages," she murmured.

The Lamanite touched his hand to a pouch at his hip. "But I do."

"We don't need your help!" Zeram spat, rising to his feet and glaring at the Lamanite.

The Lamanite's jaw tightened, yet he spoke in even tones, "As you wish. The child will not die. I merely wanted to ease his suffering."

Turning away from Zeram's glare, he nodded to Jonas. "Your son is a brave boy."

"He is not my son." Her voice shook.

The Lamanite tilted his head.

"His mother died giving birth to him, and now—"

Her words cut off as a blade of fresh agony sliced into her heart.

"And now his father, too, is dead," the Lamanite finished for her, glancing toward Pacumeni's still form where it lay at the base of the wall. "The one for whom you were weeping. The ruler of your people."

The Lamanite turned back again, meeting Elizabeth's eyes. His dark eyes softened. "He was dear to you."

"They were betrothed," Zeram spat. "They were to wed in a month!"

"His name was Pacumeni," she choked. "I loved him."

Pity filled the Lamanite's eyes. Elizabeth turned away from him, fixing her gaze on the faint motion of Joshua's breathing. Her childhood friend lived, and her wounded heart clung to that one comfort.

"What do you mean to do with us?" Zeram demanded. "Take us back as your prisoners? Is that why you saved his life? Do you plan to offer him as a sacrifice later?"

"I have no wish to sacrifice anyone."

"Then what are your intentions for us?" Elizabeth asked.

The Lamanite hesitated. "I will do nothing to you."

"Nothing?"

"I have no reason to harm you," the old warrior said.

"You will leave us here?" she said.

"I will let you leave the city. After that," he waved his hand in weary dismissal, "you may go where you will."

Suspicion thickened Zeram's voice. "Why would you help us?"

The Lamanite heaved a breath. "The gods are drunk with blood, and you are no danger to me. Your comrade is injured, and *you*," he glowered at Zeram, "are a mere boy."

"I am a Nephite warrior," Zeram insisted. "And you are a—"

"I tore your weapon out of your hands and could have killed you if I wished, whelp," the Lamanite snapped. "Still your tongue,"

Zeram's jaw tightened, but he did not speak.

The Lamanite bent to retrieve Zeram's sword. He straightened, the blade grasped in his hand as he held it out, hilt first.

"You will need this."

With a scowl, Zeram took it from him, examining the blade as if he imagined some mischief done to it. Finding none, he glanced up at the warrior in disbelief.

"Why would you give this back to me?"

The Lamanite did not answer. Instead, he stepped around Elizabeth, lowered himself to one knee at Joshua's side, secured the cloak about him once more, and gathered the unconscious Nephite in his arms.

"Follow me," he commanded.

"Wait." Elizabeth rose, Jonas upon her hip. The Lamanite turned.

"What of Pacumeni?" She drew backward. "I won't leave him. If I do, his body will be desecrated by your people."

"On my honor, his body will not be harmed. I will see to it myself. I will bury his body where none can harm him or despoil him further."

A breath caught in Elizabeth's lungs. "You would do that?"

"I swear it," he replied, his eyes searching hers.

"Elizabeth," Zeram urged, touching her elbow. "Come on."

Elizabeth pulled away from Zeram's grip and glanced back. Pacumeni lay as if in peaceful sleep.

Her grief twisted afresh and she wanted to run back to Pacumeni, lay down upon the cold stone at his side, and never rise again.

Instead, she turned away, her cheek touching the top of Jonas's dark head. His arms clung about her neck, and she could feel his tears wet against her throat. She looked up, meeting Zeram's somber eyes. He found her elbow again, and this time, Elizabeth did not pull back. She turned her head as she went, her eyes fixed on Pacumeni's silent form. At last, the fog enclosed his body like a silver pall, veiling it from her sight.

Chapter 10

Coriantumr stretched comfortably against the back of the woven reeds of the chair he had commanded to be set at the crest of the palace steps. He heaved a sigh as he gazed out over the darkened plaza and the prisoners huddled there. He snatched up his cup from its place on the armrest beside him and sipped the heady wine, letting the tart warmth slide down his throat.

Lylith moved along one line of bound Nephite warriors at the base of the stone stairs. She paused each step, drawing flat corn cakes from the bag she carried over one shoulder, and pressed them into the outstretched hands of the prisoners she passed.

How gracefully she moved in the mist that partly shrouded her, Coriantumr mused. Like a goddess.

As if sensing his eyes on her, Lylith glanced up. Coriantumr grinned and lifted his cup in salute. She frowned and turned away, returning her attention to the prisoners.

Curse Shemnon and his wretched *honor.*

One day, he would find a way to rid himself of the old man. The greater part of the troops looked up to Shemnon, but Coriantumr would find a way. He took another thoughtful sip. And with her advocate gone, he could—

"My lord."

Coriantumr whipped forward, a curse upon his lips for having his reverie disturbed, but his angry retort died as two guards shoved a bound Nephite to his knees at Coriantumr's feet. The two guards hovered behind the man, their javelins ready lest the prisoner bolted.

"Here is one of the men who knows the sign," one offered.

"Ah, yes." Coriantumr rose.

"Peace to you, friend." Coriantumr addressed him in the Nephite tongue, striding round the prisoner before coming back to stand in front of him. "Speak your name."

The prisoner glowered and muttered a curse beneath his breath.

"I wish to speak to the leader of your brotherhood," Coriantumr continued, his tone congenial. "Will you tell me who he is?"

"No."

Rage boiled in Coriantumr's heart at the prisoner's defiance, but he merely smiled. "Perhaps you could deliver a message to him, then. I wished to thank him for sending your emissary before the battle. He came to us from the river valley, cloaked and hooded. We never saw his face. A resourceful fellow. Because of his coming, the lives of your brotherhood, those who know your secret signs, have been spared. For now."

"But so have countless others," the man spat.

"Ah." Coriantumr rolled his eyes skyward. "I dared not tell my second-in-command our pact, nor the men under him. Such an agreement would smack of dishonor to him, and he would not be so agreeable as I in keeping your secret. What matters to you is that you and yours survived. You cannot say I did not honor my end of the agreement just because a few others lived as well."

"A *few*?" the prisoner scoffed.

"Your friend described your chief judge to me."

Despite the distrust in his eyes, the prisoner leaned forward. "*And?*" he demanded.

"I found him," Coriantumr said. "And though the coward tried to flee, I ran him down, cornered him against the city wall, and killed him."

The Nephite sneered.

Coriantumr studied the kneeling man. "But it is a mystery to me how your *messenger* found his way out of this city at all, with the gates and walls so heavily manned."

"He's like a ghost," the prisoner said. "He could pass through walls of rock if he wished, and return again through the same stones."

Coriantumr came to face the bound man again. "What is your secret?"

"We have many secrets, few of which you need to know."

Coriantumr's fists clenched at the man's impudence. "Very well, then. Allow me to bestow this small gift as thanks for your aid."

Coriantumr snatched an obsidian knife from his belt and lashed out. The prisoner jerked back, but not quickly enough, and the blade sliced upward across his face. With a cry, he crumpled, clutching at his face with his bound hands. Blood seeped through his fingers.

A curse, taut with fury and pain, burbled from the man's lips.

"Take this worthless rat away!" Coriantumr ordered.

He wiped his bloody knife on the hem of his kilt and returned to his seat. He took up his cup of wine again as the Lamanite soldiers dragged the writhing man away.

"Do not cringe like a turtle trying to hide, boy!" The Lamanite flashed an annoyed glance at Zeram as the shadow of the eastern gate loomed closer through the heavy fog. The gate stood ajar, and through the gap, Elizabeth could see a column of light-gray mist. "Straighten your back."

Elizabeth studied the shadows that moved on the walkway above it.

"And you." The Lamanite nodded toward Elizabeth. "Keep the little one as still as you can, and walk like a man."

Elizabeth drew in a deep breath at the Lamanite's orders, her eyes fixed upon the narrow opening through the half-closed gate.

"Why are you doing this? What do you have planned for us?" Zeram asked.

"Do not speak!" the Lamanite hissed.

"Halt there!" a voice in the Lamanite tongue called from the top of the wall. "State your purpose for approaching the gate! Our bows can find their mark despite this wretched fog if you are not given leave to be here."

Straightening his back as well as Joshua's heavy form would let him, the Lamanite called out, "On orders from Lord Coriantumr, we have come to scout the riverbank."

"Captain!" The man's tone changed as the dark shadows on the wall stiffened. "We were not informed... Of course you may pass! Forgive us."

"You are fulfilling your duties well, my young comrades," the Lamanite called. "There is no need for apology." Without a glance to Elizabeth or Zeram, he started forward.

Elizabeth followed him, keeping Jonas's head tucked against her shoulder. His breath felt quick and warm against her skin, his arms tight around her neck.

Thank the heavens the child knew not to cry.

Risking a glance beside her, Elizabeth caught sight of Zeram's expression. The youth's face struggled to remain stoic, but his eyes betrayed uncertainty.

A heavy silence lay beneath their footsteps as they passed through the close opening. Then the gate fell behind them, and only a sea of silver mist lay before them.

"Continue to walk as if you have nothing to fear," the Lamanite instructed as the thoroughfare began to slant downwards. They were descending into the river valley of the Sidon, east of the city.

Her grief had muted to a throbbing ache, pierced now and again with splinters of pain. Elizabeth's body felt weighted, as if chains dragged at her. A numb stupor enshrouded her mind, as thick as the fog that surrounded them. Her aching heart clung like a drowning thing to her need to protect Jonas, and to help Zeram and Joshua. Without them, she would have no purpose, no feeling at all. She followed on the man's heels, sheltering Jonas in her arms as the sound of flowing water increased.

Faint light seemed to glow in the air about them. Perhaps sunrise neared, though Elizabeth could not be certain, for she had lost track of time.

The bridge spanning the river grew visible now, stretching across the darker ribbon of water. The Lamanite warrior paused.

"What lies along here?" he asked, pointing to a narrow path that broke off from the main road and wended northward along the west side of the river.

"The boat house," Zeram said. "For taking messages to the land of Bountiful."

"Good," the Lamanite said. "You will find a boat faster than anything else to take your wounded friend and yourselves to safety."

He turned off the wider road, and Elizabeth followed, with Zeram close behind.

As their group rounded a jutting outcropping of stone, a faint orange glow flickered through the misty shrouds. The Lamanite jerked to a stop, and as he did, a whiff of smoke wafted through the moist air. Elizabeth turned toward Zeram. The flickering light gleamed off his face.

After a moment, the warrior resumed his steps. Elizabeth followed, Zeram at her side as the fog withdrew, revealing the smoldering skeleton of what had been a small boat house.

The wooden supports that had held the building above the water level remained intact, holding up much of the blackened flooring that had not crumbled to the ground.

Elizabeth's steps faltered, then stopped. Her eyes roved over the long, sleek boats lined face down, side by side upon a slope of sand where the river lapped, their peaked bellies shattered in, the hacked scars of Lamanite axes.

Zeram cursed and kicked at a charred fragment of wood that lay smoking on the ground. He picked up something from beside one of the shattered boats. A single oar, undamaged. But what good would one oar do them in the midst of these broken wrecks?

"We will have to make a travois for Joshua," Zeram said as he turned to Elizabeth with hopeless eyes. "We'll cross the river and try for Gideon. But I don't know if Joshua will be able to last—"

"Wait." The Lamanite's voice arrested their despair. His head jerked toward the charred remains of the hut and to a darkened space between two support beams that still upheld the smoking floor.

Elizabeth looked. Between the wooden supports lay a slender boat almost invisible in the shadows that sheltered it.

Zeram scrambled over the shattered remains of the other boats. He dropped to his knees, grasped the stern of the boat, and wrenched on it. The vessel scraped over the earth as he dragged it out into the light and down onto the sand toward the steady flow of the river. Its smooth, unmarred belly gleamed.

With a heave, Zeram pushed the boat over onto its hull and tossed in the single oar. The Lamanite lowered himself to one knee and lay Joshua's unconscious form down in the boat's belly, then rose again.

Elizabeth reached out and touched Joshua's cheek. It felt warm and slick with sweat. "Joshua."

He stirred at her touch, and his lips moved.

"Take this." The old warrior unlatched the fat pouch from his belt and held it out to her. "This has dressings and herbs to kill the evil in his wound. There are also herbs and bandages for the child's ankle to lessen the swelling and pain."

"Thank you." As her fingers clasped the soft leather bag, the old warrior's fingers closed over hers, and a faint sensation that she knew him fluttered through her thoughts.

"I wish that I had a salve for the wound upon your young heart," he said in his own language, his eyes softening. "I too know the pain of losing my beloved to death."

Elizabeth's throat grew tight. "Your wife died?"

"Many years ago. Giving birth to our son." He swallowed. "The child also died."

"I am sorry," Elizabeth said, unsure what more she could say.

"What of our kindred still in Zarahemla?" Zeram asked.

The Lamanite turned. "I will do what I can for them."

A discontented breath broke from Zeram's throat. "I still do not understand why you are doing this," he murmured in the man's tongue. "Your own people would think it disloyalty."

"Mercy to those who can do me no harm is disloyalty to no one," the Lamanite said. "What good would keeping you four as prisoners do for my people? What harm would releasing you do?" He heaved a sigh. "Come. You must go now."

With that, he grasped the stern of the boat, and Zeram joined him. Together, they shoved the craft down into the water where the current caught the bow, tugging it as if the boat itself wished to get away. As the men pushed it farther and the pull of the current strengthened, Elizabeth waded into the shallows. She lifted Jonas, setting him upon the seat above Joshua's head. Jonas hissed in pain when his injured ankle bumped the edge of the vessel, but he made no other sound.

Elizabeth scrambled over the edge of the boat, the Lamanite's pouch clutched against her as she settled beside Jonas. She circled an arm about the little boy and tucked her legs beneath her, her skirt dripping.

Zeram, soaked to the waist, leaped into the stern. The boat rocked with his weight as he snatched up the oar.

His eyes met Elizabeth's, but he did not speak as he dipped the oar into the current and pushed the boat toward the swift center of the river with a determined stroke. Elizabeth glanced back toward the misty shore as it fell away and sought out the Lamanite warrior as he watched them from the water's edge. She had not known him before today, yet as she watched him slip away into the fog, she felt as if she were losing a comrade—a friend, even. And she realized she had never asked his name.

Chapter 11

Distant calls of night animals. Voices hushed and murmuring. And then a soft hand brushed against his face, sweeping him to full consciousness. Cold, sweet air filled Joshua's lungs as he opened his eyes.

Dark outlines of trees passed above him, framing a sky scattered with stars. Something cradled him as it swayed in gentle, rhythmic motion. The murmur of water lapped near his ears.

A cloak enfolded him. A slender form, soft and warm, nestled beside him, a hand against his face.

From the stars overhead and the shadows of trees against the night sky, Joshua realized he was traveling northeastward.

He lay in a boat as if in a cradle. How…?

He stirred, wishing to sit up, but a spear of fire lanced through his chest, and a hiss of pain broke past his lips.

He heard a faint gasp, and the figure beside him stirred. The hand drew back from his cheek and a face moved into his view, silhouetted against the bright points of stars. He could not discern her features, but a feather-soft lock of hair tumbled out of the darkness and brushed his chest. His nostrils drank in the sweetness of her scent, and he knew her.

Elizabeth, his lips moved, but her name would not come forth.

"Zeram," Elizabeth gasped, her shadow looking up and away. "He's awake."

Joshua opened his mouth and tried again. "Elizabeth," he groaned.

"Lie still, Joshua. Don't move." Her face bent near his own. Another lock of hair tumbled down and brushed his throat. Trails of warmth shivered through him as the coolness of her hand caressed his forehead.

"How…?" he murmured as her hand drew back.

"We are on the river," she said. The movement of her hands in the darkness showed her binding her loose tresses back. Joshua wished she would leave them unbound—he had enjoyed the feel of her hair against his skin. "On our way to the northward lands near Bountiful. Zeram is here. And Jonas." She sighed. "Jonas is sleeping, thankfully."

"Zeram?" Joshua choked out.

"I'm here, Joshua." Zeram's voice, laced with weariness, came from the stern of the boat, accompanied by the splash of a paddle.

"You're wounded, Joshua," Elizabeth murmured. "Don't move."

A hand beneath his head tipped his face up as something blessedly cool pressed against his parched lips.

"Drink," she said, and he obeyed. Sweet water trickled into his mouth.

As the water skin moved back from his lips, another thought rose in his foggy mind.

"What happened?" He struggled to rise, but a piercing pain in his ribs and Elizabeth's hand against his chest forced him back. He flinched, then with effort asked, "What became of the battle?"

"Zarahemla fell to the Lamanites," Elizabeth said, her voice soft with misery.

Joshua's heart clenched as a sense of desolation fell over him. Despite the pain the movement caused, he lifted his hand to his chest and found her small hand. He squeezed, and his sorrow eased a little as her fingers answered his own.

"Then how did we come to be here?"

"An unlikely friend gave us aid."

"Who?" he asked. "How...? My last memory...Where did you...?"

"Hush, Joshua," she soothed. "You must rest. You're badly hurt. But I won't let you die." Her voice softened. "I couldn't endure losing you as well."

Elizabeth's words stopped him. Something was wrong in what she had said.

"Where is Pacumeni?" he demanded.

Silence met his words. Even the steady dip of Zeram's paddle stilled.

"Oh, Joshua."

A shard of grief pierced his heart at Elizabeth's tone even before she whispered, "Pacumeni is dead."

At these words, anguish and guilt struck him in a crushing wave, and in spite of his weakness, a sob wrenched from his lungs. Spasms of pain tore through his body, but he didn't care. After all his oaths and promises, he had failed.

"No, Joshua," Elizabeth pleaded as her hand pressed against his chest. "Don't move. You'll tear your wound open."

"I gave him an oath!" Joshua's sobs jerked from his throat. "I told him he would live. I failed him, Elizabeth! I failed *you*!"

"Hush, Joshua. You failed no one." Pain laced Elizabeth's voice, yet her fingertips felt gentle as they touched his cheek. "Here," she insisted. "Drink more."

The water skin touched his lips again, and he swallowed. Disgusted that he should, Joshua felt better as the cool liquid slipped down his throat.

"We don't want to lose you," she whispered as she drew the water skin away. "*I* don't want to lose you. My dear, brave friend."

"I would do anything for you, Elizabeth," he murmured.

"Then rest for me," she pleaded. She bent over him. "Rest."

Joshua surrendered to her words, like a child exhausted with weeping, and let his eyes close. The rhythmic splash against the sides of the boat and the pulsing grief in his heart faded as unconsciousness claimed him once more.

"You failed," Coriantumr said, his voice like a snake's hiss. His eyes fixed on the small stone idol in his hand rather than on Shemnon. "You did not bring back the head of their chief judge as I commanded you to do."

Shemnon's jaw knotted. Coriantumr held an image of one of the gods, and Shemnon recognized the serpentine figure of Kukulcán, its feather-etched form twined in a death grip around a bearded figure clearly meant to be Nephite. The sight struck Shemnon as unjust. If the gods willed that they conquer Zarahemla, so be it. But why gloat? What purpose did it serve?

Shemnon's eyes fell from the small idol in Coriantumr's hand to the stone tiles beneath his feet, his thoughts recalling the face of the Nephite maiden who had spoken his own tongue with such ease. Shemnon knew he had defied Coriantumr by letting her and her friends go and by burying her dear one instead of returning with his head. Even so, he regretted nothing. The body of her beloved would never be found by his enemies.

"Shemnon, do not ignore me!" Coriantumr roared, lunging to his feet, the stone figure clenched in a white and mottled fist.

Shemnon lifted his head and studied Coriantumr's angry features in the torchlight.

"Where is the wretch's head?" Coriantumr demanded.

"His name was Pacumeni," Shemnon replied.

Coriantumr scoffed at this. "You have disobeyed me, and in so doing, you have dishonored the gods!"

A small gleam of unease flickered in Shemnon's heart.

The two guards who stood at the feet of the dais glowered at him. Shemnon did not turn, but he felt the malice in the eyes of the other guards behind him, burning into his back.

The muscles of the guards in front of him bulged beneath skin a lighter hue than his own, showing them to be sons of Nephite dissenters, kinsmen to Coriantumr or to the king.

But Shemnon's heart only grew all the more determined.

"You know nothing of honor, my lord. And the gods have had more than enough blood."

"Enough?" Coriantumr shouted. "The gods have not *begun* to slake their thirst, old man! On the morrow, I will take the greater part of my army and march toward Bountiful. I will sweep through these lands like a plague."

A wave of anger swelled in Shemnon's chest. "Bountiful knows you are coming. Do not underestimate them. You will not find them so unprepared."

Coriantumr's eyes narrowed. "Those are the words of frightened old women. Zarahemla is crushed. It makes little difference whether Bountiful knows I am coming. Once the sow is speared through, it is a small matter to hunt down her squalling babes one by one. Any Nephite not swift enough to escape me will die."

Shemnon's stomach knotted at Coriantumr's words. "Even the children?"

Coriantumr pushed himself forward on the stone throne, his blue eyes cold and fierce. "Anyone I must to serve our king and our gods. Mercy is for fools like you, Shemnon. I have no use for it. It is cowardice."

"It is not cowardice to face a strong warrior who has a weapon in his hands," Shemnon said. "But I will take no part in the murder of children and women, Nephite or otherwise."

"So be it." Coriantumr rose from the throne, his eyes narrowed to dangerous slits.

He lifted his hand. In a moment, Shemnon felt his arms snatched in fists of iron and wrenched behind his back.

He jerked at the painful grip of the two guards behind him, yet as much as he struggled to pull away, their fists tightened like vises.

A sneer curled across Coriantumr's face as he dropped down the steps and stalked forward, the idol still clasped in his hand. "You have defied me for the last time," he snarled.

"I have never—"

Coriantumr's fist plunged into Shemnon's stomach with the force of a battering ram, and Shemnon's breath burst from his lungs. The men on either side of him twisted his arms all the more fiercely as he staggered.

Coriantumr smashed the back of his hand across Shemnon's face, and his head bobbled to the side, the acrid taste of blood sliding down his throat.

"Your continued defiance has been a disgrace to our people!" Coriantumr growled.

"*My* people have never been yours." Shemnon managed to lift his heavy head to meet Coriantumr's burning eyes. "We have only ever been dogs for your sport, to send out before you into battle, to kill and be killed, so you can take the glory."

Coriantumr slammed his fist into Shemnon's abdomen again, splinters of pain stabbing through his core, tearing the last of his breath from his lungs. Shemnon's knees buckled.

This time, the guards let him fall, the stone floor scraping the palms of his hands as he caught himself.

"You are guilty of insubordination," Coriantumr fumed. "And I strip you of rank."

"I am guilty of nothing," Shemnon snarled."The men will not support it. They will rebel against you when they learn what you have done to me."

"They will know nothing of it."

Shemnon managed to glance up, seeing the sneer curled across Coriantumr's face.

"Do not fear." The Nephite dissenter sneered. "I will take good care of your daughter."

Shemnon's heart leaped in fear. "Talilia?" he gasped. "You will not touch her!"

"Who will stop me? Shall the gods come to your aid?" Coriantumr turned his back upon Shemnon and started toward the throne.

In a mocking tone, he added, "Or perhaps the Nephites' god, since you love them so well?"

Desperation gave his weakened limbs strength, and Shemnon lunged forward with a roar of fury.

Coriantumr spun back.

Shemnon caught a glimpse of his face, etched with fury, his arm a blur of motion before a sharp crack exploded through the side of Shemnon's head, and he crumpled.

The stone idol had struck him like a club, Shemnon realized, before his thoughts sputtered like a candle and flickered out.

Chapter 12

"You must push now!" Lylith glanced up from where she knelt. The young woman's face dripped with sweat, her nut-brown hair askew about her girlish features. Her eyes pled with Lylith over the swell of her belly. Weak firelight flickered off the walls of the thatch hut about them. Lylith's eyes trailed to the face of the woman who supported the girl's shoulders, then to the other women who knelt nearby, watching in silence. Beyond them, a boy, too young to be a soldier, tended the small fire in its hollowed-out place on the floor, his back to them. A small group of children, their faces streaked with dirt and tears, huddled among their mothers.

"No," the girl sobbed. "Just let me die."

Lylith's eyes shot back to the woman at the girl's side. The woman returned Lylith's gaze.

"Come, Mara," the woman cajoled as she brushed a cloth against the girl's flushed face. "You are young and strong. You won't die."

"I want to die, Lady Pazia," the girl sobbed. "Riyad is dead."

"Come now," Lylith ordered. "Push!"

The girl shook her head. "I can't."

"You can, Mara," Pazia insisted. "Your husband is here beside you, even if you can't see him."

The girl turned her eyes to Pazia's. The despair seemed to ebb a little. But then her teeth clenched as another pain gripped her.

"Come, Mara, push," Lylith commanded, and Mara obeyed. Lylith shot a look at Pazia, a hopeful grin coming to her lips. "The child is coming."

Her eyes turned to the girl's face. "Push again. Harder!"

The girl's face contorted, and a screech tore from her.

Lylith's heart leaped as the baby's head appeared, followed a moment later by the plump little body. A relieved gasp escaped Mara, and she fell back against Pazia's arms.

"The child is here." Lylith heaved a breath. "Bring me that basin."

A little girl scurried near and carefully placed a wooden basin of water next to Lylith. Pazia came to her side and helped the girl with the afterbirth as Lylith busied herself with the baby.

"A boy," she declared as she worked. A murmur moved through the group.

But something was wrong. A pang of worry knifed through her.

"Why isn't he crying?" the baby's mother asked.

Lylith bent her head, pressing her ear to the baby's chest. His heart beat. Faintly. But he wasn't breathing.

She bent over the baby, rubbing his chest gently. Still, he didn't cry.

A moment later, pounding sounded at the door before it shoved open, streaming light into the dim room.

"What is going on?" a voice demanded in the Lamanite tongue as a warrior stepped into the shadows of the hut. "What was that noise?"

Lylith glared into the blinding light that outlined the officer and several others. "Get out!" she shouted. "You have no business here. Leave now, or my father will hear of your foolishness!"

She turned back to the baby. "Breathe," she ordered. "Do not do this to your mother. She's suffered enough!"

"Why isn't he crying?" the girl asked.

"Forgive us my lady," the soldier said, subdued. "We–"

"I said get out!" she shouted over her shoulder.

The officer nodded, and the men began to turn away.

"Wait!" one of the men called in the Nephite tongue just beyond the threshold, and the two men on either side of him hesitated. Lylith's eyes shot to the speaker, who stepped beneath the doorway. Her lips parted. In the glare of the light, she had thought the men were all Lamanite warriors, but this man's wrists were bound together.

"Let me help."

"There's nothing you can do," she snapped. "Get him out."

The soldiers nodded, grasped the prisoner's arm, and began to turn him away.

"Please. I'm a healer."

Lylith hesitated. She glanced toward Pazia. Pazia nodded. "His name is Tuloth. He's a skilled physician."

"Very well." Lylith nodded to the officer. "But you must cut his bonds, for he will be no help otherwise."

The Lamanite officer snatched Tuloth's arm and turned him. "Do not attempt to escape." The man took Tuloth's bound wrists, pulled an obsidian blade from his belt, and slit his bonds. "We will wait outside the door."

The man named Tuloth came to her side as the door scraped shut behind him, and dropped to his knees at her side. He dipped his hands in the basin and hastily cleansed them before reaching for the baby.

"Stillbirth?" The baby seemed so tiny in his large hands.

"His heart beats, but weakly. And he is not breathing."

The man nodded, then bent over the baby. Placing his mouth over its nose and mouth, he gave a measured breath. The baby's chest rose slightly.

As he drew his mouth away, the baby released a wail. Color began to warm his body.

Sighs of relief rippled through the room. Pazia came forward with a cloth and gathered the baby from the man's arms. The baby's wailing eased as his mother cradled him.

Tuloth stood slowly and turned away. "I should go now."

"Wait." Lylith scrambled to her feet.

He turned, and for the first time, she saw his face clearly.

"Yes?" He looked to be a Lamanite, but his garb appeared Nephite-made. His hair, black as obsidian, fell unbound about the strong angles of his face, framing dark eyes.

For a fleeting moment, Lylith became painfully aware of her appearance, her tangled hair, her rumpled tunic.

"You are an Ammonite, an ally of the Nephites."

The man studied her with mild curiosity before a faint smile touched his face. Lylith felt foolish for her obvious assessment.

"I am," he returned, his tone laced with gentle humor.

"You saved the baby. Breathing life into him—I haven't seen that before."

"No doubt you too would have convinced him to draw a breath."

"Perhaps. I have been able to save some infants in that state, but others…"

She ended her words, but from the understanding in his eyes, she did not need to finish.

"We cannot save them all."

She glanced away and nodded.

A hand touched her arm, gentle despite the strength in it. "You are a skilled midwife. I can tell."

Lylith looked up, and her heart grew warm at the approval she saw on his face.

He drew in a breath, studying her features. He gestured toward the closed door. "Forgive me, but I am most curious. You are not a born Lamanite, but they obey you so readily."

"My father is a great captain."

"A dissenter from the Nephites?"

"Well, he…" Lylith stopped.

The Ammonite did not press her for an answer. "You know my name is Tuloth, for Lady Pazia has already spoken it. But what is your name?"

Her heart gave a painful thump. "Talilia."

"Talilia," he echoed. "To light the way. It is the Nahuatl tongue."

"My father liked the sound of the word, and gave it to me as my name."

A shy smile touched his lips. "It is well chosen, for your eyes shine like sapphires."

Heat warmed her cheeks, and she found herself returning his smile.

"Do not say I cannot pass! Open this door!"

The voice doused over her like freezing water as the door burst open. Coriantumr marched into the room, light streaming about him.

Lylith bristled, her hands clenching.

Coriantumr eyed Tuloth up and down with dismissive eyes before turning to Lylith.

"Here you are, Lylith," he said. "I disapprove of you consorting with prisoners like this."

She could hear the women behind her hurrying the girl and her baby away, and she heaved a breath, grateful that Coriantumr's wrathful eyes remained upon her.

"They needed my help. My father wouldn't disapprove."

"Your father?" he scoffed. "You have been too long at your work. You have not heard the news."

"What news?"

"Your father has returned southward with a contingent to report our conquest to King Tubaloth. He left you in my care."

Fear crackled through Lylith at his words. "You lie. Where is he?"

"What *if* I lie?" Coriantumr lowered his voice to a dangerous hiss. "What can you do?"

At his words, her hand snapped upward, striking Coriantumr across the cheek.

"What did you do to my father?" she shrieked.

Coriantumr turned back, his features contorted in fury. He lifted his arm, his fist a blur as it swung toward her face.

Lylith flinched, but another hand snatched Coriantumr's wrist in midair, jerking him to a stop.

The sinews of the Ammonite's arm bulged beneath his skin with the effort it had taken to halt Coriantumr's blow.

"Wretch," Coriantumr seethed as he jerked his fist from Tuloth's hold.

"Do not strike her," Tuloth hissed.

Lylith furrowed her brow. What madness possessed Tuloth? Coriantumr could kill him!

Coriantumr's jaw grew knotted. "Lieutenant Zamir!"

A warrior appeared in the doorway. He bowed his head and slapped his fist to his chest.

"Bind the healer. Get him out of here. He is making a nuisance of himself."

The soldier stepped into the hut, drawing a strap of leather from a pouch at his side. Without looking up, he began binding the Ammonite's unresisting hands.

"And spread the word that the greater part of my army will march out within the hour toward the land Bountiful."

"Zamir." Lylith fixed her eyes upon the young Lamanite. "You know my father. He has always been fair to you, has he not?"

Zamir furrowed his brow, glancing from Coriantumr to Lylith, then nodded hesitantly.

"Coriantumr has done something to him. He—"

Coriantumr's iron fist snatched her wrist, and pain silenced her words. He said nothing, but the threat in his grip felt real.

"He has returned with a small contingent to report our victory to the king," Coriantumr said. "He left his daughter in my charge. Her mind is weakened from all she's seen. I fear she may be going mad. Keep her here with the scum, if she likes them so much. See that she wants for nothing, but do not believe her ravings, and do not let her leave." Coriantumr's eyes slid over her, his gaze causing Lylith's skin to crawl. "I have plans for her when I return."

"She doesn't want you."

Tuloth's voice was a soft, but determined growl. The Ammonite pulled his bound hands away from the young warrior and faced Coriantumr.

Coriantumr stepped to Tuloth, his face inches away. "I could kill you in an instant, Ammonite."

Tuloth met Coriantumr's gaze with equal fire. "I will not remain silent when you speak to her dishonorably."

A sneer slid across Coriantumr's lips. He glanced at her. "It appears you've gained a champion, Lylith."

Tearing her focus from Coriantumr, she fixed her eyes upon the floor.

Coriantumr turned to the guard. "The Ammonite will make the journey with us. We will need a physician."

Lylith's eyes shot up. "No." She reached toward Tuloth. "Coriantumr, please—"

"Get him out." Coriantumr shoved her away from the Ammonite.

"Yes, lord," Zamir murmured without looking at Lylith.

The soldier grasped the Ammonite's arm. Tuloth kept his eyes on Lylith until the doorframe blocked him from her view.

Coriantumr cast a cold glance toward Lylith. "Don't expect to see him again."

Lylith sucked in a breath. "If you hurt him…"

Coriantumr stepped out, jerking the door shut. A bolt slammed.

"Coriantumr!" She pounded a fist against the door. No one answered.

Tendrils of cloud glowed golden in the eastern sky, and the darkness of night gave way to the shadows of early morning as Elizabeth trudged behind Zeram, Jonas hitched upon her back. The pack of herbs and bandages which the old Lamanite warrior had given her hung over her shoulder, bouncing against her hip. Weariness sank to the center of her bones. Her feet felt as if lead encased them, and her eyes burned from lack of sleep.

She turned to the travois Zeram tugged along, weighted with Joshua's unconscious body. The little sled, constructed from vines and tree branches, scraped over the rough ground, complaining as it went. Their faithful boat remained behind, drawn up on the north edge of the river they had left a few hours before. Joshua's eyes remained closed and his face expressionless as he lay on his makeshift bed. His arms rested motionless on the cloak tucked about him, and now and again, a soft groan escaped his lips as the travois bumped over an uneven portion of the path.

Elizabeth lifted her gaze from Joshua to Zeram. His hair clung like plaster to his head, rivulets of sweat trickling down his face and neck. Sweat drenched his uniform, visible above the collar of his heavy quilted armor, and his straining arms gleamed. If they did not take a rest soon, he would collapse from exhaustion.

"Zeram, it is near dawn. We must change Joshua's dressings."

Zeram nodded. He staggered to a halt and lay the travois horizontally on the path.

"We must be quick with this," he said, "and move on again as soon as we can."

He reached for the pouch hanging across her shoulder. But instead of handing it to him, she slung Jonas's sleeping weight from her back and passed him into Zeram's arms.

"I'll treat Joshua," she said. "You rest."

She wondered if Zeram would argue. Instead, he nodded, stumbled to the edge of the trail, and sagged down against a tree trunk, cradling the drowsing boy on his lap.

Elizabeth dropped to her knees at Joshua's side. The strong angles of his face gleamed with sweat, and his brow felt warm against her fingers as she smoothed the damp locks of hair away from his forehead. Weariness and sorrow pulled at her, yet she could not give in to her weakness or grief. Joshua needed her.

She drew back the cloak, loosening the knot that held the thick bandaging in place. Steeling herself, she peeled back the strips of cloth and lifted away the bloodied leaves Zeram had used to dress the wound some hours before. A cruel line lashed across Joshua's bare chest, the ragged edges of the deep cut barely knit together. "Oh, Joshua," she choked.

A faint breeze fluttered down the path. She looked up as it stirred Zeram's sweat-dampened hair and Jonas's dark locks. Like a playful child, it found its way to her, catching at her hair and swirling about her, cool and welcome, tasting faintly of the sea. Elizabeth drew in a breath of the well-loved scent. Perhaps Joshua could taste the tang of the sea and knew somehow that he was nearing home.

She smiled at the thought as she opened the Lamanite's pack and removed the last of the dried leaves that would draw the evil out of the wound. Joshua's flesh tensed beneath her fingers as she placed the leaves over the torn skin, but she did not pause. She pulled out the last sheet of clean, white fabric and laid it over the wound. She knotted the strips of cloth over his ribs once again.

"Joshua." She turned her eyes to his expressionless face. "Please live."

But he did not hear her, or did not seem to. With a weary sigh, Elizabeth trailed her hand down the length of his forearm until she found his wrist. She pressed her fingers against the skin, finding the weak pulse that thumped like a slow, steady dirge.

"Elizabeth," Zeram hissed.

She turned toward him to see the alarm on his face, then twisted to look in the direction his eyes were fixed. Her mind, slow with weariness, struggled to understand as she caught glimpses of javelin points rising in the air like stripped corn stalks, and the movement of many forms through the forest growth. She rose, ignoring the wave of dizziness that swept over her.

Glancing over at Zeram, she saw him shoot to his feet.

"Take him." He strode to her and shoved Jonas into her arms. No hint of weariness remained on Zeram's face.

The rasp of his sword reverberated off the trees around them as Zeram drew it forth and strode several paces forward, his eyes fixed upon the bend in the path.

"They've followed our trail," Zeram said. "Whoever *they* are."

He pointed the tip of his sword at the bed of the path. Two parallel marks where the earth had been scraped by the dragging legs of the travois stretched out behind them along the path until they disappeared around the bend. "Jonas, go hide," Elizabeth ordered. She set the little boy down on a clump of grass and shoved him toward the shadowed undergrowth. "Wait until I call for you."

"No!" Jonas grasped her hand, and she struggled to pull away.

"You there!"

She spun at the surprised voice. Her eyes fixed upon an indistinct figure shadowed in the pale light. A man had just come around the bend and stopped in the center of the path, motionless as a statue as he studied them.

Elizabeth's heart dropped. Though the man spoke in the Nephite tongue, his Lamanitish accent reverberated through the trees.

Behind him, a cluster of several other men rounded the bend in the path as well, stopping at the sight of her small group. They wore breastplates of quilted kapok, helmets gleaming in the waning light of the forest.

Beside her, Zeram's sword arm drooped. The blade fell from his hand to the trail with a soft thump as if it had grown too heavy for him. He staggered several steps forward like a tottering child taking its first trusting steps toward its father.

"Captain Thobor?" Zeram asked.

"Upon my life," the man said. "Zeram, son of my friend Jacob the elder! You've grown much!" Glancing over his shoulder, Thobor called to someone beyond the bend, "Jacob, come quickly!"

Tension rushed from Elizabeth's limbs, for she recognized him now—Captain Thobor, a converted Lamanite and one of the most trusted officers in Bountiful. A new figure appeared around the bend, clad in a uniform similar to Captain Thobor's.

"Zeram!" the man cried in a voice too youthful to be Zeram's father as he rushed forward and enveloped the young man in a fierce embrace. "My nephew! Thank the heavens! Your parents have been sick with worry for you since the news came!"

Nearer now, the younger soldier's features became clear, and Elizabeth remembered him. Jacob, the son of Aaron, often called *the younger*, for his sister's husband carried the same name. He had been Joshua's friend since they were boys, the two often inseparable comrades, with Zeram as their loyal follower.

"And Elizabeth, daughter of Nathan," Thobor's gentle voice called out as he turned compassionate eyes upon her.

"Yes," she whispered.

Thobor took a step toward her. "And the child?" He offered a sympathetic nod at Jonas who still clung to her skirt.

"Jonas, son of Pacumeni." She gestured weakly to the unconscious figure upon the travois. "And Joshua, whom you know. Son of Antipus."

"Upon my life," young Jacob said as he pushed away from his nephew. He moved to the travois and knelt. "Joshua?" He touched his friend's brow. "It's me, Jacob." But though the steady rise and fall of his breathing continued, Joshua did not respond.

The other men of the Nephite patrol spread out, their sword belts clattering as they studied the weary travelers with curious eyes.

Jacob looked up toward Elizabeth. "My wife Rachel will be relieved to hear you're safe, Elizabeth. Do you remember her?" Jacob nodded toward Thobor. "Thobor's sister? You and she were friends."

Elizabeth did not speak. He meant, perhaps, to help her feel at ease, but his friendly demeanor did not comfort her. Nothing could.

Jacob seemed unoffended by her silence and simply turned his eyes back upon Joshua, studying the bandaged wound. "A gash across his ribs," he said. "How deep?"

"It struck bone," Zeram said. "But we have herbs and bandages."

"You've done well thus far," Jacob said. "How did you get here?"

"It would take time to explain," Zeram said. "We've come a long way."

"And we bring unhappy news," Elizabeth murmured. She dropped her eyes, studying the earth of the path beneath her feet.

"We heard Zarahemla was attacked," Thobor said.

"She was overrun within hours," Zeram added.

Jacob nodded. "We've heard nothing else until now. All the city is in fear, not knowing the fate of friends or kin."

"Then—" the words jerked from her throat, "you don't know that Pacumeni…"

Seeing her falter, Zeram spoke for her. "Chief Judge Pacumeni, to whom Lady Elizabeth was betrothed, was…killed in battle."

A collective breath of grief escaped the soldiers. On the ground, Jacob winced bitterly. He shot Elizabeth a look of fierce apology, then dropped his head, striking a fist against his thigh.

At the soldiers' palpable sorrow, the weariness of the past days and her own grief came full upon Elizabeth's shoulders like a sudden crushing weight. Her knees buckled and she felt herself crumpling, but not before Captain Thobor moved to her and caught her arms.

She collapsed against the warrior's stiff armor as a wild sob jerked from her. She covered her face with her hands as the sun rose, filling the forest with light, which, through her tears, she could not see.

Chapter 13

88 BC, Land of Ishmael

Shemnon's jaw clenched as he paced before the closed door of his hut like a caged jaguar, helpless in his frustration.

How long had it been? He glanced skyward. Keza's pains had begun that morning, and now the sun lowered beyond the trees on the far side of the village. Her pains had not been this long with Hana. What was wrong?

"Baba?"

Shemnon looked down at his daughter, who tottered to him, taking one of his fingers in her small hand.

"Mama?" she queried, her brow furrowing in worry and confusion.

"Mama is sick." Shemnon reached down and lifted her precious weight into his arms. "Do not worry. Grandmama is with her."

This seemed to satisfy the little girl. She rested her head against his shoulder, her hair soft against his face.

A moment later, the soft rustle of cloth brought Hana's head up again. Shemnon turned to see his mother, Delia, beneath the doorway. Her wise, patient face looked drawn as she beckoned to him.

"Keza?" He shifted Hana to his other arm and started toward the hut as fear clenched his heart.

"The child," she murmured, "is dead. He did not draw breath."

A fist seized Shemnon's throat. Only yesterday, he had felt the child kick against Keza's belly and had laughed over the strength of it. How could the child be dead now?

"Are you sure?" he demanded, to which his mother nodded.

He clutched Hana more closely to him. Others had suffered similar losses, and if Keza recovered, if he could care for her and comfort her, the loss would not crush him.

"What of Keza?" he asked "She is going to recover, yes? She will be—"

But his mother's countenance only fell further. Dread settled in Shemnon's stomach.

"I have done all I can," Delia managed to whisper. "I cannot stop the bleeding."

Shemnon's heart fell like a stone. He let his mother take the little girl from him as he staggered into the shadows of the hut, his eyes finding Keza's slender form where she lay upon their pallet of woven reeds. A coverlet had been pulled to her waist, and her dark hair billowed about her as she gazed down upon a tiny form nestled in the crook of her arm.

"Keza," he murmured, dropping to his knees at his wife's side. He touched a finger to a lock of hair that lay against her sweat-dampened brow. "Look at me, dearest one."

Her dark eyes looked up at last and met his. "I have lost our son," she whispered. "And now, Ixtab will take me."

Shemnon's heart tore within him. "No," he said, his voice breaking. "You will be saved. I will not let you die, Keza. You will be weary for a time, but you will recover."

"I have lost our son!"

"You are the one who matters now!" Shemnon hissed, grasping her free hand in his. "You must stay. With Hana. With me, Keza."

"I want to," she said, her eyes pleading.

"Then stay," he begged, his heart tearing at every beat. He bent over Keza, encircling both her and the silent infant in his strong arms. Tears filled his eyes, but Shemnon did not heed them as he pressed a kiss to her brow. Her skin felt so cold.

A hand, gentle as a butterfly's wing, touched the heated sinews of his jaw. He caught it and held it there, willing warmth into her flesh. Keza's eyes brimmed with tears.

"Where is our son now?" she pleaded. "I must find him. I must care for him. Is he in paradise? I do not want Ixtab to gather me there unless he is there as well."

The question gave Shemnon pause. He did not know what had become of the child's soul he had felt with such strength yesterday. How could he answer what he did not know?

"Turn your thoughts away from the death goddess and onto me," he insisted. "From the day your grandparents brought you to my father's dwelling to speak of marriage, from the moment I saw you and touched your hand, I wanted no other. I have never wanted any other but you."

"Despite my being the unwanted child of a Nephite?"

"That has never mattered to me, Keza," he murmured. "You matter to me. I love you."

A weary smile touched her lips. "Dearest Shemnon," she breathed. "I love you too."

He leaned over and kissed her pale lips. Her soft mouth answered his, her slender hand rested on his muscled arm. Shemnon's heart swelled within him. She was his whole world. Everything precious to him held her at its center.

Then, in a moment, she was gone.

He felt it as her hand fell from his arm, and her sweet lips no longer answered his.

With a numbness closing over his heart as if half his soul had been torn from him, Shemnon released her limp form and straightened.

He heard his mother's footsteps and felt her gentle hand on his arm.

Shemnon ignored her, his eyes upon the figure that had once been his wife.

"Mama?" Hana whispered. The innocence in her tone spoke clearly that she understood nothing of what had happened.

At once, he burst to his feet, his heart a fist of fire within him.

"Shemnon."

He looked up to see fear in his mother's eyes.

"Do not speak, Mother," he pleaded. "I...I cannot..."

His eyes strayed to the corner where his obsidian-edged scimitar leaned, wrapped in leather. "I must go."

"Where, my son?"

"I do not know. Away."

His mother's voice grew frightened. "You would not do harm to yourself to join her?"

Shemnon continued, barely hearing his mother. "I will go to another city. Far from here. I will find new duties. I will send my earnings to you. Hana will want for nothing."

"Shemnon. She will want for her father."

Shemnon turned toward his mother, his chest tightening at the sorrow he saw on her face and the child cradled in her arms.

"Baba," Hana said, reaching a hand toward him.

Shemnon spun away toward the corner where his scimitar leaned, but stopped when he felt his mother's hand on his arm. "Hana needs you," she pleaded. "We need you here."

"I cannot stay, Mother." He did not look back at her. "My pain is without fathom."

"There must be one god somewhere who knows your honorable desires and who cares."

Shemnon leaned down and grasped the handle of his scimitar, smoothed and well-worn from use. He hefted its comfortable weight, letting the sheet of leather tumble away from the gleaming black blades. "No god understands, Mother. None care."

He glanced back at the figure on the pallet. She and the silent child lay as if asleep, Keza's face as beautiful as he had ever seen her. He turned to his mother, and Hana who studied him with large, dark eyes, ignorant of her father's agony.

He reached out to the child and touched the silk of her dark hair. He could see Keza in her eyes. Her small hand grasped his finger.

"Perhaps the god of the Nephites understands," Delia whispered. "I have heard others in the village talking of the Nephite missionaries. Sons of their king who gave up their inheritance to come to us. King Lamoni believes them, and he is not a fool."

Shemnon snorted bitterly and drew his hand from his daughter's grasp. "Lamoni has lost his mind. I will not hear their words."

"Shemnon, please do not go away."

"You will watch over Hana?" he asked, turning toward the door.

"I will watch over her for as long as I am able."

He opened his mouth to speak, but then he shook his head and plunged out the door.

Shemnon opened his eyes to darkness, the dream retreating into the mists of his memory.

But had it been a dream, he wondered, or was he dreaming now? Had he died and fallen into the treacherous entrapments of Xibalba? He blinked and drew in a sharp breath of cold, musty air. He could still hear an echo of Coriantumr's laughter lingering like a malignant spirit in the darkness about him, but he knew as he listened to the echoes of his own breathing that he was alone. The voice echoed only in his thoughts.

He lay on hard stone, crumpled as if he had been flung there like rubbish. A dull pain throbbed on the side of his head and neck. Shemnon heard the sound of trickling water from some unseen corner of the room.

Coriantumr had struck him with the small idol, the memory faint as if it had happened years in the past. A wave of vertigo swept over Shemnon as he pushed himself to his knees. He faltered, steadying himself with his hands against the stone beneath him until the dizziness passed. Burning pain lanced through his neck and head and he grit his teeth. He touched a hand to the sore spot, feeling crusted blood. He still lived, so he had not fallen into the underworld. Where, then, was he?

The echo of trickling water suggested a closed chamber.

Groping outward into the darkness, Shemnon's fingers came to a stop against something firm and grainy. And wet.

Shemnon pressed his fingers against the cool dampness, then brought one hand near his face and touched the insubstantial moisture to his lips. It tasted drinkable, though gritty.

Pushing himself along the wall, it grew dry, and smoother, like masoned stone. Shemnon followed the wall with his hands, crawling slowly as he went. He met an abrupt stop where a corner came together, then followed another stone wall, the slow drip of water moving away behind him.

And then something new met the tips of Shemnon's fingers. It too felt smooth like masoned stone, but softer, and almost warm against his fingertips. Wood.

Trailing his hand along the grainy surface, his fingertips followed the long seam that ran in a vertical line between the wood and the wall of stone. Extending his other hand in the opposite direction, Shemnon found a similar crack between wood and stone. A door.

Now if he could find a latch… With this faint hope, he began trailing his hands back and forth across the surface of the wood. He paused when the fingers of one hand touched upon a smooth square. A metal plate bolted into the wood. Nothing more.

Was he abandoned here, left to waste away in darkness until starvation claimed him?

The thought weighed upon him, thick and tangible like the very darkness about him. But this thought did not dominate the greater part of his fear. He was a warrior. He could face even the most painful death with resolve. But as he remembered again the merciless look in Coriantumr's eyes when he had spoken of slaughtering Nephite women and children like pigs, and of his vile intentions toward Talilia, a heavy blackness formed in the pit of Shemnon's stomach.

His frame shuddered as his mind echoed with the screams of little ones mingled with their mothers' cries of anguish as Coriantumr's gleaming blade flashed in his thoughts. Shemnon could do nothing now but plead to whatever god condescended to hear him that Coriantumr's bloody cowardice be stopped.

Shemnon pressed his brow against the wood. Could his gods hear him in this void? Would *any* being hear his plea in this dark pit?

Despair began to settle upon his heart like a pall, suffocating, stifling him. The gods of which he had been taught from childhood were too self-serving to hear the pleas of one broken warrior. What god, even among the gentler ones, would stoop to be the advocate to one so fallen and disgraced?

But then in the midst of his misery, a faint memory touched Shemnon's heart.

There must be one god somewhere who knows your honorable desires and who cares.

His mother's words rose from Shemnon's memory like a beam of light gleaming through darkness.

Shemnon mulled it over in his mind. Could truth exist in such words? Would the god of the Nephites hear the words of a Lamanite whose hands still bore the stains of the blood of Nephite warriors? He did not wish to plead for himself, but for the women and children of these people, and for Talilia. Shemnon swallowed against the thickness in his throat.

"God of the Nephites," he began. The words spoken in the stiff, difficult tongue of the Nephites echoed in the air about him.

"God of the Nephites, hear my words, I beg you," he continued. "I am Shemnon of Ishmael, a Lamanite. I am unworthy to speak to you, for I have slain many of your sons. But I ask not for me. I ask for your daughters and their little ones. I ask also for my child, Talilia. She was called Lylith daughter of Pachus among this people. But she is my child now, and I cherish her as I would my own seed. I beg you to stop Coriantumr, for I cannot."

Shemnon drew in a breath. The darkness did not change. The same steady drip continued to echo through the room, unaltered.

Yet in spite of this, a slow, comforting warmth, like sunlight rising over the rim of the world, fell over him. He did not understand the peace of the feeling, yet he welcomed it, for it seemed somehow familiar, like a well-loved memory from long ago or the voice of a trusted friend he had not heard in many years.

He lifted his eyes to the darkness above his head, seeking for…what, he could not say. And though he saw nothing, he knew, somehow, that the Nephites' god had heard him.

Elizabeth startled awake at the touch of a hand on her shoulder. She looked around, disoriented, then realized she had fallen asleep in the wooden chair beside Joshua's bed.

"Elizabeth."

She blinked at the silhouetted figure above her. "Zeram." She sat up and released Joshua's wrist. His arm remained motionless upon the coverlet.

Zeram cleared his throat. "I've just come back from speaking with Captain Lehi. He's the chief captain over the armies here in Bountiful. He wanted me to tell him all I'd learned since we escaped from Zarahemla." He shrugged. "As you know, I had very little to tell him. Captain Lehi says Chief Captain Moronihah has a plan to head off the Lamanites and has given Bountiful's soldiers orders to march out." He looked toward the curtained window. "They say the Lamanites are slicing through the land like a scimitar's blade, sparing no one."

Elizabeth sat up straighter. "What do you mean, *no one*?"

For a moment, Zeram looked older, no longer a youth, but a war-weary soldier. "I mean what I say, Elizabeth. The only survivors are those who can outrun them. Whoever leads them is a madman."

Her heart tightened. "What about the man who was kind to us? He would never hurt a...child."

"He wasn't the whole army, Elizabeth. And he wasn't the leader."

Elizabeth studied her young friend's raw, angry eyes before she asked, "Are you marching out too?"

Zeram shook his head. "I was ordered to stay here with the reserves. And I won't forget my oath to Pacumeni to watch over you and Jonas as long as you need me."

Elizabeth heaved a breath of relief even as her heart clenched at the mention of Pacumeni.

"You shouldn't be alone," Zeram said. "Not with all that has happened. Jonas is staying with Esther, Captain Thobor's wife."

Elizabeth hugged her arms to herself, remembering Esther, with her kind eyes and long, dark hair. "She'll take good care of Jonas."

"She says you're welcome in her house," Zeram continued. "Or you can come stay with my family. My mother Miriam would be pleased to have you. You need someone to watch over you."

"But who would watch over Joshua?"

Zeram turned to study Joshua's face, and for the briefest moment, Zeram's lower lip trembled. A moment later, he drew in a breath and squared his shoulders.

"The healers are well trained," Zeram said. "And you need—"

"I need to stay here beside him," Elizabeth insisted. "He needs me."

A glimmer of the little boy she remembered sparkled in Zeram's eyes, and the corner of his mouth drew up in a slight smile. "I forgot how stubborn you can be."

The distant blast of a conch shell horn reverberated off the stone walls before dying away.

Zeram turned. "That's the signal for muster," he said. He moved to the window and pushed the curtain aside.

"Now other women will fear for the men they love," Elizabeth said.

Without turning back, Zeram nodded.

A deep weariness settled upon her, and Elizabeth sank against the back of the chair, her eyes turning to Joshua's face. *Did* her presence aid his healing? She grasped his hand where it lay upon the coverlet and gently squeezed his fingers. "Joshua," she whispered. A moment later, though she saw no change upon his face or in the rhythm of his breath, she felt a slight pressure as his fingers squeezed in response.

Joshua became aware of the touch of slender fingers upon his wrist. The pain in his chest had muted, no longer a sharp fire, but a steady throb. A thin coverlet lay over him, and his limbs—heavy, unmoving—rested at his sides. He could taste the air—sweet, cool, and laced with the scent of the ocean.

Ignoring the pain in his chest, he breathed deeply. This was no feverish nightmare. He was in Bountiful again. He was home.

Joshua opened his eyes and blinked as the wooden ceiling beams came into focus. The room glowed in the warmth of a small lamp resting upon a shelf on the wall. On the other side of the room, a curtain fluttered with the breeze. Beside him, he felt another movement of air, softer and warm, against his arm, and the press of fingers against his wrist. He turned his head. Elizabeth slept at his side, curled up in a wooden chair beside his bed. His lips parted as he studied the fair curves of her sleeping face. One arm rested on his bed, her hand on his wrist as if to keep a measure of his heartbeat even in her sleep, and her face turned toward his own as if she had been watching him when her eyelids closed.

"Elizabeth…" he whispered.

She stirred, but did not awaken.

Joshua lifted his free arm and slid it toward her. Slivers of pain crackled across his chest, but he ignored them as he reached for Elizabeth and brushed his fingertips against her soft cheek.

"I wish I had saved him for you," Joshua whispered. Misery tightened his throat. Pacumeni should have been lying here, with Elizabeth awaiting his recovery, hoping for a life at his side. Joshua should have been the one to die.

"*Why?*" Joshua breathed to the flickering shadows upon the ceiling. Tears filled his eyes. "Why do *I* live? Why could you not have saved Pacumeni instead?"

But no answer came as the lamplight stirred, setting the shadows to flutter like falling leaves down the wall.

Chapter 14

The sky glowered hot and brassy. Beneath his armor, Coriantumr could feel sweat trickling down his limbs. Far to the west, he could see the gray-green forest that bordered the yellow grassland, distant mountains rising up like pyramids skirted by wisps of cloud. To the east, the river valley of the Sidon wended northward, barely visible through the haze of dust that hovered over his men as they marched across the grassy plain. Coriantumr chuckled under his breath. This war was proving even easier than he'd thought.

His gaze rose to the slope of the hill before him, and his thoughts turned forward. The thrill of coming battle throbbed through his veins. The Nephite city of Aaron waited just beyond this knoll. The survivors from the towns and villages he had encountered along the way had fled here. Coriantumr sneered. The fools had merely prolonged their doom.

The high stone walls of the city of Aaron rose above the haze as the crest of the hill drew nearer. From the turrets, white standards with dark letters fluttered against the sky. Coriantumr brushed a hand across his brow and grinned. This city was little more than a walled village, a mere pause on his triumphant march to Bountiful.

"You," he barked at a lieutenant marching at his side. "My shield."

"Yes, my lord." The young man drew Coriantumr's leather-bound shield from across his own back, then darted to the overlord's side.

Coriantumr extended his left arm, and the soldier fastened the shield to it. The thick leather strap held firm against Coriantumr's forearm as he gripped the smaller strap in his fist.

The youth hesitated, his eyes on Coriantumr's face.

"What is it?" Coriantumr demanded. "Go back to your place."

"My lord, what has become of Captain Shemnon? Why has he not led us since—?"

"I have led you from the beginning," Coriantumr spat. "Be gone."

"Yes, lord." The young man hurried away.

A weak breeze wafted from the east, fluttering the guidons scattered here and there above the heads of the men. It brushed over the summit of the hill, clearing the haze a little, and as he lifted his eyes, Coriantumr's stride faltered.

Upon the crest of the knoll stood a man. How long he had been there, watching them through the haze, Coriantumr could not say. The man held a sword in one hand, a shield upon the other, and he wore the armor of a Nephite soldier. Feathers fluttered upon the man's helmet. For a moment, Coriantumr's heart chilled at the Nephite's fearless stare. Then rage flared hot within him. This lone Nephite could be overrun with ease.

Lifting his sword high, Coriantumr shouted to the sea of warriors behind him. "Run him down! Slay him before he can reach the city!"

The man turned and darted down the other side of the hill, disappearing from view. A cry rippled over the wave of soldiers as they broke into a jog, their energy renewed, the pounding of their feet like the throb of a drum.

But as the crest of the hill neared, a vibration trembled through the ground like a faint earthquake. Coriantumr faltered. All about him, his men began to slow and many halted, glancing about, uncertain. Coriantumr stopped, his gaze frozen upon the ridge.

From the other side of the knoll, a low roar began. A line of helmeted heads and armored bodies appeared over the crest. Their evenly spaced guidons flashed in the sun.

Coriantumr's eyes widened as he took in a sight his mind refused to believe. Had he not subdued the greater part of the Nephite armies in Zarahemla? Where had all these troops come from? Against his will, Shemnon's warning echoed in his mind. *Bountiful knows you are coming. Do not underestimate them. You will not find them so unprepared.*

He had mocked Shemnon's words then, but he felt no humor now. Through the swirling dust, these forms seemed as specters risen from the dead, the souls of the men he had killed returning to torment him. But as the rolling cry of their voices reached his ears, Coriantumr realized, a sickness growing in his stomach like a swell of black tar, that these were living men—not ghosts, but Nephite warriors in their full strength.

Coriantumr wished it had been the demons, but he could not back down. He could not surrender. He had come too far and done too much. For glory, for the praise of the king, and for the gods for whom he had already spilled so much blood, he must fight. Pushing his forebodings into the pit of his stomach, Coriantumr lifted his shining Nephite-forged sword, waved it in the direction of the oncoming army, and shrieked, "Attack!"

⋈

"Something is happening." Tuloth's muscles strained beneath the weight of his pack, and the words hurt as they passed his lips. A strap across his forehead aided him as he balanced the pack, but did not make the weight any less.

He glanced beside him at the young, stone-faced Lamanites who had been assigned as his guards. "Can you not sense it?"

"Lord Coriantumr commanded you not to speak to us," one soldier reminded him.

Slowed by the heavy bundle of rolled leather and tent pegs he carried on his back Tuloth turned to the youth. Pity and annoyance mingled in his heart. "Do you not sense it?" he repeated. "Something has changed."

The soldier beside him furrowed his brow. In the distance, mountains clad in green rose out of the vast haze of dust that rested like a thick brown cloak across the plain.

A muted roar vibrated through the low haze, followed by the clatter of weapons. The boy's lips parted.

"They have met the Nephites," another guard said, shrugging. "Lord Coriantumr said we would come upon their city of Aaron today."

"But this is not the siege Coriantumr expected. They are battling on the plains," Tuloth said. "They are fighting hand to hand. The Nephites would not come out to meet their foes unless they knew their forces outmatched Coriantumr's."

"What do *you* know of battle, Ammonite?" one guard scoffed. "Your Nephite god will not even let you hold a weapon!"

In an instant, Tuloth spun on the soldier, swift in spite of his heavy burden. His hand flashed out before the young man could react. With a jerk, Tuloth pulled a short knife of chipped obsidian from the youth's belt. In the same moment, his foot swept beneath the young man's heel, so that the young soldier stumbled and fell back onto the ground. The other soldiers and the bearers nearest them gawked at what had just happened, but none drew near, cowed by the iron in Tuloth's gaze.

"I have killed more men than all your kin combined, boy," Tuloth growled, the gleaming black blade clenched in his fist. "I know more of war than you ought ever to know."

"But that is mine. How—?" the youth stammered as he scrambled backward, his eyes filled with fear.

But rather than advance on the frightened soldier, Tuloth turned his attention to his left wrist bound to the strap of his pack with a short strip of leather, giving him only a few inches of movement. He slid the knife beneath the binding and sawed until the leather broke with a snap.

With one hand free, Tuloth pushed the thick leather strap from his forehead and let the oppressive pack fall to the ground with a thump. Holding the knife now in his left hand, he worked the blade beneath the binding about his right wrist until it too snapped, crumpling to the ground like a dead snake. He straightened with a relieved groan.

"I wish you good fortune," Tuloth said, "but I am going now."

"You can't simply leave," one warrior protested, gripping his spear and stepping forward. "Lord Coriantumr's orders—"

"Since leaving Zarahemla, Coriantumr has commanded you and your kin to slaughter innocents," Tuloth spat, turning his eyes on the young warrior who had spoken. "Do you feel no shame in following him? I do not care what his orders are."

The young man gulped and lowered his spear. The other soldiers shifted their weight, glancing at one another.

"I do not need this anymore."

Tuloth flung the knife so it plunged blade first into the ground between the knees of its owner. The young warrior gasped and scrambled further back.

Tuloth nodded southward. "If I guess the thoughts of Chief Captain Moronihah, he will have another army waiting when you try to retreat to Zarahemla. You will find yourselves in a vise. The battle will become unimaginably fierce, but if you ask for mercy, they will give it to you."

With these final words, he turned and strode away through the high brown grass toward the green line of forest in the distance.

He glanced behind him. The fallen soldier rose on shaky legs, pulling his knife from the ground his face filled with nervous distrust as he and the other young warriors watched him go. Many of the bearers also followed Tuloth with their eyes, but none moved to stop him. Tuloth lifted a hand in farewell, then turned away.

⌐⊗⊠⌐

Coriantumr's face twisted with frustration as he staggered through the shadows of the trees. He had lost his shield, his helmet, and had cast aside his shredded, useless armor long before, but his right hand still clenched his sword. His leg throbbed like pulsing fire where a blade had grazed him. Drops of blood trailed down his chin and dripped onto his chest from the long gash on his cheekbone.

Curse those wretched Nephites. Where had this army of uncountable men come from? They fought like rabid jaguars with a fury Coriantumr had not expected. They could not be beaten back any more than the sea, and now his men retreated southward in scattered disarray. Some were in the plains, others in the cover of the forest, but everywhere, the Nephites pursued them. His own guards had all fallen or surrendered, and now he staggered through the forest alone, hunted like an animal.

He stumbled over something on the ground half-hidden beneath the leafy fronds of a fern. His eyes fixed upon the motionless body of a Lamanite warrior. Coriantumr stumbled past it only to see another fallen Lamanite. He spat upon the corpse and continued on. May they and Shemnon—and all the Nephites—rot in a dung heap.

A movement down an incline to his left, a rustle in the undergrowth, set his senses on edge, and Coriantumr halted. He held his breath, clenched his sword, and crept forward a few paces, his eyes seeking for the movement he had caught through the trees. Then he saw the source of the soft noise, and narrowed his eyes.

The Ammonite, weaponless and alone, strode along a narrow animal trail that meandered southward through the shadows. Stains of sweat and dirt smudged the man's tunic, and he carried nothing—no pack, not even a water skin. He moved with the confident pace of one who knew his destination and did not doubt he would reach it.

Coriantumr sneered. The fool would not make it home.

Cold laughter rose through the trees behind Tuloth. He spun around as Coriantumr lurched from the shadows, his eyes glowering like an angry jaguar. He looked like a corpse that had dragged itself out of the grave. His right hand, caked in dried blood, clutched his metal sword.

Tuloth's chest tightened.

"Well?" Coriantumr stepped forward. "Aren't you going to fall on your knees and call out to your one true god, like all your people do before they die?"

"I can pray in my heart." Tuloth stepped backward. "And I do not intend to die today."

Coriantumr snorted. "Eager to get back to that harlot Lylith?"

"Her name is Talilia, and she is no harlot."

Coriantumr staggered forward again as Tuloth continued to retreat.

"You fool. You have no idea who she is."

Tuloth backed away, keeping his distance from the Nephite dissenter, but as he stepped backward, the tangled roots of a thick tree caught his foot, and he stumbled to the ground. Seizing the chance, Coriantumr lunged, his blade lifted, glinting in the waning light.

He swung the blade, but it struck a low hanging tree limb with a crack, and jerked to a halt, buried deep in the wood. Coriantumr cursed and wrenched on it.

Scrambling frantically, Tuloth struggled to rise, but Coriantumr left his embedded blade and smashed his boot into Tuloth's stomach.

Pain flared through Tuloth's abdomen. His elbows buckled, and his head struck the gnarled roots. His mind swam in agony, like a drowning swimmer whose head could not breach the surface of the water. With a satisfied sneer, Coriantumr stepped back to his trapped sword. He snatched the hilt and jerked so furiously that the branch cracked, and the whole tree shuddered like a creature in pain.

Forcing breath into his straining lungs, Tuloth tried to rise, but the treacherous roots entangled his limbs, and he could not get up.

"Your god won't let you fight me." Coriantumr strode back and shoved one foot into the center of Tuloth's chest. "And you cannot flee."

Far above Tuloth, the woven branches of the trees stood out dark against the green light that filtered through the canopy. Something rustled amongst the branches and fell down through the air. At first, it seemed to be a length of thick rope twisting in the dim light, but in a moment, Tuloth made sense of it.

Coriantumr raised his sword.

"Look out—" Tuloth choked. "Get back—"

"Nothing can save you, fool!"

The viper plunged ever closer, dashing leaves aside and snapping smaller twigs.

Hearing the snapping branches, Coriantumr lifted his head just as the mottled brown viper tumbled onto his shoulders, tangling his flailing arms like coils of thick rope. With a muffled cry, Coriantumr staggered backward. His sword fell and clattered among the gnarled roots.

A feral shriek erupted from his lips. As the viper bared its fangs and lunged toward the throbbing artery in Coriantumr's neck, Tuloth, helpless, shut his eyes and turned away.

Chapter 15

Weariness penetrated to the center of Chief Captain Moronihah's bones as he dropped onto the bottom-most step of a ravaged building not far from the palace of the chief judge. From where he sat, he could see the upper walls of the palace, but not the plaza itself, for which he was glad. To his left, perhaps half a league away, the massive east wall rose into the air. A group of Nephite soldiers stood in a cluster behind the battlement, gazing together out over the land beyond. If they knew the chief captain of all the armies could see them, they would be standing lengths apart, planted like stalwart trees in the crenels, not clustered together like nervous schoolboys. The last several days though, had been enough to make the strongest weak, and he understood their need for the nearness of their companions.

Behind him, steps rose up to what had once been an oaken door, now nothing more than a gaping wound, hacked to splinters by Lamanite axes. If he had felt less weary, he would not have wanted to sit with his back toward such darkness, imagining unholy, wicked things hiding in the shadows beyond.

Moronihah stabbed the point of his sword into the ground and dropped his forehead onto his hands folded over the pommel. He studied his feet—the bands of his boots wound halfway up his muscled calves, the blood on the leather dry now. If he narrowed his eyes, he could imagine the splatters were mud.

Away from the prisoners, and the remnants of battle, not needing to keep up any pretense of godlike strength, Moronihah allowed himself the luxury of tears. Despite the silence about him, the battle still echoed in his thoughts. He closed his eyes. "Father, was it like this for you?"

If only Moroni his father still lived, he would have led this war, and Moronihah would not feel the weight of responsibility—and of guilt.

"Captain Moronihah?"

Moronihah jerked his head up to see one of his aides approaching. He shot to his feet. "Lieutenant Kalen."

His voice came out broken, and the young officer glanced away as Moronihah brushed a fist beneath his eyes, sweeping away remnants of wetness.

"What Lamanites we captured are all gathered, sir, but we don't know if any are still secreted away," Kalen said. "You shouldn't be alone."

Moronihah nodded. "You're right, Kalen. But I'm a bit disobedient, aren't I?"

The young man smiled. "I have varied news, sir, good and bad."

Moronihah squared his shoulders. "The good?"

"We've received word that Pacumeni's betrothed, Lady Elizabeth, and his son, Jonas, are alive. They and an officer and one of the young recruits reached the northern cities by boat. They're in Bountiful now."

Moronihah smiled wearily. "Pacumeni's kindred will be relieved. And the bad?"

A scuffle beyond Kalen's shoulder drew Moronihah's attention.

"This, sir."

Two soldiers, flanked by several more, approached, a prisoner between them. The man's wrists strained against leather bonds as he struggled between the two guards.

The man wore Lamanitish garb, though his skin bore a lighter hue than a pure Lamanite. The man's eyes found Moronihah, and his lips drew back from his teeth like a snarling dog.

"He was encouraging the other prisoners to rise up against us," Kalen explained, "to fall on our swords rather than agree to leave in peace."

Moronihah drew in a breath, studying the prisoner's angry features. "Why were you trying to persuade your kin to die needlessly?"

"I have no kin," the prisoner spat.

"Speak your name and rank," Moronihah commanded. "Under whom do you serve?"

The man spat at Moronihah, and Moronihah stepped back, the spittle striking the dirt at his feet.

The Nephite guards growled. One shoved the man in the legs, forcing him to his knees, then lifted the pommel of his sword to cuff the man's head.

"Don't hit him," Moronihah ordered.

The guard nodded, his face grim, and stepped back.

In spite of this act of mercy, the man continued to glare, malice in his eyes.

"Why would you want a rebellion?" Moronihah demanded. "You are our prisoners. We outnumber you. Your weapons are gone. You cannot hope to leave alive, except in peace."

"All I want is to see you Nephite dogs rotting in a cesspit." The man's eyes flashed to the steps behind Moronihah. "Or locked away, dying slowly with the demons in the dark." He sneered. "Like the worthless weakling who would not stomach Coriantumr's orders."

Moronihah glanced over his shoulder, imagining the fiends of his childhood fears clawing their way through the broken door.

A roar jerked Moronihah's attention back to the prisoner, who leaped to his feet in an explosion of fury. He shoved one guard off balance, then swung his knotted wrists, bashing the other guard in the face. As the soldier fell, the prisoner wrenched his sword from its sheath with his bound hands.

"Stop him!" Moronihah rushed forward, fearing that the prisoner would bring the blade down upon the stunned guard.

Instead, the man swiveled the weapon in his hands so the blade pointed against his own belly and collapsed upon it with a grunt.

Moronihah staggered to a stop, his stomach twisting.

The guards scrambled up, unhurt, as the others gathered around the unmoving body, muttering their disbelief.

"Sir…" Kalen's face had paled. "Forgive me. I—"

"It's not your fault." Moronihah understood the young man's emotions. No matter how many times he saw it, violent death still filled him with sick horror.

"What do we do now, sir?" Kalen asked.

"There's nothing we can do for him." He gestured to the body. "But perhaps..." He gazed up through the gaping doorway. A faint sense of urgency stirred in him. He did not fully understand it, but it grew stronger as he gazed into the darkness beyond. "Come with me."

He strode up the steps and stooped through the hacked entrance. The shadows closed over him, and at first, he could see nothing of the empty interior. He heard his own footsteps and Kalen's as the younger soldier ducked in behind him.

An empty room materialized as his eyes adjusted to the dark. The chamber seemed unremarkable. As he cast his gaze about, a narrow set of stone steps to his right came into focus, descending down into the earth.

"This way." The eerie echo of his own voice came back at him as Moronihah started down the darkened steps. He wished he had brought a torch.

As they descended, the shadows deepened. Moronihah shuddered, a palpable chill in the air as their steps echoed off the stone walls.

Moronihah stumbled before he realized the steps had ended at a level floor, but Kalen's hand steadied him, and Moronihah regained his footing. He peered into the darkness of the small chamber where he found himself. The room appeared empty except for a wooden door in one wall, a shadow against lighter stone.

Two iron brackets had been bolted into the wood, and two more brackets had been fastened into the stone wall on either side of the door. Between the brackets lay a long, thick slab of wood. A serpentine rope twined around the beam, bound fast.

"No one has been down here for days." Moronihah touched the grainy wood of the door.

"What do you think we'll find here, sir?"

Even in the darkness, Moronihah could see the concern in Kalen's eyes.

"Let's find out." Moronihah drew his sword from the sheath and sliced it through the knotted rope. Loosened, the rope slithered off the beam and tumbled with a hiss to the floor.

Moronihah slid his sword back in its sheath. "Help me lift this beam."

The two men lifted the slab out of the brackets and let it fall with a heavy thump.

Flinching, Moronihah grasped one of the cold metal brackets and pulled. The door scraped open, revealing an archway of yawning darkness before a musty smell struck his nostrils.

Tensing his jaw against his fear, he stepped through the archway into the void.

"Is anyone here?" His voice filled the close room. He heard the soft scuff of Kalen's boots as the younger soldier stepped through the door behind him.

"Sir, there," Kalen whispered. "To the left."

Moronihah turned his head. A shadow lay beside the wall. Moronihah stepped closer and lowered himself to his knees beside the still figure.

"Can you speak?"

The form stirred. "Water," a ghostly voice pleaded in the tongue of the Lamanites.

Kalen's water skin was off his belt and in Moronihah's hand in a moment. Moronihah loosed the cork. He slid his hand beneath the head, shorn in the manner of Lamanite warriors, though short stubble brushed against his fingers. He had been here for several days, at least. Why would they do this to one of their own?

He tipped the leather skin.

"Drink," he ordered, and the shadow obeyed.

"How long have you been here?"Moronihah asked as he drew the water skin back.

"Days. Weeks. Light is but a memory."The man shook his head. "What has become of my daughter?"

"What is your name and rank?"Moronihah asked. "Who did this to you? Why?"

The man stirred. "By the accents of your speech, you are Nephites."

"We are, sir."

"You have reclaimed Zarahemla?"

"We have."

"What of Coriantumr?"

"He was found among the slain."

Silence followed Moronihah's reply, and he recalled the words of the other prisoner...*the worthless weakling who would not stomach Coriantumr's orders.*

Had this half-dead man argued against Coriantumr's senseless brutality?

"What of my child?"the man pleaded. "Coriantumr meant to do her harm."

"I give you an oath that we will do all in our power to find your daughter and restore her to you. For now, drink more."

The man obeyed as Moronihah tipped the water skin to his lips again. Then he spoke. "And what will you do with me?"

"We will make you well. Then you may return to your own lands."

"You will let me live?"

"That is our intention."

The man trembled as if he wept. "You know what honor is."

"No better than you do, sir." Moronihah murmured. "What is your name?"

"I have none."

Behind him, Kalen shifted his weight.

Moronihah furrowed his brow. "But surely—"

"Who I was before no longer lives, and we do not speak the names of our dead."

Chapter 16

Light sifted through the linen curtain, illuminating the room where Elizabeth sat beside Joshua's bed, the coverlet drawn to his waist. His eyes were focused on the ceiling, his fingers woven together behind his head. With painstaking care, Elizabeth loosened the knotted strip of wide cloth around his ribs, revealing the wound upon his chest. Her throat tightened as she studied the lines of the gash, the edges knit more firmly than before.

"How is it?" Joshua asked, his eyes still on the ceiling.

"Better." She rolled the old bandage and dropped it into a basket at her feet. "How do you feel?"

"Not as strong as I wish." He heaved a breath. "But the pain is less."

A breeze stirred at the window, fluttering the curtain with playful fingers before making its way into the room.

Glancing up at Joshua's face, she noted the faint smile, the deepening rise and fall of his breathing as he drank the sweet sea air.

"What do you think became of that Lamanite who saved my life?"

She shrugged and looked away. "I doubt we'll ever know. If he lived, he returned home. If not…" She let her words fade. It made her a little sad that she would never know the old warrior's fate. She wished she had asked his name.

"Much time will pass before the land is safe again, and then months will go by before the season is right for travel," Joshua murmured. "What will you do during that time?"

"Watch over Jonas." She paused. "And you."

She felt his eyes upon her, but a strange timidity would not allow her to look at him. Instead, she turned to a small table beside her, picking up a bowl half filled with a healing salve of crushed herbs. She scooped out a portion and reached to smooth it over the healing wound.

As she touched him, his flesh tensed beneath her fingers. Elizabeth flinched and drew her hand back.

"Forgive my clumsiness, Joshua." She set the bowl down. "I'll fetch a healer."

But as she moved to rise, Joshua's hand shot out and caught her wrist. "Don't go, Elizabeth." His warmth seeped into her from his fingers. His gaze found hers. "Not even the most skilled healer has hands as gentle as yours."

Her lips parted, something in his gaze quickening her heart. Drawing in a deep breath she nodded and lowered herself again to her seat.

"How would you know that my hands are the most gentle?" She salved the wound as she spoke. "This is the first time anyone has treated you while you were conscious." She gathered up a bandaging cloth and lay it over the healing skin.

For a long moment, Joshua remained silent. Elizabeth finished the last knot on the bandage and ventured to glance up into his eyes.

"I knew." He drew in a breath, studying her with softness in his gaze. "Somehow."

She held his eyes for a long moment before the sound of children's laughter filtered through the fabric of the curtain. Elizabeth looked toward the sound and rose to her feet. She moved to the window, pushing the curtain aside as the bright daylight streamed in.

Elizabeth's eyes trailed to an alcove across the street between two small shops where a group of children played a game of kickball with Zeram, his golden hair tied back in a tail. A smile touched her lips when she recognized Zeram's smaller companions. A little girl named Dayani, the daughter of Thobor, whose wife, Esther, looked after Jonas. A boy named Aaron, Zeram's younger brother. And little Jonas himself, dancing from one foot to another.

Dayani's dark braids swung about her neck as she stole the ball from Zeram, who pretended helpless dismay. Dayani kicked the ball to Aaron. He passed it to Jonas, who kicked it into a small basket set against the side of a nearby wall.

Jonas threw his arms skyward, whooping, and Elizabeth smiled. She hadn't seen him laugh since Pacumeni's death, and her heart warmed to see the child happy again. She ran a thumb over the grainy surface of the window ledge, her heart full of both sweetness and pain.

A breeze brushed over her shoulder and into the room. A soft sound, almost like the notes of a distant flute, seemed to float in the wind.

The agony of your own heart is fading too, my love, and you are healing, as you should, a voice seemed to whisper as the wind caressed her skin and brushed through her hair.

Elizabeth's grip tightened on the curtain. The voice seemed so real.

"Elizabeth," a man's voice breathed behind her. A hand touched her shoulder, sending trails of warmth shivering over her skin.

With her free hand, she covered the larger one upon her shoulder, running her thumb over the lean fingers. "Pacumeni..." She turned, her eyes fixing upon Joshua, who stood behind her.

He wore the pale linen kilt the healers had garbed him in, the thick cotton bandaging wrapping most of his chest. His face furrowed with the effort it had taken him to rise, and his firm shoulders rose and fell as if he had put himself through a great strain.

"Joshua." Her hand remained upon his as her other hand released the curtain. The fabric fell back, bathing the room again in muted light. "The physicians said you shouldn't be on your feet. Not yet."

"I'm sorry, but I thought I heard music. And almost... a voice." He paused. "Pacumeni's voice."

Elizabeth's lips parted. "So did I." A broken sigh escaped her. "But please. You need rest."

He looked away, despondent, and his hand fell from her shoulder.

"I don't want rest. I want to be useful again, Elizabeth. I cannot bear this *waiting*. I failed in my duty before, and—"

"You didn't fail, Joshua. You did all that was in your power."

The honed lines of Joshua's jaw grew taut with frustration, and his eyes gleamed with unshed tears. "It wasn't enough. If I had the power to choose, Pacumeni would be here, and I would have been the one to die."

"Joshua, do not say such things!" A tear pricked her eye and spilled over her lashes, trailing down her cheek. "I mourn Pacumeni too, but you sin in your wish, for Pacumeni isn't here, and *you* are. I would *never* wish for your death even if it would bring him back!"

His gaze, deep as the sea, delved into her own. "Forgive me, Elizabeth. I didn't mean to make you cry."

"I know," she said before she moved to him and circled her arms around his chest.

His arms tightened about her as she settled her head beneath his chin. The bandage felt stiff against her jaw, and through it, she could hear the steady beating of his heart. A fragment of a memory flashed through her thoughts of a time not long before his death when Pacumeni had held her just like this. But Joshua was not Pacumeni. The comforting feel of him wasn't the same, nor the musky scent of him. And though she missed Pacumeni with a pang that stung to the core of her soul, still Elizabeth did not wish this man who held her to be anyone else but Joshua.

"You are my dearest friend in all the world, Joshua. I never want to lose you."

Joshua's arms tightened. "Nor I you, Elizabeth," he whispered.

ᗡ⋈⋉

Light flickered through Shemnon's eyelids as he rose from oblivion. He lay on his back, a coverlet drawn to his chest.

"He's waking," a feminine voice murmured in the Nephite tongue. Feet pattered upon stone, and cloth rustled as someone knelt at his side. Small hands grasped his own.

"Father? Can you hear me?"

Talilia, Shemnon tried to say, but no sound came forth.

"Drink a little, Father," she pleaded.

A strong hand, not Talilia's, slid beneath his neck, tilting his head as a bowl touched his lips.

Shemnon swallowed, warm broth slipping down his throat.

As the bowl drew away, he tried once more to speak.

"Talilia," he said, his voice grating. "My bright candle. You are safe."

"I am, Father." Her grip tightened. "And so are you."

"Where are we?"

"In a house of healing," a man's voice answered. "And here, we will see to it that you are made well."

Shemnon opened his eyes to wooden beams crossing a ceiling high above him.

At his side sat Talilia. Her worried smile reflected flickering lamplight.

Beside Talilia and nearer to Shemnon's head knelt a man whose hands held a wooden bowl. This man appeared Lamanite, though he wore the garb of a Nephite. His unshorn hair lay smoothed back and tied behind his head, trailing to his shoulder in a long tail.

"Greetings, Tuloth, son of Zadock of Shemlon," Shemnon murmured.

Tuloth smiled. "You remember me, sir."

"Few could forget you. It seems your Nephite god has been with you after all." Shemnon turned his eyes back to Talilia.

"This, Father," Talilia murmured, gesturing behind her to a figure on the edge of the lamplight, "is the chief captain of the Nephites. He and his lieutenant found you."

The man moved into the circle of light, offering Shemnon a nod. Though his face appeared young, almost boyish, he wore the uniform of a chief captain.

"I am honored, sir. I am Moronihah, son of Moroni."

Shemnon's heart gave a heave of emotion.

"Son of Moroni? The great Nephite captain?"

Moronihah inclined his head. "Yes, sir."

Shemnon studied the beams in the ceiling. A Nephite, the very son of Moroni no less, had shown him mercy. Shemnon had once hated the name. But now, he lived because of the kindness of the man's son.

His throat tightened with emotion as the old belief of the dishonorable Nephites crumbled like an old stone wall, tumbling into dust, leaving nothing but throbbing emptiness behind. "You saved me, and yet it would not be unjust if you slew me. I owe you a debt I cannot repay."

"You owe us nothing but an oath of peace, sir," Moronihah insisted. "And when you are well again, you will be free to return to your own lands."

A sigh escaped Talilia. Her eyes darted to Tuloth's face before her gaze fell away.

Shemnon's eyes trailed to the Ammonite who knelt at her side. Tuloth's eyes lingered on Talilia's face, the tenderness in the young man's expression unmistakable.

"My child…" Shemnon's throat thickened as he reached for and grasped Talilia's hand. "This is the land of your birth. You should remain here." His eyes moved to Tuloth. "Begin a life here."

Her brow furrowed at this, and her hand squeezed his. "Where you go, Father, I will follow. You would not wish to leave me?"

"Never, my daughter." Shemnon's throat tightened. "For I do not intend to return to the lands of my own birth. Here, you should stay. And so, also, shall I." His gaze moved back to Tuloth, noting the relief upon the Ammonite's face.

Shemnon turned his eyes to Moronihah. "I have done great harm to your people. Even so, will you permit me to stay and try to repay my debt?" His hand felt like a stone weight as he lifted it.

"If you wish to stay in peace, you are welcome." Moronihah reached down, clasping Shemnon's proffered forearm. "But your daughter honored your wish not to tell us your name without your leave, and we do not know what to call you."

Shemnon released Moronihah's grip. He had spent his strength, and his arm fell to his side as he sank back against his pillow.

"We do not speak the names of our dead. But if you must, you may call me—" Shemnon searched his mind. "Amasa."

Chapter 17

A breeze, filled with the sweetness of growing things and the tang of the sea, wafted through the orchard where Elizabeth stood at the base of a sapota tree.

She plucked another plump fruit and dropped it into the cloth bag that hung over her shoulder nearly filled with the potato-sized fruits. Grateful for the cool breeze in the heat of the afternoon, she lifted her face and studied a passing cloud, white against the blueness of the sky. Peace had come to her heart, and she was content. Yet even so, a lingering sorrow remained, hidden in the corners of her soul.

She would have been Pacumeni's bride for several months now. Perhaps she would already have borne his child. But now, that would never be.

The soldiers had restored Zarahemla, along with the smaller cities the Lamanites had plundered, and but for the dead who could not return, all was as it had been.

The wind brushed over her face, sliding through her unbound hair like a gentle hand, rustling the cloth of the mantle she wore about her shoulders and her light tunic beneath.

The world still had beauty and goodness in it.

"Elizabeth!"

A thrill of pleasure shot through her at the voice, and she turned.

Joshua stood on the edge of the road that wended past the orchard and toward the city walls rising above the treetops. A blue cloak hung over one sturdy shoulder, and the cloth of his new uniform rippled against his chest. The emblem at his shoulder marking him as a lower captain caught the sunlight.

She raised a hand. "Joshua!"

He waved in return, something white in his hand. "Esther said I would find you here!" He turned off the roadway, striding toward her beneath the dappled shadows of the rows of cultivated sapota trees. "I bring news!"

For a fleeting moment, a faint warmth stirred within Elizabeth's blood as she watched Joshua move toward her, his strength and grace evident in his stride, the light and shadow of the waving branches dancing off his lean form.

But just as quickly, into her mind came a memory of Pacumeni coming toward her in the same manner, smiling upon her just as Joshua smiled now, and the yearning faded like an elusive scent upon a breeze.

Rallying, Elizabeth set her bag at the foot of the tree and darted toward him. "What is it?"

Joshua stopped an arm's length from her. The breeze stirred his dark hair, loose about his face. "A runner just came from Zarahemla."

Elizabeth's eyes darted to the folded parchment in his hand, then back to his eyes. "And?"

"Word has come of the election." Joshua grinned. "The people chose Helaman over Gadianton as our new chief judge."

Elizabeth smiled at his words. "I'd hoped he would win." But her thoughts sobered, and her smile eased. "I wonder what Pazia's feelings are, with her husband in a post that has caused so much death in her family."

Joshua nodded. "I've thought on the same things." His next words came with effort. "As her husband has, it appears. This came to me from Helaman himself."

Paper crinkled, and Elizabeth's eyes moved to the folded piece of parchment in his hand, bearing the seal of the chief judge.

"He believes that young Pahoran's murderer still lives, and is but one of a larger group." Joshua's brows knit. "For myself, I suspect he's right."

He held out the crumpled missive, his expression uncertain. "You may read it."

Elizabeth took the parchment, opening the folds.

To Lower Captain Joshua, son of Antipus, peace be with you.

May I first congratulate you on your promotion. It is well deserved. And may this letter find you in good health. Pazia sends her greetings to Elizabeth, and to Jonas. We pray daily for you all, that God's blessings and comfort may be with you in Bountiful.

And now, Captain, to the key purpose of this letter. As you may already be aware, I have received the appointment to the judgment seat, and will have taken office before this missive reaches you. I pray that I will lead this people as God wills me.

In recent days, my mind has dwelt much upon the secret society that I believe was responsible for the murder of my brother-in-law, Pahoran the younger. I fear that they are not gone as many hope, and I fear also the poison of the words and deeds of such men. Not for myself alone, but for all our people. Such men, if left unchecked, would lead our nation to falter and ultimately destroy itself.

I know that you were as a brother to Pacumeni, and that you were a loyal guard in the palace when he lived. I also know that you have taken up duties in Bountiful.

Elizabeth swallowed hard as her eyes trailed over the next words.

But I would beg you to consider returning to Zarahemla to take up duties here again. I cannot think of any man better suited to the post I wish to offer you. And I assure you that if you accept, the service you perform would be of lasting benefit to our people.

I remain in your service, Helaman, son of Helaman, Chief Judge, Zarahemla

She returned the parchment and struggled to smile. "He wants you to serve in the palace again. That is a great honor, Joshua."

"It is." His jaw knotted as he tucked the letter into his cloak.

Elizabeth's eyes trailed to the east border of the orchard where the wall of the untamed forest rose; tall trees and dense undergrowth that grew unbroken, save for one narrow trail that wended through the trees toward the sea. She knew every curve of that path, every tree, root, and stone along its course. Joshua had first taken her on that path when they were children. How many times had they followed it together since?

"What do you intend to say?" she asked, turning to meet Joshua's eyes. Blue as the sea beneath a clear sky, and filled with a tangle of unreadable emotions.

"I'm not certain yet."

Elizabeth bit her lip. "What would make the choice difficult?"

"Bountiful," Joshua answered before his eyes turned away, fixing on the same path Elizabeth had studied. "And everything here. The forests, the shores, and..." His gaze returned to her face. "Would *you* ever return to Zarahemla, Elizabeth?"

Elizabeth's heart quickened at the softness of his tone.

"Jonas must be taken home, and it would be my duty to see him there. He belongs with his kin, much as I love him. But I would not stay long. I loved Zarahemla, but—"

Joshua shifted nearer, his fingers brushing the back of her hand. "But it wouldn't be the same without Pacumeni," he said.

Elizabeth's throat tightened. "It wouldn't." She turned her hand toward his, allowing his lean, warm fingers to weave through hers as they had so often done when they were young.

"Will you come with me to the shores, Elizabeth?" he asked.

"I would like that."

Joshua led her toward the wall of wild trees and the narrow path that disappeared through them. As she and Joshua stepped from the edge of the cultivated orchard into the shadows of the forest path, sound grew muted.

Elizabeth drank in the heavy air that hovered beneath the canopy, her heart weighted with a mingling of both peace and sorrow. As if he sensed her need, Joshua released her hand and circled his arm about her shoulders. A thrill shivered through her as he drew her closer to his side.

"I remember you brought me here when we first became friends." Elizabeth slipped her own arm about his sturdy waist.

"I've known this trail for as long as I can remember. It was the first thing I wanted to show you," Joshua said. "My parents often brought me here when I was small." His hand gently squeezed Elizabeth's shoulder.

"After my mother died, my father would come alone, sometimes, before he went to war." A deep breath escaped him. "He missed her."

Companionable silence rested between them as they continued on, blue water beginning to peek through the thinning trees. The earth beneath their feet softened, soil giving way to sand.

At last the trees drew back to reveal a long curve of white sand stretching far and away southward. Before them, foam-crested waves rolled against the edge of the sand, the ocean extending into the infinite distance.

A breath caught in her throat as she took in the scene, and together, they drew to a stop.

Elizabeth stepped away from Joshua's side into the sunlight. The breeze off the sea trailed cool fingers through the loose strands of her hair.

"I remember that first day I brought you here," Joshua said, "and the moment we stopped at this spot."

He stepped to her side, and his arm brushed her shoulder, sending a shiver of warmth through her.

"You said something in the Lamanite tongue. I didn't understand the language then." He turned to her, his voice softening. "I never asked what you said that day. Do you still remember?"

Elizabeth gazed over the water and murmured in the tongue her mother had taught her, "'*Your heart and my heart are one.*'"

She turned to him, and noted the deep breath that swelled his chest as he studied her face.

"Meaning that what is dear to me is dear to you," he translated.

"Yes." Elizabeth grew still for a moment, studying the depths of his eyes, the way the sunlight upon his hair caused it to glimmer like liquid obsidian as it fell about the honed angles of his face. He did not touch her, but his nearness sent trails of warmth through her body. Letting her eyes move over his features, her gaze came to rest upon his mouth, and she wondered why she had never noticed before how perfectly formed his lips were.

Her gaze fell to his shoulder, and she marveled anew at the quiet strength Joshua possessed, hands that could slay an enemy in defense of his people, yet hold her hand as he would a priceless treasure.

"I remember many other days as well," he said, and she lifted her eyes to his face. He grinned, and she returned it, the laughter of two children racing toward the water echoing in her thoughts.

"Do you remember our races to the water?" she asked.

"Of course." He chuckled. "And I remember how you cheated and ran first! Yet I would still beat you." A boyish grin touched his lips.

She snorted. Then on an impulse, she gathered up her skirts, turned, and dashed toward the surf. "But this time, I *will* beat you!" she shouted.

"*Cheater!*" Joshua cried and his feet pounded after her. He wrenched his cloak from over his shoulders and flung it away as he sprinted past. Within moments, his warrior's legs had far outdistanced her own. The foam splashed up around him, and he plunged headfirst into an oncoming wave.

"Joshua, your sandals!" Elizabeth laughed, gasping as she pulled to a stop at the water's edge.

His head surfaced, bobbing with the swells. He tossed his head, flinging water from his hair as he turned toward her and waved his arm, whooping in merriment. "I won!" he crowed. "Again!"

Elizabeth pulled off her sandals and tossed them higher up on the dry sand, then drew off her mantle and flung it in a heap upon her discarded sandals. She started toward the water as a wave rolled up the beach and hissed, cold, over her bare toes. Joshua's breathless laughter rang out across the water. A smile curved Elizabeth's lips as she gathered her skirt about her knees and waded farther into the shallows.

"But *my* shoes are still dry!" she called out, laughing.

Joshua scowled at this, then swam to the shallows and waded to her.

Elizabeth's laughter receded though as Joshua rose out of the water. His hair streamed and his wet shirt clung to his chest, taut against the sinuous muscles beneath it. Her heart quickened and she dropped her gaze, hoping he would not see the color in her cheeks.

Balancing in the surging water, Joshua lifted one foot and attempted to unlace the leather knot of his sandal, but it would not come free for him.

Giving up on the knot, he pried the soaked sandal off, and then the other, before tossing them with a wet plop higher up on the sand.

"Your sandals *are* still dry, Elizabeth," he agreed before he cupped his hands into a wave as it surged about his knees. He flung it at her in a shining arc and she gasped, throwing up a hand as the water struck her in cool spatters. "But now *you* aren't!"

"You scoundrel!" She lifted a foot, kicking a sheet of water back at him.

At this, an ominous smile spread across his face. "Is it war, then?"

"Now, Joshua." Elizabeth backed away as he sloshed toward her through the knee-deep water. "Don't—Ah! No!" she wailed as Joshua lunged near, scooped her up in his arms, and with a wild laugh, plunged into the next wave. The water, cold and silent, closed over her head, stifling her further protests.

As the water rolled back, Elizabeth rose and sucked in a breath, gasping and laughing, clinging to Joshua as the waves buffeted them. Her hair streamed water and her tunic clung tightly to her body. As she caught her breath, she slowly grew aware of the way she and Joshua held one another. Joshua's hands about her waist steadied her and held her close, her body pressed against his in the thigh-deep water. Her hands clung to the damp cloth of Joshua's tunic, the corded muscles of his firm chest evident against her fingers through the soaked cloth. Water surged about them, but with Joshua's arms around her, she was secure. Her heart skipped a beat, and emotions—nameless, yet sweet— simmered in her blood.

Quieting, Elizabeth lifted her eyes to find Joshua's. His features had sobered as well, as if he felt what she did. She retreated a step. A look of pleading filled his eyes, and at her hips, his hands tightened for a moment as if he wished to restrain her and keep her with him. But as she resisted and drew further back, his strength eased, and he let her slip out of his arms.

Alone, the waves rocked her, and the chill of the water caused her to shiver.

"You're cold." The playful tone of his voice had faded. He extended his hand. "Come. Let's find a pleasant place where we can sit in the sun and dry."

She studied his upturned palm, his lean fingers. A warrior's hand. Strong, yet gentle. The hand of a friend, of a man she trusted with her life.

She reached out and slipped her smaller hand into Joshua's. Together, they rose out of the water onto the sand.

Chapter 18

Elizabeth stirred where she lay asleep upon Joshua's cloak spread beneath the trees at the edge of the sand, the shadows now reaching almost to the water. Joshua, who held a flat stone in one hand as he sat cross-legged beside her, shifted his eyes from the foam-crested waves to study her.

Elizabeth. He breathed her name.

She lay on her back, her knees bent slightly. Grains of sand still clung to the hem of her tunic, and to her smooth calves as they tapered down to her small feet, her toes peeking through her sandals. One ankle crossed over the other. Her mantle lay folded beneath her head as a pillow. One of her small hands lay in repose across her slender stomach while the other, with fingers curled, rested against her cheek. Her breasts rose and fell with each breath, and her hair shimmered like gold where it spilled over the folds of his cloak in luxurious whorls. All but for one lock which trailed down the side of her face.

Shifting his weight, Joshua reached a hand and caught the errant curl between his fingers.

Tingling pulses raced along his nerves as the lock of her hair slid between his thumb and forefinger, smooth as silk. He let his hand linger there, hovering a fraction above her cheek, content with drinking in the peaceful tranquility of her sleeping form and the silken touch of her hair.

Elizabeth shifted, and her cheek brushed the backs of his fingers.

Just a feather's brush. Even so, she drew in a tremulous sigh and opened her eyes.

Joshua withdrew his hand and sat back. Her eyes blinked as they contemplated the fanning leaves overhead before trailing downward and resting upon him. His throat grew dry as he returned her gaze, noting the quickened intake of her breath and the soft shimmer of her hair as she shifted her head to study him more directly.

"How long have I been asleep?"

"About an hour."

She sat up, the cloth of her tunic rustling with the motion. Her hair fell about her shoulders in tousled locks. The corner of her tunic shifted to one side, exposing part of her shoulder and the edge of one frail collarbone.

Her pulse beat steadily beneath the smooth flesh of her slender throat.

Joshua swallowed, the blood throbbing in his own veins.

"And you have been watching over me all along?" she asked.

He tightened his fist around the small rock and tore his gaze away from her, fixing instead upon the waves that hissed against the sand. "Yes," he said. "It gave me time to think."

Elizabeth curled her legs beneath her. "What about?"

Joshua couldn't speak, and instead, he turned his eyes to the rock in his hand, white flecks scattered across its black surface.

He squeezed the rock one last time, then turned his eyes toward the blue of the water. Pulling his arm back, he flung the stone with a furious burst of energy. Over the wide stretch of sand it sailed to the water where it skipped off a rolling wave, then disappeared beyond a ridge of foam.

"I wish…" As his eyes found her face, his voice fell silent.

Elizabeth's jade-green eyes looked toward the water, her cheeks a gentle rose pink, her lips softly parted. How unutterably alluring she was. How he wished he could slide his fingers into the richness of her hair…

"What do you wish?" she whispered.

Joshua swallowed hard. "I wish that I was stronger," he murmured.

Elizabeth's lips parted, and she turned to look at him as a confused expression touched her face. Her gaze flitted over his arms and chest before lifting again to his eyes. "There is none stronger than you."

"I don't speak of physical strength." He turned his gaze away. "I wish… that I could make you happy."

"Joshua."

Elizabeth's voice caressed his heart like a healing balm, even as the sweetness of it stung. Cloth rustled as she shifted near and touched his arm.

Trails of fire pulsed through his blood from the spot where her fingers pressed. He drew in a breath, drinking in the scent of her, her closeness an exquisite agony to him.

"I *am* happy, my friend."

"Not as happy as you would be if Pacumeni still lived."

Her fingers trembled where they touched his arm, and he dared not look at her.

"Joshua, please. Do not speak this way. You cannot change the past."

He cringed at the pain in her voice, but he continued, "Had I died fighting beside him—"

"Then I would be bereft of you both!" Elizabeth hissed, her slender fingers tightening on his arm. "Do you know what that would have done to me?"

"Had I died and he lived," Joshua persisted, "he would be here with you now." He turned to her, finding her gaze near to his own as she leaned toward him, her eyes damp.

"He is not, Joshua, and you are," she said.

"But you loved him, and he loved you." Joshua lifted a hand to her cheek. "And life is empty without such love."

Elizabeth lowered her eyes. The breeze fluttered her hair about her shoulders. After a moment, she lifted her gaze. Her eyes shimmered with unshed tears. "But how can my life be truly empty when you are in it, Joshua?"

Joshua could not say what caused his actions, but something in her misted eyes, in her trusting expression, something in the way she tipped her face toward his, compelled him. Without thought, Joshua bent his head and brushed his lips against her own.

Elizabeth wondered why she did not withdraw when Joshua bent over her, his warm mouth so unexpectedly capturing her parted lips. She only knew, as the music of the sea whispered at the edge of the sand, that deep within herself, she did not wish to pull away.

With Joshua's lips tentatively caressing her own, she became intensely conscious of his nearness, of his strength, gentle and controlled.

Something in the way his hand cupped her cheek, in the way his lips moved over hers, something in the closeness of him, in his sweet, musky scent, compelled her to lean nearer, to return his timid caresses. Joshua was her friend, her dear one, and she did not want his kiss to end.

His hand trembled upon her cheek.

"Elizabeth," he breathed against her lips. His voice trembled through her, startling her back to reality.

Elizabeth's eyes flew open. She gasped and thrust herself away. Joshua's gaze fixed with uncertainty upon hers. She still tasted the sweetness of his mouth, still felt the warmth of his hand cupping her cheek. And even now, passions she had never imagined she would feel again coursed through her blood as she gazed into Joshua's face. She swallowed, regretting that she had ended the kiss.

"I'm sorry." Joshua's sea-blue eyes tore away from hers. "I shouldn't have—Elizabeth, forgive me."

"Why did you kiss me, Joshua?"

"Because I..." Joshua's eyes lifted to hers, fraught with guilt, before they fell away again.

Elizabeth jerked her eyes from his face, her heart convulsing. "I must go." The words tore from her like a knife's blade that had been thrust into her and then wrenched out again. "Esther expected the fruit hours ago."

She scrambled to her feet, snatched up her crumpled mantle, and turned away.

Elizabeth hurried toward the path that led back the way they'd come, wetness blurring her eyes. As she reached the path, she paused and glanced back.

Joshua remained where she had left him, sitting beside his rumpled cloak where she had slept. His hair, loose about his shoulders, fluttered in the wind. His sturdy arms lay folded across his knees, and his head drooped as if in deepest weariness.

Her heart breaking within her, Elizabeth turned and plunged into the forest.

Evening cast a crimson mantle across the sky over Bountiful. The shadows of night crept from the east like a dark mist.

Within the shadows of the forest, Joshua sat on a fallen log, the flicker of torchlight from the battlements of the city wall barely reaching him.

The memory of that brief moment Elizabeth had given him earlier, the fragrance of her, the warmth of her cheek beneath his fingers, the taste of her pliant mouth, all ravaged Joshua's senses, leaving him exhausted. Wounds delivered by the blows of enemies felt nothing like the barbs driven into his soul by the memory of her soft eyes, the sweetness of her lips, and the knowledge that he lacked the power to deliver her from her sorrow. He could not bring Pacumeni back, nor take his place.

He had no right even to try. He could do nothing for her, just as he had been unable to save the man she loved.

The shame of his own weakness throbbed in his heart like a hammer on an anvil. It had not been his right to take advantage of her sorrow, for surely it had been Pacumeni she had imagined when she allowed Joshua that brief kiss. She would not have kissed him back otherwise.

Why did you kiss me, Joshua? Her question echoed in his thoughts.

"Because I love you." He finished the words he'd been unable to speak to her earlier. "Not as a sister, not merely as a friend."

In his thoughts, her eyes grew sad. *But I can't love you in return*, he imagined her saying. *My heart is Pacumeni's. Forever.*

To hear such words would have torn his soul, and for that reason, he had been unable to speak.

Joshua turned his eyes from the sky and drew his iron knife from its sheath at his side. With a grunt of frustration, he plunged it into the rotting wood of the log beside him. The knife sank to the hilt. Leaving the blade embedded, he glanced skyward, studying the clouds that stretched from the west to the east in flames of red and gold. A sight he had gazed at often before, but tonight, the beauty of it did not soothe him.

Perhaps if he banished Elizabeth from his mind, stopped tormenting himself with thoughts of her, his longing would fade, and he would find another woman who could fill his heart as he had resigned himself to do when Pacumeni had been alive. But Joshua cast this thought away, repelled at the idea. Could he move on and allow his heart to accept another when somewhere in this world, Elizabeth remained alone? No. Not anymore. Not for as long as he could draw breath.

Letting his eyes trail in the direction of the gate, he imagined Elizabeth, beautiful and sad, her gaze fixed on the brilliant sky. Would she never have anything to cling to but memories? He could not make everything well for her again. He could never trade his life for Pacumeni's, nor fill his place. But neither could he deny his own feelings for her.

Perhaps it would be best to take Helaman's offer, return to Zarahemla, separate himself from her, and take his longings for her with him. Painful as it would be, it would be for the best.

With a wrench, Joshua tore his knife from the crumbling wood, tearing the log nearly in half before he thrust to his feet. He clapped his knife in its sheath and started back through the trees toward the southern gate and the torchlight that flickered along the darkening parapet.

Lamplight flickered off the walls of the small room Elizabeth shared with Jonas. She sat before a wooden table, her elbows resting on the surface. Jonas lay curled up on his mat, his body no more than a small lump beneath his coverlet, his breath deep as he dreamed. Her own mat lay untouched in the other corner.

Elizabeth's eyes moved over the words upon the scroll of scripture unrolled before her, a story of a conversation between Moses and his father-in-law Jethro, but she could not keep her thoughts on the words, her mind flickering between images of Pacumeni and Joshua. Tears sprang to her swollen eyes while in her mind she studied the familiar expressions of each man.

With all the ardor of first love, she had loved Pacumeni, certain that he would be the one bright star in her sky for all her life. When he had died, so had all of the life and passion of her heart. Or so she had thought before today. Now, Joshua's power, the masculine scent of him, the tenderness in his eyes, the feel of his fingers cupping her face, the taste of his mouth, his goodness and honor, his strength and beauty—all that he was tumbled through her thoughts with merciless clarity and throbbed through her blood.

Why had he kissed her? Had mere pity compelled him? Had he done it without thinking, not knowing how else to comfort her? Equally befuddling, why had she kissed him *back*? How could she feel such tender stirrings for him when less than a year ago, he had been nothing more than a dear friend?

"Elizabeth?" At a muffled voice beyond the shutter, she lifted her face.

Elizabeth rose and drew the window open.

Zeram, clad in his uniform, stood in the square of lamplight. His chest rose and fell as if he had been running. Despite her heavy heart, Elizabeth gladdened at the sight of the youth. His tall frame and broadening shoulders filled most of the window. He was becoming a man before her eyes.

"Zeram." She managed a smile for his sake, certain he could see her red-rimmed eyes. "What are you doing at this hour?"

"I come from the west gate," he gasped. "I was on duty there when Joshua came. He told me to give you this," Zeram held out a square of folded parchment. "He said it's urgent."

Elizabeth's breath faltered as she recognized her name written in Joshua's hand.

She took the parchment and turned it over, breaking the stiff waxen seal. The paper crinkled with the faint trembling of her hands as she unfolded it.

To Elizabeth, my dearest friend, peace be with you. By the time this message reaches you, I will have gone.

The breath froze in her lungs.

"What does he say?" Zeram asked.

Elizabeth looked up, but could not speak. Dropping her eyes, she continued to read.

I beg your forgiveness for the suddenness of my choice to take Helaman's offer and return to Zarahemla. I'm starting tonight, and I intend to go quickly enough that I will be in Zarahemla by evening tomorrow. I feel no need for rest, and think it best not to delay.

I know, my friend, that you wish for an explanation. Zeram will too when he learns the contents of this letter. I can only say that I do this because I believe it is what is right. Forgive my weakness of words. I wish—

Here, Elizabeth noted a minute strain in the characters, as if Joshua's quill pressed more firmly against the parchment.

—that I could say more to you than that.

My thoughts and prayers remain with you. Say goodbye to Jonas for me, and Zeram. He is growing into a fine soldier. And you are a fine woman, Elizabeth, of whom I am certain your father, mother, and all your kindred are proud.

Your friend, Joshua

Elizabeth's heart twisted as she looked at Zeram.

"He's taking Helaman's offer." She handed the letter through the window. "He's going to Zarahemla."

Zeram scanned the parchment, his brow furrowing. "Tonight? Why the sudden haste?"

At this, tears filled her eyes, and though Elizabeth struggled to blink them back, one escaped her lashes and tumbled down her cheek.

Zeram's eyes filled with concern. "What's wrong?"

Elizabeth met the youth's gaze. "I know why he left."

Zeram's brows furrowed.

"There is a… misunderstanding between us." Elizabeth halted. "There are things I should have said and didn't, foolish things he—I— we both did. And now we… Oh, Zeram, I don't know what to think."

Zeram studied her, perplexed. "Joshua's your friend, Elizabeth. Surely there's a way to end this…*misunderstanding*, whatever caused it."

Elizabeth brushed a hand beneath her eyes, then let it fall against her skirt. "He's already gone."

Zeram lifted his palms in a plaintive gesture. "Yes, but you should go to Zarahemla yourself. Take Jonas, and I will go with you. The land is safe again, and the season is good, so there are plenty of traders and other folk making the journey. I'm sure my father will give his leave. I can return to Zarahemla and continue my training. Jonas can rejoin his kin, and you—" His tone grew firm. "You're older and wiser than me. I've always looked to you as my teacher, but if what I say holds any weight with you now, I think you should find Joshua once we're there, and…" Zeram shrugged. "Talk to him."

Elizabeth turned her head toward her desk and looked at the scroll she had been reading before Zeram came. Her eyes stopped on a line of gentle advice Jethro had given his son-in-law, Moses: *"Hearken now unto my voice, I will give thee counsel, and God shall be with thee…"*

Her heart still ached, but something in Zeram's words mingled with the words of the scripture before her and settled on her heart with a peace she found undeniable. *God shall be with thee…*

"Yes," Elizabeth agreed softly. "I think I should."

Chapter 19

The stone steps rising up to the palace of the chief judge scraped under the soles of Joshua's boots as he neared the open doors. Two guards stood on either side of the opening, spears in hand. Behind him, commerce in the market hummed beneath the lowering evening sun. Voices of merchants filled the air amid the bleating of flocks, and the scent of sheep mingled with the smoky smells of cooking fires.

Nearly at the crest, Joshua paused and turned to study the scene below him. Few visible signs remained of the war that had ravaged the city less than a year before. The thought comforted and pained him in the same moment.

"What would you feel if you were to see this, Elizabeth?" Joshua murmured. Her face formed in his thoughts as clearly as if she stood beside him, her bright eyes uplifted to his. The taste of her soft mouth returned unbidden to his thoughts.

"Lieutenant Joshua?" a man's cheerful voice called.

Joshua turned as one of the door wardens strode forward.

"Captain Micha." He swallowed hard.

"Are you well?" Micha chuckled as Joshua climbed the last of the steps and stopped before the old captain. "You seemed lost."

Beyond the old soldier, the other guard remained in his place. *Abram*, Joshua remembered. One of Elizabeth's old students. The youth grinned as their eyes met, though he remained at his post.

"I'm fine, sir." Joshua offered Micha a salute. "Only lost in my thoughts."

The older man's eyes moved to the insignia on Joshua's shoulder. "Ah, but you're *Captain* Joshua now." Micha returned the salute before reaching out to clasp Joshua's forearm.

"And Abram has risen in rank as well." Joshua nodded in approval to the young guard who stood beside the doorway. "A sergeant now, I see. Well done!"

"Thank you, sir," Abram, taller than Joshua remembered, beamed at the praise. He shifted his weight. "I hope to be an officer before the year is out."

"No doubt you will be," Joshua returned.

The throne room doors began to creak open, and the murmur of men's voices followed, mingled with tapping feet and rustling cloaks. Helaman's council with the lower judges had ended for the day.

"And how is Lady Elizabeth, sir?" Abram asked. "Is she well?"

Joshua's heart gave a fierce throb at the mention of her name. "She is."

Abram glanced past Joshua's shoulder as if expecting Elizabeth to be climbing the steps behind him.

"But she remained in Bountiful. For now," Joshua added.

"That *is* a pity." A smooth voice grated on his nerves as Gadianton strode onto the veranda and stopped as his fellow judges continued past him. "Zarahemla's beauty is lessened without her, would you not agree, Captain?"

A half-step behind Gadianton stood Kishkumen, his snake-like guard.

The two men traded an amused glance as Gadianton continued, "We all felt great relief when the news came that she had arrived in Bountiful with such a devoted... protector as you, Captain. Doubtless you have used these many months since the war to comfort her, and help her forget—"

"Pacumeni could *never* be forgotten," Joshua returned, his jaw burning as the sinews tightened beneath his skin. His right hand clenched into a fist as the hum of the marketplace faded from his senses, and nothing but Gadianton's features filled his gaze. *How satisfying it would be to put my fist between those arrogant eyes—*

"True, Captain Joshua," called a woman's voice. Like a gentle breeze tempering the heat of the sun, Lady Pazia, clad in a cream-colored mantle, glided between the two men and stopped, poised like a queen. "And aptly put."

"My lady." Gadianton bowed graciously to Helaman's wife. Joshua's eyes narrowed.

"Pacumeni didn't rule long, but he was a noble man." Pazia turned to face Gadianton with a courteous smile. "And my little brother…" Here, Pazia's words took on a bite. "May very well be remembered until the ending of the world."

After hesitating a moment, Gadianton managed an easy, "Of course. No one could forget him, my lady." His expression remained unflustered as he turned away, and with Kishkumen at his shoulder, descended the steps toward the plaza.

Joshua glowered after him until he felt a gentle hand on his arm. He turned. The steel in Pazia's gaze dissipated, replaced by a smile, though Joshua could see that her eyes gleamed with tears.

"This is a marvelous surprise, Joshua." Pazia brushed a hand beneath her eyes. "You have come to answer my husband's request?"

"Forgive me. I should have sent word ahead."

"There is nothing to forgive. Come. Helaman will be pleased to see you."

With a nod of farewell to Micha and Abram, Joshua followed Pazia's lead through the doorway into the inner corridor.

"How are Jonas and Elizabeth?" Pazia asked.

Joshua faltered at Elizabeth's name. "Both well," he said. Out of the corner of his eye, he saw Pazia turn her head.

"And young Zeram? From the letters he's exchanged with Nephi, he seems well."

"His home and kin are in Bountiful, and he has been glad to be with them. I expect he will return soon though, to complete his training."

She nodded. "I am sure he will come to Zarahemla when Elizabeth and Jonas do. He seems a faithful youth. He would not break his oath to Pacumeni." Her last words broke faintly.

Joshua nodded, remembering his own oath to Pacumeni, still unfulfilled.

Pazia stopped Joshua within the doorway of the throne room, gesturing that they should wait a moment. Helaman stood at the base of his throne, speaking with two lower judges who had lingered.

"Forgive my emotions when I spoke to Gadianton." Pazia pursed her lips, her brow furrowing. "He is a man of great intelligence, but—"

"I understand, my lady," Joshua returned. "You cannot be faulted any tears. You've suffered much this past year."

"No more than any other woman of this city. I still have my husband. And both my sons live. I'm very blessed. But I miss my father, and my brothers. Little—" Pazia faltered. "Little Pacumeni especially."

"As do I." Joshua's words thickened as he spoke. "Pacumeni was a great man. And the greatest of friends."

Pazia lifted her eyes, offering him a grateful smile. "You are a great man as well, Joshua." She studied his face, and her eyes grew thoughtful. "You are like Pacumeni in so many ways."

Joshua glanced away. "But I'm not him."

"True," Pazia agreed and fell silent for a moment before adding, "And those who love you would not have you be." He looked up to see her gentle eyes boring into his. "Including Elizabeth."

The sound of nearing footsteps freed him of his need to respond. He lifted his eyes to the two lower judges who nodded to Pazia and to him as they passed through the outer doors onto the veranda. As the men departed, the guards pulled the outer doors shut, closing out the crimson evening light.

"Joshua, you've come!"

Helaman's face bore an expression of pleased surprise.

"Peace to you, Your Eminence." Joshua offered the new chief judge a salute.

"And to you, Captain Joshua." Helaman returned the salute before he strode forward, his hand extended. "You came faster than I expected. You've accepted my offer?"

"I am ready to do anything you request of me, sir," Joshua returned, clasping Helaman's forearm.

"Good." Helaman studied his face a long moment, then turned to his wife. "Sweetheart." He gathered her hands. "I must speak with Joshua alone."

"Of course." Pazia smiled.

Joshua glanced away as she rose up on her toes to kiss her husband. She drew back, offered Joshua a final nod, then turned and glided through the throne room doors, the echo of her footsteps fading as she went.

Helaman studied the empty doorway with a tender expression that made Joshua's thoughts turn again to Elizabeth. His very soul ached for the sight of her. But what good would it have done to stay in Bountiful, seeing her every day, unable to declare his heart to her? And if he did speak his heart? She would only be wounded by his words, for she loved another. Such foolish actions could do neither of them any good. What precious threads of their friendship remained, he dared not damage.

"Joshua."

Joshua lifted his eyes to the face of the man who was now both prophet and chief judge.

"We have much to discuss." Helaman turned his gaze to the guards standing to one side and the other in the doorway. "And we need greater privacy to do so."

"Of course, sir."

"Come." Motioning for Joshua to follow him, Helaman strode out into the corridor. Torches set in sconces along the length of the long corridor flickered off the walls as well as the stalwart forms of the guards who stood as still as statues, spaced at equal distances between the torches.

Joshua turned and studied Helaman's face. Joshua had known him for years both as the prophet and as a wise friend, but the man seemed different now that he had the added responsibility of the judgment seat. Helaman's eyes held a weighted look that had not been there in the days when Pacumeni had been alive. Responsibility and loss had taken their toll, but they had also strengthened him.

"Thank you for returning to Zarahemla, Captain," Helaman said as they made their way down the corridor, his face fading in and out of shadow as torches neared and then passed. "I know I wasn't forthcoming in my missive about the task I wish to offer you. I'm grateful for your trust in me."

"I've always trusted you, Your Eminence. Whatever you ask of me, I am ready."

Helaman nodded and ran a hand over his mouth as if contemplating some troubling thought. "Pacumeni did say you were one of the most loyal soldiers he has ever worked with."

"He spoke more highly of me than I deserved," Joshua returned. "I did my duty, as any soldier should."

Helaman met Joshua's gaze. "You were, and are, much more than just a dutiful soldier, Joshua. You would not merely sacrifice your life— you would sacrifice the deepest desires of your heart to do what is right."

The two men stopped outside the door that led into the chief judge's private office.

Joshua studied Helaman's eyes in the dim light. "My desire is to do what God wishes of me. And what you and our people need from me."

The somber weight in Helaman's eyes eased a little. "And that, son of Antipus, is why I sent for you. Come. We have much to talk about." He lifted the latch and drew the door open.

Joshua obeyed, stepping into the room.

A desk sat in the center of the room, a wooden chair beside it. The shutter had been closed over the window, striations of evening light leaking through. The single clay lamp upon the desk spluttered a faint flame. Little had changed since that fateful day when he had last been here with Pacumeni, and a pang of nostalgia gripped him.

"Even in here, Joshua, we must keep our voices low." Helaman's tone filled with gravity as he dropped the latch into place. He strode past Joshua and stopped at his desk, dropping a hand to its surface before he turned, his face grave. "The real duty for which I called you back to Zarahemla entails much secrecy, and great risk." He paused. "To you."

Joshua's chest tightened, but he squared his shoulders and met Helaman's gaze. "You have but to tell me what you wish of me."

Helaman smiled wearily. "As much as we would wish to believe it, Joshua," he murmured, his words measured and even, "I don't think those who murdered Pazia's eldest brother are gone from among us. I have thought much, and prayed much, and it has come to my mind that this secret faction means to seek my life also.

"Yet my greatest fear is not for my own life as much as it is for our people." Helaman's voice grew somber. "These subversives have no righteous desires, and if they gained power, there is no telling the depravity they would bring upon this nation."

Joshua gave a nod and shifted his weight.

"Understand that I do not give this as an order, Joshua, but rather as a request. If you refuse it, I will not count it against you."

Helaman's eyes gleamed like steel. "But there are few men I trust as I trust you. I know you to be—"

"I will do it." Joshua heard courage in his words that his heart did not feel.

Helaman stepped back at Joshua's bold acceptance. "Do you know what you're agreeing to?"

"You wish me to find these dissidents, gain their trust, and infiltrate their ranks." Joshua finished in a fierce whisper, "You wish me to be a spy."

Helaman drew in a deep breath. "Yes."

Joshua gave a terse nod. "I understand, Your Eminence."

Helaman studied Joshua's eyes for a long moment. "Very well," he said at last. "For the greatest chance of success for your mission, and safety to you, heed these instructions. Your story, for now, will be that you have taken a distant post at the western watchtower newly built in the south wilderness. Tonight, you will go out the south gate as if to journey to that post. You must say to any who ask that the need is so great that I wish for you to go without delay. But when the night has reached its midpoint, I want you to discard your uniform for this disguise and double back to Zarahemla."

From behind his desk, Helaman drew out a bundle of worn cloth, a pair of worn sandals atop a tattered, rolled-up cloak. Along with the bundle, he drew out a soldier's pack, and pushed both across the desk to Joshua. Joshua stuffed the tattered bundle into the pack, tying it shut. "Let no one see the contents of that pack."

"Yes, sir."

"You will arrive back in Zarahemla at daybreak. Blend in with the crowd coming to the market. Captain Micha will be at the south gate, performing an inspection. He will be watching for you. Do not speak to him openly, but follow him.

"Micha will speak to you only when you are both certain no one can see you. He will give you more instructions, and directions to a small room in the poorer quarter of the city. It has already been secured for you under the name of Akish, son of Saul. The area is inhabited mostly by hirelings and laborers among whom I suspect this group is recruiting. Do all you can to find out what they know of any secret bands founded by the traitor Paanchi."

Helaman studied Joshua's face. "No one else will know the truth of this besides you, me, and Captain Micha, who will deliver correspondence between us. He will see to it that any needed communication reaches me. Even our dearest kindred will not know. Not even Pazia."

Joshua's brows knit, and he looked away from Helaman. "Nor Elizabeth," he murmured, his throat constricting.

"She will not," Helaman agreed.

Joshua shifted his weight as a long moment of silence passed.

"Forgive me if my words are intrusive," Helaman said. "But what *are* your feelings for Elizabeth?"

At Helaman's question, Joshua's heart faltered in his chest. "Sir, such a question has nothing to do with the threat of these subversives, or the task I have taken."

"True." Helaman folded his hands behind his back. "But chief judge though I am, I have not forgotten my obligation to the Lord's children, of whom you are one. Your loyalty to Pacumeni was more than mere duty. He was a brother to you. And during your friendship, he grew to love a woman to whom you were also fiercely devoted, and, I would guess, in love with even then."

Joshua's breath stopped in his lungs. "Sir—"

"I know of the request you made to be transferred, Joshua," Helaman continued. "And I can only respect you for it, guessing as to the reasons behind it. At that time, leaving would have been the honorable path. Now, however, you should perhaps choose a different course of action. After all, Elizabeth is capable of healing. She *can* find happiness, and love, again. As the true friend I know you are to her, certainly you wish that for her."

"More than anything."

"Then answer me this, Joshua," Helaman said, his eyes filled with compassion. "Do you love her?"

At the bold question, Joshua paused, his mouth opening before he gathered his wits enough to speak.

"How *I* feel doesn't matter, for she does not love me. I am nothing more than a friend to her. That is all I will ever be. Her heart is still Pacumeni's."

"Has she *told* you this?" Helaman pressed.

"Not in words, but—"

"There are few men in this world like you," Helaman cut in, the insistence in his tone tempered by the deep caring Joshua could see in his eyes. "You are selfless, and truly noble-hearted. And Elizabeth, daughter of Nathan, is no fool. She has seen it for herself. Memories have their place, but don't let what is in the past rob the future. Such a thing wouldn't be fair to you. Or to Elizabeth. Do you truly think she could never learn to love you?"

Joshua studied the floor, the straight lines and squares of intersecting stone tiles where Pacumeni had once walked. "Sir." He looked up. "Just before I left Bountiful, I forgot myself." He swallowed. "I kissed her, sir. And she pushed me away."

Helaman's countenance remained unchanged. "Immediately?"

"Ye—" Joshua stopped himself, remembering. "No. Not immediately. But perhaps for those few moments, she imagined Pacumeni—"

"She knows who you are, Joshua."

The sinews in Joshua's jaw tensed, and he cast his gaze to the floor.

Helaman drew in a breath. "Elizabeth cares for you. Deeply, Joshua. Enough that she would not encourage your hope if she feared she did not love you as you deserved. And I know that your regard for her is such that you would never seek to make her your own if you did not think you had truly won her heart. This regard that you and Elizabeth share can become, in the right time and under the right circumstances, the foundation of a good and godly love. *If* you both wish it to be."

Joshua lifted his eyes, and spoke. "Sir, do you speak these words as the prophet, or as the chief judge?"

"As your *friend*." Helaman's eyes grew warm. "As your father would, or hers, were either of those noble men still living."

Joshua blinked wetness from his eyes. "I will think on your words, sir."

Helaman paused as if he wished to say more before he nodded. "That is all I ask. You are dismissed."

Joshua offered him a crisp salute, which Helaman returned.

"May God be with you, Joshua. In *all* you have before you."

"And you, sir."

Joshua slung the pack over his shoulder, strode to the doorway, and opened it.

In the corridor, Joshua paused to regain his wits as the latch fell into place behind him, then started down the corridor. Several paces away, a torch flickered in its sconce, illuminating the silhouette of the nearest palace guard. As he neared, his eyes lifted to the man's face, noting a scar that knifed up the guard's cheek and over the sunken space where an eye had once been. Despite the scar, Joshua recognized the soldier's familiar features.

"Oren," he greeted, and drew to a halt.

Oren's good eye jerked to Joshua's face, his expression startled, before he smiled. "Sir! Peace to you." He saluted.

"And to you, Oren." Joshua returned the salute. "You are well?"

"Aside from this war wound, yes, sir." Oren gave a rueful chuckle, lifting a hand to the scar upon his cheek. "I was caught in the thickest fighting before this took me down." He heaved a sigh. "But I lived, and I can still serve. Is all well?" Oren's gaze fell to the pack Joshua carried.

Joshua hesitated. "I have accepted a post of command at the westernmost watchtower in the south wilderness. The need is urgent, and His Eminence wants me there right away."

Oren grinned. "Good fortune to you, sir."

"And to you, Oren." Joshua nodded, then strode on.

Chapter 20

The evening sun fell in a slant through a bank of clouds that sat low on the western horizon as Elizabeth and Zeram paused at the crest of a knoll. Elizabeth caught her breath as they looked down upon Zarahemla. The tall stone battlements, flags fluttering, gleamed almost like gold beneath the lowering sun.

"Elizabeth?"

She turned, meeting Zeram's eyes.

"Are you all right?" he asked.

Her gaze slid to Jonas, his gray eyes like Pacumeni's. The little boy clung to Zeram's shoulders hitched on the youth's sturdy back.

"It doesn't look any different," she murmured.

Zeram turned and contemplated the city. "Like the war never happened," he agreed.

"Except it did," Jonas said.

Elizabeth smiled sadly. "It did." She reached out, brushing Jonas's cheek before the three of them turned and continued on.

The open gate grew larger as they drew nearer amid the throng of folk eager to enter or leave the city before the sun set.

A cluster of soldiers stood upon the ramparts over the gate, and a pair of guards stood on either side of the open portal, upright javelins in their hands as they studied the passing crowd with dispassionate faces.

But as Elizabeth's small group neared the base of the steps, her eyes met the gaze of the young guard who stood to the right, and his familiar features brightened.

"Zeram!" Nephi called out. "Elizabeth! Jonas!"

"Nephi!" Zeram shouted, letting Jonas slide to the ground as Nephi jogged toward them, his javelin bobbing beside him.

Nephi reached Zeram and threw his free arm around his friend. "You're back!"

"What did you think?" Zeram chuckled, pushing his friend to arm's length. "That I'd stay away forever? You're not that lucky."

Nephi snorted at the joke. He stood taller now than Elizabeth remembered, and a faint scar marred his cheek.

"Did you get our missive?" Elizabeth asked.

"Mother said it came just this morning," Nephi said. "She'll be pleased to see you."

He dropped to one knee to embrace his small cousin. "And you, Jonas! You're bigger than I remember! The last time I saw you—"

His words cut short as he realized his mistake, and his smile faded.

"Was when Abba died," Jonas finished.

Nephi rose and turned his eyes toward Elizabeth. "Lady Elizabeth, I...I'm sorry."

She shook her head. "Don't be, Nephi."

Nephi gnawed his bottom lip. "I, um..." His brow furrowed. "I know where he is buried."

Elizabeth's heart twisted.

"A Lamanite who stayed behind—he didn't return with his kinfolk— he showed me and my father and several others where he buried..." his voice softened, "Uncle Pacumeni."

A wave of comfort washed over Elizabeth's heart and she glanced at Zeram who smile faintly. The Lamanite had kept his promise.

"I would like to see it one day," she murmured, her gaze finding Nephi again. "And meet this man who showed you where it is."

"I'll see that you do," Nephi said. With that, he lifted his eyes to the officer who stood above the parapet.

"Sir," he called, "permission to take my friends to the palace?"

"Granted," the man called down, and Nephi turned back.

"Come on," he said, his cheer beginning to return.

He reached down picked up Jonas, hefting his little cousin to his back. "It's near time for the evening meal. Mother wouldn't wish for you to miss it."

"How is Joshua?" Elizabeth asked as Nephi guided them through the gate.

"I don't know," Nephi said over his shoulder. "Captain Joshua arrived days ago, but he came and left without me seeing him. Father sent him to a new outpost in the south wilderness." He offered an apologetic grin. "I'm sure he's fine."

Zeram glanced toward Elizabeth, and the two traded a silent look.

"Father had several watchtowers built in the south wilderness in the last few months," Nephi continued, unaware of the exchange. "He wanted Captain Joshua to command one of them."

Elizabeth's steps slowed. Joshua wasn't even here.

The thought filled her with loneliness and disappointment, followed by a prickle of guilt. After all, why *did* she miss Joshua so much?

She mused over this as the sights and sounds of Zarahemla surrounded her—roasting meat from somewhere nearby, the sound of the crowd, the taste of the air. All of it recalled to her mind images of Pacumeni.

If she still missed him, what did she feel for Joshua? How could she truly love *two* men?

Joshua deserved a woman who loved him with the whole of her heart, not a portion of it. He was brave and strong, gentle and wise. And so fiercely beautiful that Elizabeth's heart fairly stopped when she thought of him.

Trails of warmth shivered over her flesh as Joshua appeared in her memory, the strong angles of his face, and the tender gaze of his sea-colored eyes. She felt his fingers against her cheek and tasted again the sweetness of his lips as the waves washed the shores of Bountiful—

"Elizabeth?"

Her eyes jerked up at Jonas's voice. The others had moved on as she had paused. Jonas looked back; now Nephi and Zeram turned as well.

Hoping her young friends could not see the heat she felt in her face, she gathered her skirt and hurried after them.

The sun beat down upon his shoulders, and a line of sweat trickled down Shemnon's back. He tapped his mallet on the flat-headed chisel he held, clipping a final imperfection off his squared block of stone, and stood back to examine his finished work. About him, the creak of ropes and men's voices sounded through the air.

Shemnon looked up, eyeing the gap in the rising wall near Zarahemla's west gate. A cluster of men stood within the gap, their muscles straining as they guided a stone block into its place between two others. With a stony growl, the block scraped between its neighbors and gave a satisfying thump as it found its place. A perfect fit.

The men straightened, lifting their fists in triumph as a weary cheer filled the air.

Shemnon drew in a satisfied breath. The months he had spent traveling between Zarahemla and the stone quarry west of the city had been exhausting, but satisfying. Stone masons had been kept busy fortifying the walls surrounding Zarahemla at the orders of their new chief judge, and they had been glad to take any man willing to perform the strenuous labor. Even a former Lamanite warrior.

Talilia had found employment as a midwife's assistant and seemed to enjoy her work, which pleased Shemnon.

And when she did not have her duties, Shemnon often saw her in the company of good Master Tuloth, which pleased him even more.

Shemnon turned his hands upward, studying his rough palms. More than a full cycle of the day-count had passed, and almost an entire year since he had exchanged his scimitar for the tools of a stone mason. It seemed a lifetime.

Still, as a cluster of younger workers neared him carrying bundles of tools, he knew that the time had not been long for them. Their conversation stilled and their eyes narrowed as they passed, suspicion hardening their faces.

Shemnon could not fault them. For all he knew, their fathers or brothers had died at his own hands.

"Master Amasa?"

A breathless voice turned Shemnon's head, and his gaze rested upon a young courier clad in a thin tunic, his chest heaving from his run. A leather bag hung crosswise over one shoulder. He studied Shemnon with guarded eyes. "I was told to find one Amasa, a Lamanite, here among the stone workers. A message has come from the city of Melek from a records keeper there."

Shemnon's heart clambered into his throat. "I am the one you seek." He set down his mallet and chisel upon the stone and came forward.

The youth dipped a hand into his bag and withdrew a folded parchment set with a waxen seal.

Shemnon nodded his thanks and took the missive.

The courier nodded in reply, then turned and jogged back toward the open gate.

Shemnon's heart quickened as he studied the salutation on the outer fold written in both Lamanitish and Nephite characters. The air seemed to grow difficult to breathe as he turned the letter over and broke the waxen seal.

Greetings to Amasa of Zarahemla, the letter read. *I am Nasser, son of Zareth of Melek. I am a records keeper to whom your request has come. It has taken some time, and I beg your forgiveness for the delay. In the archives of this city, I have found records of one whom you claim as kinswoman, one Hana, daughter of Shemnon, who matches your query, born in the Lamanite land of Ishmael forty years ago, on twelve calli in the month Toxcatl, and brought to these lands with the people of Ammon, having been the ward of her grandmother, Delia, who was converted by the preaching of Ammon and his brethren.*

Regrettably, Delia died in the lands of the Lamanites shortly after her conversion.

Shemnon's throat tightened, and his fingers gripped the parchment.

He had not expected his mother to be living still, but to have died so soon after her last letter to him... A fist of regret settled in his stomach. He should have gone back as she had asked him to.

Hana, however, the letter continued, *was brought north and raised among the people of Ammon. When she became of age, she departed these lands. Our records indicate that she was taken to wife by a son of the Nephites and went with him to dwell in the city Mulek, in the east, near the great city, Bountiful.*

Having said that, I regret to end this epistle with word that your kinswoman, Hana, daughter of Shemnon, died of sickness thirteen years ago in the 29th year of the judges in the city of Bountiful. I am able to give you only this sad news, for records of her death were sent here to Melek as she had lived here in her youth.

Aside from these, there are few other records in Melek, for we have no records of her husband's name or the names of the children she bore. These may be obtained from records keepers in Bountiful, and I have sent to them of your request. You should receive news of Hana's husband and children within the month.

I am sorry for the sorrow this news brings, and hope that word may come swiftly from Bountiful and bring recompense to you.

I remain in your service, Nasser, son of Zareth of Melek.

For a long moment, Shemnon could do no more than stare at the words upon the parchment.

"Master Amasa, are you well?"

He turned to look into the eyes of the overseer, Jubal, a thick-armed man who studied Shemnon first with impatience, then with a trace of sympathy as he took in Shemnon's wilting expression.

"Are you well?" he asked again, his tone less harsh.

Around him, Shemnon grew aware of other workers pausing in their duties to focus their attention on the exchange between their overseer and the Lamanite.

"Years ago, she— But I only learned just now—she *died*."

He bit back a sob that threatened to escape his throat. He did not wish this crowd of Nephites to see his tears.

Jubal's eyes dropped to the parchment in his hand, then rose again to Shemnon's face.

"I'm truly sorry." Jubal's voice sounded distant, almost disembodied. "I wish that…"

The overseer cleared his throat. "You may take the rest of the day for yourself."

Shemnon felt himself nod, but he did so without feeling, as if he stood outside himself.

He turned away.

He did not look back as he passed the wooden barriers of their work area and moved beneath the shadow of the west gate onto the wide thoroughfare that led toward the center of the city. His eyes turned down, refusing to meet any glance.

He had no wish to go home. Talilia was away fulfilling her duties and would not return until evening fell. What friend could he turn to, what sympathy could he find in this city of Nephites who saw him as an enemy?

Shemnon lifted his eyes, gazing up the wide street toward the great palace in the distance where dwelt Helaman, both ruler to the Nephites and prophet to those who called themselves Christians, their advocate between them and their one god.

He dropped his eyes to the ground as he remembered the peace he had felt when he had called to the Nephites' god from the darkness of his prison.

If the chief servant of such a god possessed a fraction of the benevolence as the master he served, perhaps he would condescend to speak to Shemnon, Lamanite that he was, about this bottomless pain in his heart.

⌐⋈⌐

The warmth of the sun caressed Elizabeth's hair where she sat cross-legged upon a sward of grass in the cool shadows of the palace garden. A pot of ink sat to the side of her parchment, her feather quill in her hand. The yellow paper already half filled with writing, rested upon the stone bench before her that served, for the moment, as her writing table.

Dearest Joshua, the letter began. *I pray that this letter finds you well. I understand that you have taken a new post in the south wilderness. I am glad for you, and hope your post brings you satisfaction. Yet if I were to be truthful, I would have to say that I miss you terribly, and that I, in my weakness and selfishness, wish you were here with me now. You may be surprised to know that I have returned to Zarahemla for a short time. Zeram and Jonas have returned as well.*

Elizabeth bit her lip, her quill poised over the parchment before she continued, *I will not be staying, though. I will return soon to Bountiful, when I can find a suitable group with which to travel. Jonas is with his kin again, and Zeram has his training. I shall miss them both, but my heart does not desire to stay. I must confess that I will also miss you, my dearest friend. Your watch post, as I have been told, is less than a day's journey south, and it was less than a month ago that I saw you last. But in my heart, Joshua, it feels as if years and leagues uncounted lie between us. My thoughts have dwelt often on you since we were last together on the shores of Bountiful.*

Elizabeth tossed the quill aside with a clatter and pressed a hand to her brow.

She could not think clearly with the ache inside her. She lifted her eyes, studying the trees and the sweet-smelling flowers that awoke so many memories of Pacumeni. But this pain that pulsed through her was not sorrow for her lost love alone. She also missed Joshua and his steady, reassuring presence with an aching emptiness that coursed through her veins, and which manifested itself very childishly on the paper before her. This letter read like the silly musings of a love-struck girl.

Pushing the parchment aside, Elizabeth looked at the second sheet before her. She picked up her quill, dipped it in the ink, and began.

Greetings to Captain Joshua, son of Antipus. I hope this missive finds you in good health.

Oh, this would not do! It sounded like a stuffy military epistle! Offering a soft groan, Elizabeth crumpled this second parchment and tossed it away.

Picking up the first sheet she had pushed aside, her eyes moved over the tender words she had written, the careful, graceful curves of the characters.

"Why did you kiss me, Joshua?" she murmured. "And *why* did I kiss you back?" Warmth and sorrow mingled and swelled within her heart as the questions swirled in her mind like leaves in an eddying wind, unable to settle to the ground. "Joshua, what does my heart feel for you?"she breathed, unable to form an answer.

Just then, the crunch of feet upon the earthen path caught Elizabeth's ears, and she looked up. A figure came toward her, a man, she could see, though not clearly, for the leaves and growth blocked a better view of him. Yet she could see enough to know that he walked as if exhausted, not looking up even as the path curved and he stood before her. He wore a shirt and kilt of Nephite make, while long, dark hair threaded with silver fell about his shoulders. He had changed. Even so, her heart leaped within her, for she still recognized him.

Elizabeth opened her mouth, though no words came forth.

Unaware of her presence, the Lamanite dropped to the stone bench opposite from her and buried his face in his hands.

"Greetings, sir," she stammered in the Lamanite tongue as she scrambled to her feet.

The man looked up and met her eyes, his expression weary rather than startled. He rose to his feet and offered her a nod of his head. "Forgive me." His words in the Nephite tongue came in slow and measured tones, though spoken with more ease than she remembered. "I did not know any others were here. I am waiting for an audience with your prophet, Lord Helaman."

But then his eyes flashed with recognition, and a sad smile drew across his mouth. "I remember you," he said now in the Lamanite tongue. "The brave Nephite maiden who speaks the tongue of the Lamanites with such skill. I am pleased to see that you are well."

Elizabeth nodded. "I too am pleased that you are well, sir."

"What of your friends? Your wounded companion?"

Her throat dry, Elizabeth nodded. "He recovered, thanks to you."

The Lamanite nodded. "And the child?"

"His injury healed fully. And he has grown like a little tree."

The Lamanite smiled. "And the brave youth?"

"He, too, is well."

"I am pleased to hear this."

Elizabeth tipped her head, uncertain what to say in the quiet that followed. "You have not returned to your own lands?"

The man looked up, his eyes deep pools of restrained emotion. "I have nothing to return to. All that is dear to me, that lives…" A breath broke past his lips. "…is here, and should remain." He drew in a breath. "What is your name, child?" he asked, speaking in the tongue of the Nephites.

"Elizabeth, daughter of Nathan."

"Elizabeth," the Lamanite repeated, saying her name with the same tones and accents her mother had used. "And you may call me Amasa."

"You kept your promise, Master Amasa," she said. "You are the one Nephi spoke of. You buried Pacumeni so his body would not be mistreated."

"I made an oath to you. It was an honor to fulfill." The Lamanite's eyes gleamed. "I also made certain to bury his flute with him. It seemed to be very dear to him."

A breath caught in her throat, and she managed a tremulous smile. "It was."

"Master Amasa?" The voice cut through her thoughts as Helaman strode around a bend in the path, standing where the path curved away toward the portico. He noted Elizabeth and gave her a smile and quick nod as he moved toward the old Lamanite, pausing an arm's length from him. "A servant said you wished to speak to me?"

The Lamanite lowered his head. "I hoped you could tell me…" He shot a glance toward Elizabeth, who dropped her gaze to the earth beneath her feet. "Where my daughter is."

Helaman's brow furrowed. "Perhaps. Will you tell me of her?"

"She was a follower of your god, but now, she…" Amasa drew in a breath, then finished in a whisper, "is dead. She died some years ago, but I only learned of it within the last hour." As if with a great weight, the old man sank again to the stone seat.

A low sigh escaped Helaman, and he dropped to the bench beside the bent Lamanite.

"Amasa." Helaman reached out and gripped the man's shoulder. "I am so very sorry for you."

"I know you are not only the ruler of the Nephites, but also the mouthpiece of the god whom she worshipped. Does…your god know where her soul has gone?"

The question tore from the old Lamanite's lips with such emotion that tears pricked in Elizabeth's eyes. She did not belong here. Turning her attention away, Elizabeth fumbled as she pressed her stopper into the narrow mouth of her ink pot and gathered up her writing things.

She looked up at the two men. As if sensing her eyes upon him, the old Lamanite's head lifted, his eyes meeting hers.

Hoping her eyes conveyed her sympathy, she offered him a faint, sad smile, then turned away, hurrying down the curve of the path toward the pillared portico that gleamed beneath the sunlight.

Behind her, the two men continued to speak, but their voices faded as she moved away through the cool greenery of the garden until she could no longer hear them.

CXXI

The empty plaza spread away from the high window where Helaman stood, studying the twilight in the sky. At last he stepped away from the view, closing the shutter on the darkening night outside with a soft clatter. His eyes burned from work and lack of rest. His limbs felt heavy as he studied the wooden surface of his desk, the sheets of parchment lying in an orderly stack on one corner. And now, he wished for nothing else but to retreat to his family's private chambers and drop into an exhausted sleep in Pazia's arms. The day had been draining, filled with councils and meetings and that one brief though emotional talk with the Lamanite who called himself Amasa.

Poor man, Helaman mused, running a hand over his face. He glanced over the room, illuminated by the sputtering flame of the clay lamp upon his desk, then lowered his eyes to the fragment of parchment Micha had furtively slipped into his hand earlier that evening.

The scrap contained no more than a few terse words, but they spoke volumes.

I have found them. Pray for me.

"Well done, Joshua." Helaman held out the parchment toward the flickering flame and watched as the corner caught, the fragment quickly consumed. He dropped it before the flame could lick at his fingertips, the last scrap devoured to a cinder before it even struck the floor.

Releasing a deep breath, Helaman obeyed Joshua's request, lowered himself to one knee, and bowed his head as scraps of ash brushed across the stone floor in a faint eddy of air.

Chapter 21

Joshua hugged the ragged folds of his cloak about him as he strode along the narrow street. The waxing moon had just set. His eyes strained through the darkness as he followed the broad back and threadbare cloak of his companion along a narrow street that wended between ancient, decrepit houses, their crumbling stone walls stained and discolored with age.

Empty windows glowered at him like dead eyes, and a tremor shivered through him. Thick steam rose up from a sewer ditch in the center of the street, twisting in the air like a tormented ghost.

Joshua reached into the loose folds of his tunic and touched the cool hilt of the knife belted against his chest, his one fragment of security in this nest of vipers he would be descending into tonight.

"Come along, boy," the thick-shouldered man said as he adjusted the cloth-wrapped package he held under one arm. "My comrades will be pleased that I've brought young blood into our brotherhood. You and I will both be rewarded well." He shot Joshua a fierce look. "If you behave yourself."

Joshua nodded.

Nissim glanced up and down the dark street. "We must take care. We cannot know what spies the tyrant Helaman might have about."

"Yes, Nissim."

"You should be warned, lad," the man said, turning to him, "that my lord does not look with favor on young upstarts who ask too many questions. You must watch your tongue, or he may lose patience and cut it out." He added as an afterthought, "If I don't do it for him so that he needn't dirty his hands."

Nissim clumped onward, picking a path through the maze of twisting streets that Joshua could never have found on his own. He pitied the man, a poor laborer with no wife or children, drawn into the secret band by the promise of power and riches.

"Ah." Nissim stopped before a low-roofed building built against the side of a massive rock that jutted up from the ground. The warped door bore an oblong scratch in the center that would have seemed insignificant to Joshua even in the light of day, but Nissim considered the mark with an expression of near reverence before he gave three short raps.

In a moment, the door scraped open a fraction, and the pocked face of an old woman, toothless and bitter-eyed, appeared.

Nissim curled his hand in front of his chest, making a strange sign with his fingers. "Nissim wishes to enter. I have brought Akish, new blood, to strengthen our cause."

"You're late. The others are gathered already." Her voice prickled Joshua's skin like the crawling feet of insects. She eyed Joshua with malevolence, but pulled the door open, the wood scraping over the floor.

Struggling to keep his face expressionless, Joshua stepped into the shadowed interior. His heart pounded as he breathed a desperate prayer. The small room leaned up against the slope of natural rock he had seen from the outside. At the back of the room, within the otherwise solid wall of stone, a ragged crevice disappeared into the rock, wide enough that a man stooped over could pass through. Joshua could see the flicker of torchlight on the sides of the crevice, and a faint echo of voices suggested that a larger chamber lay beyond the narrow passage.

"Put this on," Nissim ordered, shoving a concave object into Joshua's hands. A mask, he realized, turning it over. A mask bearing the features of a snarling jaguar. Nissim had already donned one himself, peering at Joshua through the carved eyeholes. Fumbling, Joshua pulled the mask over his head, obliterating his peripheral vision.

"Follow me," the old woman said.

Repressing a shudder, Joshua stooped and followed her through the narrow stone cleft. The passage slanted downward, the voices growing louder as he went. At last the crevice opened onto the stony floor of a large cavern, and he straightened, gazing about him at the walls of a natural cave. Before him, a crowd milled about a large flat stone rising in the middle of the room like a dais upon which an orator might stand. Several torches burned in brackets encircling the platform.

"Do not gawk, boy," Nissim said, shoving Joshua a little to make way.

Saying nothing, Joshua turned and edged along the wall, making room for Nissim, who moved forward and joined the crowd that pressed around the stone platform. The old woman shuffled away, disappearing into one of several shadowed alcoves at the back of the chamber where the torchlight did not reach.

Left to himself, Joshua shrank against the wall, the rough, uneven stone at his back.

Most of the other men wore masks as he did, and this brought a fragment of comfort to Joshua, for he could remain hidden without drawing attention to himself.

"Peace to you, sir," an unexpected feminine voice said from not far away.

Joshua turned, startled, his eyes coming to rest upon a young woman who must have materialized from the alcove where the old woman had disappeared. The flame of the clay lamp she held fluttered in the air that stirred about the large chamber, flickering off the soft curves of her face and form. "I have not seen you here before. I am Sharai."

Joshua's heart quickened as she glided toward him, her movements fluid and graceful in the faint light of her lamp. Her hair spilled in unbound curls over the linen tunic she wore. Her face, fine-boned and lovely, lifted to study his.

"Our band is fortunate to have gained one so young and strong as you," she said. "What is your vocation, Master…?"

Joshua found that his tongue could barely work. "Akish," he managed to say. "I'm a stone cutter."

"Akish," she repeated.

Her fingers reached out and touched Joshua's forearm. He gulped hard as the feather-soft touch of her fingertips trailed over his shoulder and brushed the flesh of his throat. The young woman smiled at Joshua's sudden indrawn breath and let her hand rest over his thundering heart.

"A stone cutter," she purred appreciatively. "I can tell." Her lips twisted into an inviting smirk. "Surely after working with rough, unwieldy stone all day, you would like to touch something... softer?"

She eased nearer, and Joshua's blood throbbed furiously in his veins. Reason threatened to leave him as a teasing smile danced across her lips. Sharai lifted the edge of his mask, studying his face in the light of her lamp. "You are as comely as you are strong, Akish."

Sharai stepped back a little and took his hand in her own. "Come with me," she said in a conspiratorial whisper. "It will be some minutes before talk of any great import begins, and there are tunnels and chambers I could show you." She gestured beyond the torchlight. "They go all through these rocks, some even beneath the city wall. None would disturb us." She released his hand, and her fingers brushed up his arm. "We could return before you were missed."

Despite the magnitude of his mission, Joshua felt a wild rush of temptation. He reflected on his years of self-denial and iron control that now seemed like a ponderous, unbearable weight that he could so easily cast off with this beautiful and willing woman.

But then from the corridors of his memory, a voice echoed, almost as if his old friend Pacumeni stood at his shoulder. *Love is stronger than evil.*

Far stronger, Joshua agreed, letting Elizabeth's face fill his thoughts, her hair spilling about her shoulders, her soulful eyes, bright as jade and warm with affection. He would *not* poison his soul. He would not make himself unworthy of her. Elizabeth's friendship, her trust and her caring, even if she never gave him more than that, mattered infinitely more to him than the garish offerings of this lovely but poisonous woman.

Joshua pulled away from the girl. "No, thank you." He tore his eyes from her and from the other women who hovered in the shadows, silent and insubstantial, like frail ghosts.

Sharai scowled, but he ignored her angry eyes and turned away. He settled the jaguar mask back over his face and moved nearer to the torchlight and to the other men.

With the mask limiting his vision, Joshua could only see the stone dais in front of him, but a cold sensation, like a bitter wind, touched his skin, and the awareness that someone watched him crawled like a worm through his heart. Joshua turned his head, glancing to his right.

Several paces away, another man stood, his face also masked. But unlike the others, whose eyes looked forward toward the rising stone, this man looked straight at Joshua. Through one hole in the man's mask, Joshua could see the glimmer of an eye. Through the other, he saw nothing but dark emptiness. A shudder trembled through him.

"My brothers! Our honored lord wishes to speak!" At the sound of the voice from the other side of the stone dais, the room fell silent. To Joshua's relief, the man turned his gaze away from him and toward the figure who mounted the platform. A feathered cloak hung about broad shoulders, and a fretted golden circlet lined with quetzal feathers rested upon his head.

Then the man turned. At the sight of his face, Joshua's chest tightened in a rush of fearful recognition, and he struggled to gain control of his thoughts against a new wave of panic.

Gadianton! Of all men, their leader was Gadianton! He knew Joshua's face. If Gadianton recognized him, Joshua would be dead in moments!

Joshua tensed as Gadianton's gaze roamed the room and stopped upon him, the traitor's eyes narrowing. Joshua willed himself not to flinch or look away, and at last, Gadianton's eyes moved on.

"My brothers," Gadianton boomed out, "Helaman, the son of Helaman, sits upon the throne in the palace of the chief judge. What say you to that?"

In answer, the cavern burst into raucous, angry shouts that rose up, filling the chamber and echoing off the walls as fists struck the air.

"What shall we do when he takes away our freedoms?" Gadianton cried. "He has claimed that his duties as *prophet* to those who call themselves *Christians* are separate from his duties as chief judge, and that he will defend our rights to worship as we choose. But we know that he is a liar! Shall we sit by, appeased by these falsehoods, until it is too late for us? What say you?"

"Usurper!" one man shouted.

"Death to Helaman!" another added.

"Gadianton should be our chief judge," shouted yet another. "Not some ignorant cleric!"

The shouting continued until Gadianton punched his fist skyward for silence.

"It warms my heart to hear that we are of one mind," he said. "To be in the midst of wise men who see tyrants for what they are, who know that it is *I* who would best govern this people!"

Cheers rose until at Gadianton's raised fist, silence fell again.

"My brothers," Gadianton called out, "be comforted to know that before the sun rises, Helaman the tyrant will be lying dead in his own blood!"

A shard of panic lanced through Joshua's heart, and he stiffened as the men in the room shouted their approval.

"Let your hearts rejoice," Gadianton continued, "for the same man who ended the corrupt rule of Pahoran the younger will put an end to the rule of the tyrant Helaman as well!"

With these words, Gadianton held out his hand and beckoned. Another figure began to ascend the flat stone. Joshua narrowed his eyes, a cold chill crawling across his skin. In contrast to Gadianton's fine garb, this figure wore a dark cloak, the hood drawn over his head so Joshua could see no more than the form of his shoulders and head. The man turned to face the gathering, flinging back the hood of his cloak.

Joshua clenched his jaw, not surprised to see the thin smirk that curled the edges of Kishkumen's mouth behind his beard, his eyes glittering like a serpent's. At his waist, the hilt of a knife tucked into his belt gleamed in the light.

"Brothers," Kishkumen called, "this night, I will go to the palace of the chief judge. I will seek out Helaman, whether he is abed or awake, and by my blade, I will end his life and the lives of any who move to stop me or who see my face. By so doing, I will make the way clear that my comrade and friend, Gadianton, may be given the rule that is rightly his." To this, Gadianton clapped Kishkumen's back in a gesture of gratitude. Joshua's stomach turned. "Will you swear as my brothers that no whisper of this will be heard beyond this chamber?"

Most of the men in the room shouted their approval, but Joshua detected a few underlying grumbles from the men clad in roughly woven garments at the fringe of the group.

"I thought you would be our chief, Lord Kishkumen!" Joshua recognized Nissim's voice. The room fell into an uneasy quiet.

"Nissim, my friend, come forward," Kishkumen ordered.

The man who had guided Joshua did as Kishkumen commanded, drawing off his mask as he came. The expression upon his weathered face filled with uncertainty, and Joshua's brow furrowed. Helpless pity clenched his heart. Kishkumen clapped a hand on Nissim's thick shoulder.

"Do you doubt Gadianton's skill to govern us well?" he hissed.

"No," Nissim stammered. "I…merely—"

Kishkumen's hand flashed to the sheathed knife at his waist. Joshua stiffened in mute horror as a muffled grunt burst from Nissim's lips. Kishkumen released his shoulder and stepped back. Nissim's knees buckled. He tumbled off the platform and thumped to the ground. No other sound filled the room as Kishkumen turned to the men and thrust his bloodied knife into the air.

"So shall Helaman be cut down before the sun returns to the sky!" Kishkumen roared to the now silent men.

As the room erupted into cheers, Joshua backed away, easing toward the stone crevice that would lead him to the open air. None seemed to notice him, all eyes fixed upon Kishkumen and Gadianton. Gadianton spoke now, shouting something Joshua could not hear.

His heart pounding in his throat, Joshua dipped through the opening. Half bent, he scrambled through the narrow tunnel, the sound and light behind him fading. At last the crevice widened into the shadows of the empty, shabby hut. Joshua straightened, and without pause, he pushed through the outer door into the night beyond.

Joshua tore off the mask and flung it away, sucking in a breath of clean air as hungrily as if he had been underwater the last several minutes. Darkness veiled the night around him, and for a moment, he could see nothing in the shadows of the narrow street as wind brushed through his sweat-dampened hair.

With the urgency of his mission weighing all the more heavily upon him, Joshua broke into a run. His feet flew over the paving stones, his cloak fluttering behind him as he dashed through the twisting streets toward the main plaza. Through breaks between the rooftops, Jacob could see the torchlight that illuminated the walls of the palace.

As he ran, his thoughts raced as swiftly as his feet. What should he do? Should he run now and warn Helaman, or should he wait in the shadows and waylay Kishkumen somehow?

In a moment, the street he followed opened and the wide plaza appeared before him, the lights of the palace flickering across the empty square.

Joshua pulled to a stop, his chest heaving. Silence filled the night, and his heart thundered in his ears.

It had been a night much like this, Joshua imagined, centuries before when Father Nephi had walked through the gates of Jerusalem seeking the brass plates of Laban. Nephi had gone, not knowing beforehand what to do, certain only that he must succeed. The welfare of generations had depended upon his success, and he had triumphed. Could Joshua do the same?

Joshua swallowed hard, his chest heaving with the weight of his task. *Father, what am I to do?* he pleaded in his mind. *Will you guide me as you did Father Nephi of old?*

No words came into his mind as he waited in the silence, but a quiet assurance descended upon him, calming his nerves and whispering to his heart that he should wait.

Joshua would have preferred a thundering voice promising victory and clear instructions on what he must do, but he would content himself with what he was given. He pulled the hood of his cloak over his head and stepped into the shadows.

He lifted his eyes to the palace, and his eyes fixed on one lighted window in the flat-roofed wing where the unmarried maid servants kept their living quarters. All the windows in a row were dark but for one. A faint yellow glow flickered beyond the curtains. A slender, feminine shadow with unbound hair passed before the window. The silhouette paused at the curtain before gliding on again.

Joshua let out a breath and let his back fall against the stone wall behind him, the chill of the gritty stones against his shoulder blades. The maiden's shadow looked so like—

"Elizabeth," he whispered softly to himself. "What are you doing tonight? Are you happy? Are you thinking of me?"

Joshua shook his head and pulled his eyes away from the lighted window, returning his thoughts to his task.

A soft wind skimmed the stones at his feet. Long minutes passed. Clouds floated across the moon.

At last, a hooded figure stepped from a darkened alleyway. Joshua's limbs tensed. Kishkumen's figure, little more than a shadow, began to glide, ghostlike, in the direction of the palace. Fighting back his fear, Joshua stepped forward, his feet deliberately clapping upon the paving stones.

At the sound, Kishkumen whirled, a metal blade in his hand obscured the next moment by the hooded robe. Joshua brought his hand to his chest, making the same sign he had seen Nissim make less than an hour before.

Kishkumen froze, then relaxed, moving nearer to him.

"A fellow brother," he said, returning the sign. "You were not at the gathering?"

Joshua's mind scrambled. "I could not come in time. My kin would question my actions. They are not followers of Lord Gad—"

Joshua paused.

Kishkumen's eyes narrowed, but not in suspicion. Instead, a conspiratorial grin crossed his face.

"I care not if you speak the name outside our gatherings, friend. That pompous fool serves his purpose, but one day, I will remove him as easily as I will remove Helaman tonight."

"You wish to kill Helaman?" Joshua asked.

"And any usurper who stands in my way."

"How will you do this?"

"You ask how?" Kishkumen scoffed. "After I, by my own hand, ended the reign of Pahoran the younger? After I took the secret way only our brotherhood knows, and gave the Lamanites what knowledge they needed to find his milksop brother, Pacumeni?"

Joshua remained still even as fury crackled through his body.

"Helaman will be dead, like them," Kishkumen seethed, "before the sun returns."

"Then let me join you." Joshua's heart hammered against his ribs as he patted his chest where his knife lay hidden. "I too have a blade. Let us go to the judgment seat together."

Kishkumen grinned in answer, exposing crooked teeth that gleamed in the darkness.

Suppressing his fear, Joshua turned and marched out of the shadows toward the lighted steps of the palace. Kishkumen followed at Joshua's shoulder.

As Joshua and Kishkumen approached the pair of guards who stood before the great doors, the two soldiers shifted their weight and drew near to one another, blocking their path.

Joshua recognized them. David and Matthew. They were brothers.

David lifted a hand to hail them. "Hold, friends," he called in a polite, though cautious tone. "The hour is very late."

"They will question our coming," Kishkumen hissed. "When the one on the right speaks, I'll cut him down. You slay the other in the same moment so neither has time to cry a warning."

Beneath Kishkumen's hood, Joshua could see little more than his mouth and jaw, a wicked grin peeling up the edges of his thin lips.

Joshua's fist gripped the hilt of his dagger. He must act now.

"For my brother, Pacumeni," he muttered. "And for Elizabeth's broken heart."

Kishkumen faltered at this, but Joshua did not give him time to react. With one swift movement, he drew his blade and swung it into Kishkumen's chest. The blade struck with a fierce crack. Warm wetness gushed onto Joshua's hand.

Kishkumen's body stiffened, then collapsed to the steps.

Joshua jerked the blade free and staggered back, a sense of bitter release washing over him. A dark stain spread across the stone beneath Kishkumen's sprawled form, trickling down the steps like spilled wine.

"What have you done?" Matthew shouted as he and his brother pounded down the steps, their spears trained upon Joshua.

Spinning toward the astonished guards, Joshua lifted his hands. "David, Matthew! It's me!"

"Captain Joshua?" David gasped as he and Matthew staggered to a stop. Their eyes darted between Joshua's bloodied knife and the crumpled figure.

"Sir, who was that?" Matthew demanded. "What—?"

"An assassin sent by Gadianton. He meant to murder His Eminence." Joshua jerked his head toward the dead man. "Get this body out of here. I must report to Helaman."

"Yes, sir," the men replied in unison before Joshua turned and sprinted up the remaining steps.

Chapter 22

Elizabeth lifted her head with a start, blinking in the light of her candle. Whose cry had that been out in the night? It had been a man's voice, and she could have sworn it had been...

"Joshua?"

Forgetting the scroll upon the desk before her, she leaped to her feet, snatched her dressing gown from where it lay on her bed, and brushed aside the curtain of her sleeping chamber. Hurrying to the door a few paces down from her own, she pulled aside the curtain into Jonas's room and cast a quick glance upon him. His little head indented the pillow, the coverlet over him rising and falling in a slow rhythm. The noise had not woken him.

Elizabeth let the curtain drop, and drew her dressing gown about her shoulders as she started toward the end of the hallway. The rooms of the other maid servants remained dark and quiet as she hurried past. But as she neared the door at the end of the hall, the clamor of men's voices, stern and uneasy, grew louder in her ears. She unlatched the wooden door and shivered as her bare feet found the chilled paving stones of the main corridor. But she did not heed the cold as she broke into a run.

The light of the torches flickered as she passed them.

Down the corridor, uniformed guards with grim faces hurried from the throne room through the outer door and clattered down the stone steps.

Bewildered, she stopped at the open doors and looked out. Soldiers ignored Elizabeth as they passed her, trotting out into the night. At the base of the steps, the men were forming into orderly rows as if preparing to march away for battle. Halfway down the steps, two palace guards hefted a heavy shape onto a stretcher. A shroud concealed the form, but Elizabeth guessed from the shape what lay beneath the cloth, and her stomach tightened.

"Lady Elizabeth!"

She spun to meet Captain Micha's stern gaze.

"You should not be here," he said.

"Captain Micha." Elizabeth's face grew hot, and she pulled the edges of her dressing gown more closely. "I'm sorry. But I heard a cry. It sounded like Joshua's voice, and I had to come and see— What happened?" She nodded down the steps toward the shrouded form. "Who is that?"

The grizzled captain heaved a deep breath as if reluctant to tell her. "An assassin." He glanced toward the throne room doors. "He tried to kill Chief Judge Helaman. We go now to capture Gadianton. Alive, if possible."

"Gadianton? What does—?"

"Sir!" a younger voice interrupted, and Zeram skidded to a stop in front of Micha.

Zeram met Elizabeth's eyes, and his brows lifted. But he shook his head, and turned his gaze again upon Micha. "What palace guards can be spared have all been summoned, but I don't know where Lieutenant Oren is." The youth jerked his thumb over his shoulder. "He isn't in the guards' quarters, and no one saw him leave."

Micha grumbled in frustration, turning away. "I haven't time for this. Oren's unexcused absence will be dealt with later. The men we have must suffice. Lady Elizabeth," Micha jerked his head toward the throne room doors. "Your questions will be answered in there."

Zeram offered Elizabeth a fleeting smile, then followed on Micha's heels as the older captain marched out into the night.

Elizabeth crossed the corridor to the throne room and eased inside.

Helaman paced at the foot of his stone throne beneath the light of several lamps, his hair askew as if he had just been roused from sleep. His face though, bore an expression of sober concentration as he spoke to a figure clad in a ragged cloak who stood a few steps away.

"Kishkumen was in league with the band of rebels?" Helaman asked.

"Yes, sir. And Gadianton as well," the figure replied in a voice whose unexpected tones gripped her heart. "Kishkumen meant to come into this very palace and slay you, tonight."

As Elizabeth watched, the man flung back his hood with one bloodied hand, revealing his dark hair and familiar features.

"And he admitted to having murdered Pahoran the younger. He also—"

"Joshua!" His name tore from her throat. She staggered forward, reeling to a stop as Joshua turned. His eyes widened.

"Elizabeth? You're here? In Zarahemla?"

"We arrived yesterday evening... Joshua, you're bleeding."

"This blood isn't mine." He took a step toward her before he stopped, holding himself back.

Elizabeth's own restraint crumbled however, and she darted across the distance he had not taken, plunging into the solid warmth of his arms.

Despite his initial reluctance to move to her, now that she was in his arms, Joshua crushed her to him, his face buried in her hair.

"Elizabeth," he choked, his voice rough. "I've missed you!"

"And I you, Joshua." Elizabeth pressed her face against his chest, relishing the warmth of his strong arms encircling her. "But I don't understand any of this."

"Kishkumen is dead." He trembled as he held her. "He and Gadianton are traitors."

Elizabeth shuddered at this new revelation. Joshua stepped back, his hands gripping her arms. She lifted her eyes, drinking in his face.

"Kishkumen meant to murder Helaman," he continued, his voice more controlled now. "I intercepted him and killed him before he could do so. This is his blood."

"But how?" she asked. "How did you know this? How did you come to be here? Nephi said you were leagues away in the south wilderness."

Joshua's eyes lifted to Helaman, who nodded. Joshua turned back to Elizabeth.

"I've been here all along, seeking the dissidents who followed Paanchi. I pretended to be one of them to learn what they knew. I'm sorry you could not know the truth."

Elizabeth studied his eyes as he spoke, the words making her knees weak as the revelation hit her like a stone in her stomach. "They would have killed you if they had known who you were."

His hands tightened on her arms. "Our nation was in peril. I had to."

"But if something had happened to you, then I—Joshua, I—" Elizabeth swallowed thickly and stepped back.

Joshua's hands, so strong moments before, let her go and fell to his sides.

"I should fetch you water to wash your hands," she said.

"No." Joshua shook his head, turning toward Helaman whose eyes moved from Joshua to Elizabeth and back again. "There is no time, Elizabeth. I must help capture Gadianton."

A sharp breath sliced into her lungs. "You're going *back*?"

"Gadianton and his followers must be stopped," Joshua answered. "The heavens only know what damage they'll do if they are not."

Elizabeth struggled to swallow the agony in her throat. "There are soldiers in the plaza—will there be a battle? Joshua, you can't—"

"I must. For our people. For you, Elizabeth. You are..." Joshua's chest swelled as his eyes softened. "You are worth protecting."

The patter of new feet echoed through the wide chamber as Pazia, her hair hanging loose about her shoulders, darted through the door.

"Helaman, the palace is in an uproar! What—?"

She stopped short as her eyes fell on Joshua and the blood coating his hand. "Joshua, son of Antipus!" A hand flew to her throat. "By all that is good, *what* have you been doing?"

"This isn't my blood, Lady Pazia. I'm unhurt." Joshua hesitated. "For now."

Pazia released a breath, but her eyes still remained wide, her frame tense as Helaman moved to her side and grasped her hands.

"Use what force you must, Captain," Helaman ordered, turning to Joshua. "Gadianton must not be allowed to escape."

"Yes, Your Eminence." Joshua spun toward the doorway, his expression hardening. Elizabeth stepped aside to let him pass, and he started for the door. But then he stopped and turned. His eyes fixed upon her.

"Elizabeth."

"Yes?"

"I—" Joshua hesitated. He met Helaman's gaze as if seeking for help, then turned his eyes again to meet hers. His chest rose and fell with fierce emotion. "Will you pray for me?"

"Yes." She nodded, her voice breaking. "I will."

Joshua stepped back, his eyes pleading as if he wished to say more. But instead, he turned and strode from the room, barking orders to the men who waited for him, his voice fading.

Elizabeth watched him go, her heart tearing as he went. "Joshua..." Her voice was too soft for him to hear. Beside her, however, Pazia heard, and she stepped forward. Her arm circled Elizabeth, lending her a soft shoulder on which to lean.

Gadianton ran a hand through his hair, then folded his arms across his chest. He turned and strode across the flickering alcove set off from the main chamber where his followers waited. Kishkumen had not returned, and nagging anxiety gnawed in Gadianton's belly like a pernicious worm.

If Kishkumen had done something foolish, if something had happened, if Helaman's guards captured him, all would be lost. The thought filled him with dread.

Gadianton lifted one hand, pressing his knuckles against his lips. It would be better for Kishkumen to be dead. After all, dead men could not be tortured into confessing their comrades' secrets. If he died, Gadianton would remain safe. But if he had been captured...

Footsteps behind Gadianton caused him to turn, furious at the unwanted intrusion. Oren appeared around the shoulder of stone that led from the main chamber. His one good eye betrayed a look of nervousness.

One of the women appeared behind Oren, and for a moment, Gadianton's frown eased. Sharai was one of his favorites. But just as quickly, his anger returned.

"I have no time for women now, Oren."

"Lord Gadianton," Oren stammered, dropping to one knee. "We must leave this place. I fear we have been betrayed."

Gadianton's eyes narrowed. "How do you know this?"

Oren gulped hard, and at his hesitation, Gadianton lunged forward. He snatched Oren's hair, forcing him to his knees. "How do you know this?"

"A man was here." Oren hissed against the pain, flinching beneath Gadianton's glare. "He stood near me. He came in with Nissim. He was different somehow."

"Different? How?"

Making a gesture toward the woman, Oren said, "He refused Sharai."

"*What?*" No man who had caught Sharai's eye had refused her before.

"And after the uproar when Kishkumen knifed old Nissim," Oren gulped, "I could see the man nowhere."

Gadianton looked up toward the girl. Sharai nodded, her eyes bright with fear.

"What did he look like?" Gadianton demanded, squeezing his fist into Oren's hair.

"I never saw his features. He wore a mask," Oren gasped.

"Useless, half-blind invalid!" Gadianton shoved Oren's head away as he turned and lunged a step toward the girl. He snatched her arm in a fierce grip. "And what of you? Did you see his face?"

"Yes," Sharai moaned, flinching in pain.

"What did he look like? Tell me!"

"H-he looked young, near m-my years. Tall, with the build of a warrior. He claimed that his name was Akish, that he was a stone mason. His hair was dark."

Gadianton's eyes narrowed, his heart climbing into his throat at her words.

"What of his eyes?" Gadianton grasped her other arm. "What color were they?"

"They..." She wilted, her eyes wide with terror. "They were blue."

A swell of rage boiled up within Gadianton and tore from his lungs in a single, wild shriek as he shoved the girl so that she stumbled and collapsed.

"*Joshua*!"

The word rebounded off the walls about him, mocking and taunting him. Because of the son of Antipus, he had lost *everything*! "I should have known!"

Gadianton drew the knife at his belt and turned on Oren. The blade gleamed crimson in the torchlight. "Pacumeni's wretched watchdog was *here*, you idiot! Joshua *lied* to you! He never went south! The son of Antipus stood beside you, in these very chambers, and you did *nothing*! Give me a reason, son of Kanan, why I shouldn't cut your heart out!"

Oren froze. He shot a glance toward Sharai, then back at Gadianton. "We know of a secret way out of the city," he blurted. "We can escape. Helaman and his guards won't find us."

Gadianton faltered at his words, though he still held his knife. "What secret way?"

"Those of us who began the band, we who followed Kishkumen until you brought your learning and wisdom to lead us, know of a tunnel to the river," Oren said. "They won't see us escape. They won't even know of our passing."

"Don't lie to me!" Gadianton snarled. "I know of Pachus's tunnel. The Nephites found it and filled it with stones and concrete years ago! Do you think I am an idiot?"

"I speak of another!" Oren winced where he knelt on the floor.

Gadianton appraised the cowering man's features. Was Oren lying to save himself? Reeling on Sharai, he demanded, "Is this true?"

She nodded. "It is. There is a tunnel. In these very caverns. It leads to the river."

"My lord," Oren pleaded, lifting his hands in supplication, "there's a natural fissure that leads to the Sidon River Valley. It was once too small for a man to go the full distance, but under Kishkumen's direction, we widened it. Only a small curtain of hanging vines and a narrow wall of stones block its exit now. They are removed and replaced with ease. We've done it before."

"Why did no one ever tell me of this?"

Oren and the girl traded a terrified look. "What matters, lord," Oren pleaded, "is that we can escape into the wilderness and build anew, away from Helaman's tyranny, then strike at him and his minions when your strength is regained."

New hope swelled within Gadianton at these words. "Then we will take this secret way," he declared, "and begin a new kingdom in the wilderness."

Gadianton fixed his glare upon the girl. "Get out, woman."

Relief washing over her face, Sharai turned and darted out of the room. Oren staggered to his feet and began to retreat also, his eye moving from Gadianton's face to the knife and back again.

"Not you, Oren."

Oren halted, paling.

"Your foolishness has cost me much." Gadianton sneered, enjoying the fear on Oren's face. "If you wish to be forgiven for this folly, I would have you do me a small service."

"What do you wish?"

"Once we are all safely away, you will return to Zarahemla. I will send a small number of men with you to make sure you fulfill your duty, and then you may rejoin our band."

Oren licked his lips. "What duty?"

Gadianton stepped forward. The young man stiffened, his eye bright with fear. "I want you and the men I send with you to go into Zarahemla and find Joshua, son of Antipus."

"And then?"

Spinning the knife in his hand, Gadianton held it by the blade and slapped the hilt into Oren's palm. "Then cut his heart out and bring it back to me."

Chapter 23

Elizabeth parted the curtain that hung over the doorway of Jonas's bedchamber and leaned against the frame. A sweet ache gripped her heart as she studied the sleeping boy; the faint rise and fall of his breath, his face peaceful in slumber.

She stepped farther into the room and sighed as she sat at the foot of the child's bed. Once, she had loved this child's father with all of her soul. But she could no longer deny the emotions that swelled within her as her thoughts turned to Joshua and the words he had spoken before he marched out to face whatever evil waited for him in the darkness.

"Elizabeth." Pazia's gentle voice sounded behind her

Elizabeth turned to see her friend standing in the doorway. Pazia's once loose hair now lay in neatly twined braids against her head.

"The maidservants have all been wakened," Pazia said as she moved near Elizabeth. "Master Tuloth and a number of other healers have been summoned. Gadianton will not be taken easily—we must be prepared to look after any wounded who come back to us."

Elizabeth forced back her own fears and stood. "I should help."

"No. Stay here," Pazia urged. "Watch over Jonas in case he wakes. And pray." She gently touched Elizabeth's cheek. "Joshua needs it. All his men do." She added with a smile, "And *you* need solitude to sort out the tangled feelings in your heart, my dear one."

At this, Elizabeth's timorous courage faltered, and she bit back a sob. "Pazia, what is going to happen to Joshua?"

Pazia drew Elizabeth into her arms. "I don't know."

"What if he's hurt? Or killed? What if I never have the chance to tell him that..." her words trailed off.

Pazia drew back, seeking Elizabeth's eyes. "That you love him?"

Elizabeth blushed at the pointedness of her friend's query and glanced away, speechless.

"*Do* you love Joshua?" Pazia persisted, her words both gentle and adamant.

Elizabeth sat down again. Jonas stirred, but did not waken. "I loved him from our first meeting—as a dear friend. I have always known the goodness of his heart, and that I could trust my life to him." She drew in a sigh. "I have always known that he would do anything for my happiness, and I would do anything for his. If that is not love, nothing else is. Yet..." She faltered.

Pazia knelt before her, taking Elizabeth's hands in her own. "Yet the sisterly affection you once felt for Joshua is changed now, grown from what it was before Pacumeni died, and you are uncertain what to think of it."

"Joshua is a wonderful man. He is honorable, and wise, and brave, and..." Elizabeth paused. "And wonderfully handsome," she finished in a whisper, her face growing hot.

Pazia smiled.

Elizabeth dropped her gaze. In a soft voice, she continued, "And he deserves a wife who will love him with all her heart. I don't deserve him if I cannot love him fully."

"Oh, my dear Elizabeth," Pazia said. "Do not think that because you once loved one man, you cannot truly love another! Do not believe that learning to love again will dishonor my little brother, or make you somehow inconstant! Pacumeni would not wish for his memory to be enshrined so deeply in your heart that it could not heal. That it could not be given to a good man who lives and breathes and walks this earth with you!"

Elizabeth's lips trembled as she studied Pazia's face through her tears.

"Lady Pazia?" A young woman's voice sounded from the end of the corridor.

Pazia lifted her head in the direction of the voice. "I'm coming, Martha!" she called before turning back to Elizabeth. "Think on what I have said," she pleaded. "And pray. For Joshua. And for his men. And for my own Nephi."

Elizabeth's lips parted. "Nephi went with them?"

Pazia smiled sadly and nodded.

"And you have set aside your worry for him to talk to me?"

"My dearest Elizabeth," Pazia murmured, "you are worth it." With that, she gave Elizabeth's hands a final squeeze, then she rose and departed. The curtain of the doorway fell shut behind her.

At the window, a breeze stirred the cloth, whispering as it entered the room. Elizabeth moved to the window and parted the thin fabric.

She could see no stars, for clouds blanketed the sky. A breeze caressed her face, sweetened with coming rain. How could the city sleep in such peace when the man she cared for above all the earth was striding willingly into danger?

Nothing but the wind whistled far and away over the city, coming to her ears like the soft notes of a distant flute.

Like Pacumeni's flute.

Elizabeth let her eyes fall shut as the faint music upon the wind flowed over her.

Elizabeth, Pacumeni's voice seemed to whisper, *a new door stands before you.*

The breeze began to fade. *Open it.*

The voice ebbed away, uttering a last faint whisper as it went, *Let yourself love him.*

She opened her eyes, stepped back from the window, and let the curtain fall shut. She returned to Jonas's side, touching a hand to his brow, smoothing a lock of hair back from features so like his father's.

Her vision blurring with wetness, Elizabeth lowered herself to her knees beside the little boy's bed. Pressing her forehead against her palms, she began to pray.

Mist fell from the sky, cooling his heated face and arms, but Joshua barely noted the drizzle. With a mighty kick powered by a rush of fury, he shattered the wooden door inward with a thunderous crash. Splinters of wood spun away into the dark interior. Hacking his sword at the remains of the door that swung madly on its hinges, Joshua lunged through the little room and scrambled down the narrow passage into the darkness, his sword ready as he emerged into the open stone chamber. The empty room, no longer lit by the light of flickering torches, was silent and dark. What little light he could see by came from the low entrance behind him.

Joshua strode farther into the room, his eyes scanning the darkness. Anyone could be hiding in the shadows or the unseen cavities that branched off the main chamber. Behind him, he could hear his men clambering out of the crevice, their weapons ready.

"Gadianton!" Joshua barked, striding into the center of the room. He found the edge of the stone dais with his free hand and vaulted up on it, heedless of the darkness before his eyes.

"Show yourself!" he shouted, but nothing more than his own voice echoed back at him.

Behind him, he heard the hiss and crackle of fire. Flickering light filled the chamber as the torches his men had brought hissed into life, illuminating the uneven walls.

Swallowing hard, Joshua turned in a full circle, his sword in his fist. Was this a trick? The last time he was here, the room had been filled with people, the air thick with light and smoke.

"They're gone." He jumped from the platform and stabbed his blade through an abandoned cloak upon the floor. "The wretches."

With a grunt of frustration, he flung the mound of cloth from his sword, where it skiffed across the stone floor and crumpled in a lifeless heap.

"They couldn't have escaped the city, sir," a youthful voice offered. Joshua glanced toward Nephi. "All the gates are watched. Men guard the walls. They may be hiding like rats in a corner, but Gadianton won't elude us for long."

"Not unless they were moles and could dig their way under the walls," Zeram rejoined, and the other men chuckled, their voices echoing in the empty chamber.

A groan on the far side of the stone platform, however, silenced the laughter. Spinning toward the sound, Joshua strode around to the opposite side of the dais.

Upon the ground at the base of the stone table lay the body of Nissim, his jaguar mask beside him. Joshua's skin grew cold. Had Nissim been lying here abandoned and in pain all this time? Nissim stirred, and Joshua knelt at the wounded man's side.

"Nissim?" He placed a hand on the thick shoulder.

At his touch, the muscle beneath the skin stiffened, and a groan escaped the fallen man as he rolled toward Joshua, a flash of something clenched in his fist. Joshua leaped backward as an obsidian blade smashed into the uneven floor where he had knelt a moment before. The end of the blade shattered, scattering shards of black glass across the stone.

"Sir!" His men hurried near, spears and swords held ready.

"Wait," Joshua commanded, holding up a hand to stay their blades.

"Cursed servant of tyrants!" Nissim groaned as he crawled toward Joshua, his tunic soaked in blood. One hand clutched the wound in his chest while the other grasped the hilt of his obsidian knife, the blade shorter now, though just as sharp.

"Nissim, put aside the blade," Joshua ordered, backing away. "You'll hurt yourself!"

"I don't need your pretended mercy, *Akish*!" Nissim seethed. "If that's even your name!"

"I am Joshua, son of Antipus. And I have no desire to hurt you, Nissim. I never did!"

"Lying whelp!" The man struggled to rise, but he stumbled and fell, catching himself with one hand. His broken knife clattered away, but he snatched it again, lifting burning eyes to meet Joshua's. Crimson seeped between the fingers that clutched the blood-sopped cloth over his chest.

"You need a physician! Do not waste your strength. I swear to you, you will be treated well."

"Ha," Nissim scoffed. "Until your judges hang me from a tree?"

"If you help us, you'll receive leniency. I'll speak for you! Put aside your knife!"

"Help you? How? By telling you how they slipped out of your hands? You won't find them, even if I did."

"Why would we not find them?" Joshua demanded. "Nissim, where are they? Where have they gone? You cannot be loyal to them after what they did to you."

Nissim's face contorted in agony. "Moles!" he guffawed. "Digging under the walls!"

Once more, he struggled to stand, trembling in weakness or fury, or perhaps a mingling of both. But his legs buckled and he crumpled again, falling prostrate on the uneven, rocky floor. His knife clattered to rest at Joshua's feet. He stirred once, then lay still.

"Nissim," Joshua called, but the man did not move.

"Sir, don't—" Zeram protested, but Joshua knelt over the fallen man and pressed his fingers to his throat. Nothing.

"There is nothing more he can do to us." A pang of sorrow lanced through Joshua as he clambered to his feet. "And nothing more we can do for him."

"Then what do we do?" Zeram's voice echoed in the silence.

Joshua looked up, barely hearing the young man's words. "Moles," he said to himself as a distant, indefinable dread began to form in the pit of his stomach, swirling like a tormented ghost taking horrific form in his thoughts. "Digging under—"

His words stopped short, and his mind flashed back to something Kishkumen had said in the plaza. *"After I took the secret way only our brotherhood knows."* And Sharai's seductive invitation to join her in the dark caverns that extended…

"Under the walls." Joshua scrambled up. Sick realization rose like bile in his throat. "Look for footprints!" he ordered. "Look where they lead."

Torchlight flickered, flinging tortured shadows off the walls as his men scanned about, searching the dust of the floor.

"This way! They lead in there."

The shout came from Nephi, who held a torch in one hand and pointed toward one small fissure in the stone wall just wide enough for a man to enter. Sure enough, several fresh scuffs and prints of human feet disappeared into the narrow gash.

Joshua strode toward the fissure and ducked his head. He grasped the torch from Nephi and held it at arm's length down the tunnel. He could not tell how far into the darkness the crevice extended. But there, within the reach of his torchlight, upon the uneven floor of the tunnel, as if dropped in haste and still smoking, lay a charred torch.

"They went this way!" Joshua exulted. He could see no lights nor hear any voices, but Gadianton and his followers could not be so far ahead that a trained eye could not follow their tracks even once they had reached the tunnel's exit, likely in the river valley of the Sidon.

On the other side of the cavern, a muffled rumble echoed through the entrance.

Joshua turned his head. "What was that?"

"Thunder, I think," Zeram said. "It's started to rain."

Joshua's heart stopped. He had forgotten the faint, cool mist that had been falling from the sky during their march here. "*Rain?*" Water would obliterate the tracks!

But just as quickly, a firm resolve gripped his heart. He would not give up. Perhaps they still had a chance. Perhaps they could still overtake Gadianton.

"Follow me," Joshua ordered. Holding the torch before him, he ducked into the narrow tunnel. Behind him, he heard the echo of his men's feet as Nephi, Zeram, and the others followed him one by one into the darkness.

Chapter 24

The remnants of the storm that had passed during the night were faded now to nothing more than thin filaments of cloud that brushed the sky. Purple shadows washed the kitchen chamber where Talilia knelt over the fire pit, coaxing a simmering coal to life with bits of dried bark. She smiled as the bark lit, causing a faint glow to flicker. As the flame grew in strength, she began to add larger twigs.

Today would be a lovely day, for she had no duties and the hours stretched before her, bright and promising. And perhaps she would see Tuloth as well.

As if summoned by her thoughts, a welcome voice called from beyond the doorway to the street. "Peace be with this house."

Talilia's cheeks grew warm. "Please. Come in."

The door swung open, and Talilia bit her bottom lip as Tuloth appeared, his tall form silhouetted against the soft light beyond him.

"Tuloth." She rose, her cheeks warm as she drank in the sight of him, his broad shoulders taking up much of the doorway. In one hand, he held a small bag, lumpy with potatoes or perhaps sweet papaya. She smiled. Almost every day, he stopped by with a gift of some kind. "Peace to you."

"And to you, Talilia," he returned. "One of the early vendors at the market had fresh papaya, and I thought you and your father might enjoy some."

He held out his small gift, and she stepped forward, accepting the weight of it.

Nearer to him now, feeling the warmth of his closeness, inhaling the pleasant, masculine scent of his skin, Talilia's heart quickened. "You need not do so much for us," she murmured.

"It is always a pleasure." A smile played at the corners of his mouth. "And I confess, I wanted a reason to come see you this morning as early as decorum would permit."

Talilia felt her cheeks reddening at his words.

"And I wished to tell you the news."

"Oh?" She lifted her eyes. "What news?"

"During the hours of darkness, the subversive group responsible for the death of Pacumeni the younger sent a man to kill Helaman too."

Talilia touched a hand to her mouth. "Is he—?"

"Helaman is unhurt," Tuloth continued. "A faithful guard slew the assassin before he could perform his task. But the man's cohorts, Gadianton among them, escaped from Zarahemla."

"How many?"

Tuloth lifted his hands, then let them fall against his kilt. "Scores."

"*Scores*?" she gasped. "How did *scores* of people leave the city without being seen?"

"They made their way out of the city by a secret pass," Tuloth said. "A narrow fissure that led from a hidden place in the old quarter of the city beneath the east wall."

Talilia's heart skipped a beat. "A tunnel? Like the one Pachus had his servants dig?"

"Yes." Tuloth's usually gentle eyes flashed with sparks. Talilia stepped forward, a hand reaching toward his arm as he seethed, "Curse Pachus and all his wretched kin. No doubt Gadianton and his minions learned from them."

His words stabbed her heart as if Tuloth had plunged a knife into her, and Talilia jerked back, agony surging through her.

Seeing her reaction, Tuloth's expression changed in a moment. "Talilia? What is wrong?"

Talilia shook her head and turned away, her throat too tight to speak.

Large warm hands covered her shoulders. Against her will, a sweet warmth pulsed through her body at his touch as he turned her toward him.

"Hope is not lost, Talilia. It is a bitter blow that Gadianton escaped, but—"

He stopped, astonishment on his face as her eyes filled with wetness.

"What is wrong?" he asked."Please, don't—"

One tear escaped the rim of her lashes and trailed down her cheek. Tuloth lifted a hand to brush the tear away, but Talilia stepped back, turning her face from him. Tuloth let his hand drop.

"I have done something to hurt you," he whispered, his voice tinged with painful realization. "Your tears are not due to Gadianton's escape, but to some foolishness of mine."

"You have done nothing foolish. You have only spoken the truth, bitter as it is."

"Tell me how I can stop your tears, Talilia. Tell me what you wish, and I will do it."

"Please just go," she begged. "And take these with you." She shoved the bag back into his hands. "I don't deserve them."

"Talilia, please—" The gentleness in his voice broke her heart. "I will go if you wish me to, but my heart aches not knowing why."

"Just go, Tuloth!" she pleaded as she turned her back on him.

Tuloth said no more, but the soft scuff of his leather sandals marked his departure.

Talilia turned. He was gone, as she had asked, but the small bag of papaya remained, sitting forlornly beside the doorway.

Beside her, the small fire she had kindled flickered lower and faded until, with a puff of smoke, it died.

As Shemnon brushed aside the curtain of his sleeping chamber and looked about the eating room, he sensed that something was wrong.

Talilia knelt beside the small fire pit, her hands shaking as she brought the flame to life. Usually she had a merry fire going now, and breakfast already warm.

"Good morning, daughter," he ventured, moving forward to touch a hand to the twined braids of her yellow hair.

"Would that it were a good morning, Father."

Shemnon's brow furrowed at the broken tones in her voice.

"Child..." he began, circling the fire pit to see her face. His brows rose at the wetness upon her cheeks. He saw a plump bag sitting in the doorway. "Tuloth has been here."

"Yes." She said no more, and she did not look at him.

Shemnon moved to her side and knelt upon the floor. "Please, child." His eyes sought hers as she turned her face down. "Speak what troubles you."

"He despises me." In the light of the tiny fire, her tears glimmered.

A smile fought to claim his lips. Nothing could be further from the truth, but seeing the earnestness in her eyes, Shemnon gentled his words. "With the way Tuloth gazes upon you whenever he is near you, my daughter, I find that most difficult to believe."

"He uttered a curse on Pachus and all his *wretched* kin."

Shemnon's faint smile died, and he swallowed hard. For the gentle Ammonite to speak in such a way, he must have been terribly impassioned by something. Shemnon's lips parted in confusion. "Why—?"

"An assassin attempted to slay the chief judge last night," she said, her words spilling forth. "He was thwarted and slain, but his cohorts escaped. They fled by some secret way— a fissure in the rock that led beneath the east wall, just like Pachus—like our tunnel, ten years ago."

"And because of this, Tuloth cursed that traitor and his kin?"

Talilia nodded.

"You are not his kin, my bright candle. You are mine."

"But I am his seed. His blood!"

"You are *my* daughter, no less than my other precious child who is lost to me," Shemnon said, his voice still gentle, though a thread of fierceness entered it. "And more than that, you are your own soul, Talilia. Tuloth knows this. I know he cares for you, and perhaps even loves you. He would not care the less were he to know who sired you."

Talilia looked up, meeting his eyes through her tears.

"Have you met Helaman?" he asked.

"No." She shook her head. "Chief Judge Helaman is a great and mighty man. One cannot often find an audience with him."

"I did."

Despite her sorrow, Talilia smiled a little. "You are unique, Father. A Lamanite who stayed behind rather than returning home? He *would* offer you an audience if you requested it."

Shemnon heaved a breath and rose to his feet. "Then come, child," he said, holding out his hand. "Come with me. I shall take you to meet him, and Helaman will speak words to you that will ease this sadness upon your heart."

Talilia studied his hand, but to his dismay, the sorrow upon her face deepened, and she looked away.

"He would not wish to speak to me, were he to know who I was," she mourned. "He would despise me too, as Tuloth already does." She scrambled to her feet.

"Talilia!" Shemnon called, but she did not look back as she hurried out the door into the rising light and vanished from his view.

⋈

Cool air filled her lungs as Elizabeth strolled along the pillared portico, the palace garden bathed in early morning shadows. It seemed an odd thing that such a morning could seem so peaceful after what had transpired in the last hours.

Her heart twisted within her as Elizabeth passed one pillar, then another.

Was Joshua safe?

When would she know?

"Elizabeth?"

The small voice, so real and near, startled Elizabeth, and her eyes jerked toward the source to see Jonas in his long linen shirt, pattering along the portico. He stopped at the sight of her, smiled, and held out his arms.

"Jonas!" She hurried to him and scooped him up. "What are you doing awake so early?"

"I saw you leave my room," he confessed. "Did you kneel by my bed all night?"

Elizabeth dropped down from the portico and sat upon the edge of the walkway with Jonas cradled on her lap, her shoulder against the pillar. "I was praying."

"What were you praying all night for?" His fists dug sleepily into his eyes.

"Many things." She brushed her finger against his cheek.

Jonas seemed content with this, for he relaxed against her shoulder and said no more.

The sound of booted feet striding along the stone tiles lifted Elizabeth's face just as Captain Micha appeared. The grizzled warrior looked weary, his uniform beneath his thick armor damp with sweat, though seeing her and Jonas, a tired grin touched his lips.

"Lady Elizabeth." He drew to a stop, wavering a little before he drew in a breath and squared his shoulders.

"What is the news, Captain Micha?" Elizabeth hitched Jonas on her hip and rose to her feet. "How many were hurt? What of Joshua?"

"None of our soldiers were so much as wounded." Micha's brow furrowed. "Though Gadianton and his band escaped."

Elizabeth swallowed, her throat dry. She accepted Micha's hand, letting him help her step up onto the pillared porch, Jonas still on her hip.

"But Joshua is unhurt?"

Micha chuckled at her repeated question. "The last I knew. He and a number of his men are still searching, but a rain in the night washed away any tracks we could have followed, and there's little hope we'll find anything. Gadianton and his followers are well out of the land now, and secreted in the trackless jungle that is Hermounts."

Micha heaved a sigh. "There is something else I came to ask you, Lady Elizabeth."

"Of course."

"Young Nephi is still with Captain Joshua, but he told me that he made a promise to you that he wishes to see fulfilled." Micha lifted his eyes to the light of the rising morning, his voice full of compassion. "Do you wish to see Pacumeni's grave?"

The sloping sides of the river valley, dotted with leafy brush and ragged stones, gleamed in the light of the morning sun that fell over them. A slight tug on her hand turned Elizabeth's eyes down to Jonas, who swung merrily along, one hand in hers, stopping now and then to pick up a stone on the path before him or exclaim over some object that caught his attention.

Beside her, Micha's graying hair blew back and forth in the wind, bare of its helmet. The folds of his palace uniform rustled a little.

Somewhere hidden in the brush on the slope above them, a brightly colored bird trilled before it took to flight, its vivid wings beating against the air as it rose.

"Oh, look," Jonas exclaimed as the bird glided over their heads.

"Watch this," Micha said, and a shrill whistle escaped his lips. At this, the bird circled back and looped above their group. A series of cries similar to the sound Micha had made escaped its throat before it turned away and dipped its wings down, descending toward the river. Its feathers skimmed the glittering water before the bird beat its wings and rose up the sloping eastern rim of the river valley, disappearing into the golden sunlight.

"I speak bird, Jonas." Micha winked at Elizabeth. "I called out 'Good morning,' and the bird replied, 'Don't distract me. I'm hungry and want my breakfast!'"

Jonas's eyes widened in childish wonder, his mouth forming a small circle before his eyes narrowed, incredulous. "It did *not*." He snorted. "You don't know what it said!"

Micha gave a hearty laugh. "Oh, you're too clever for me, Jonas." He ruffled the small boy's hair. "Clever like your father was at your age."

Elizabeth found herself smiling at the thought before Micha's features sobered again, and he nodded ahead toward a small grassy hollow where the path widened, surrounded on three sides by walls of stone. Lush vines trailed over the walls, many hanging down over the rock faces like curtains. Their leaves stirred in the breeze, filling the air with the faint aroma of growing things. Jonas's hand tightened within hers. One part of the curtain of vines had been savagely torn away, revealing a narrow crevice disappeared into darkness. Torn vines lay scattered amongst a tumble of stones at the entrance of the crevice.

"This is where the people of Gadianton made their escape," Micha said, nodding toward the dark cavern. "That leads back beneath the wall into the city.

"But here," Micha gestured to a low mound of stones on one side of the crescent-shaped hollow, "is where Pacumeni's earthly body rests. And this is what I brought you to see."

Thick grasses and flowers that had escaped trampling rose among the stones, wavering in the breeze that flowed along the river valley.

A single flat stone had been placed upon the ground at the head of the mound, and careful marks had been scratched upon its rough surface.

Her heart quickening, Elizabeth stepped nearer. She touched a hand to her throat as she recognized the markings, figures that her mother had taught her when she was a child.

Emotion gripped her as she read the etched characters. *A noble man lies here.* And beneath the epitaph, in simple, phonetic characters evenly etched, the single word, *Pacumeni*.

A sweet ache gripped her heart for a moment before easing into a warm wave of gentle peace. She turned her eyes to Jonas, who stood near, understanding in his eyes.

"Amasa the Lamanite buried your father here." Micha placed a hand on Jonas's head.

"The same man who helped us so many months ago," Elizabeth added. "Do you remember him, Jonas?"

Jonas nodded.

"I was among those he brought here," Micha said. "Amasa seems like a good man."

"He is," Elizabeth agreed. She knelt beside the stone, the surface cool and rough beneath her fingertips as she traced the indentations of Pacumeni's name.

The sound of footsteps along the path lifted Elizabeth's head. A woman drew near, her face downturned. Tawny hair lay neatly twined in braids upon her head, and a broken sigh escaped her as if she had been crying.

"Peace to you, friend," Elizabeth greeted.

The woman stopped and lifted her head. Her blue eyes, red-rimmed, met Elizabeth's.

"And to you." The woman sniffed, coming forward more slowly. "Forgive me. I did not know any others were upon this river path so early in the day."

"There is no need for apology." Elizabeth rose to her feet. "I am Elizabeth, daughter of Nathan, and this is Jonas. And our guard, Captain Micha."

The woman looked away. "I am... Talilia, daughter of—" She fell silent, her eyes lighting upon the narrow crevice in the wall of rock. "This must be where Gadianton and his comrades escaped."

"It is," Elizabeth said.

"It is in a different place, but it looks the same," Talilia murmured, her voice morose.

Elizabeth smiled, uncertain what Talilia meant. Perhaps it didn't matter. "Your name is lovely," Elizabeth offered. "Talilia. To illuminate the way."

"You know its meaning." Talilia smiled briefly. "My father gave it to me—" Her face fell again. "But I will never be free of my past, no matter how much—"

A sharp gasp from Micha cut Talilia's words off, and Elizabeth's face jerked toward their guard. Her heart leaped into her throat at the arrow that protruded from Micha's side, and the look of fear in his eyes that fixed wildly upon hers.

"Micha!" she shouted as a shriek burst from Jonas's lips. The little boy snatched Micha's arm, trying to help him keep his feet as the old warrior toppled to his knees.

"No," Micha choked. He seized Jonas's tunic and shoved him toward Elizabeth. "Forget me. Run. All of you. *Run!*" His expression crumpled, and his body tumbled to the earth.

A gasp jerked its way out of Elizabeth's throat as five men appeared around the jutting wall of rock enclosing the small grassy bay. They stopped, fixing their eyes on the two women with the boy at Elizabeth's skirts. Every drop of blood in her screamed for her to flee, but these strangers blocked her escape. A day's growth of beard roughened the men's faces, and cold flint filled their eyes. Bows and quivers of arrows hung across their backs, their tunics dirty and torn, damp with sweat. Their eyes looked red and wild as if they hadn't slept in a week, and their chests heaved as if they had been running. The last man, fierce-looking with a vicious scar slashed across his face, gripped a bow in his fist. The hilt of a sheathed dagger on one hip caught in the sunlight as the man stepped over Micha's inert body as casually as if he stepped over a felled log.

This man seemed chillingly familiar to Elizabeth as his good eye flashed from her to the small boy half-hidden by her skirt then to Talilia, and back again. He traded grins with his companions and stepped forward.

"What have we here?" The man chuckled, looping his bow across his back. Elizabeth's heart gave a wrenching thud at his voice. "What spoils to bring to Lord Gadianton!"

"Lieutenant Oren?" she gasped.

"*Lady* Elizabeth," he returned in a mocking tone. His eye flashed over Jonas, a look of disgust claiming his face. "And Pacumeni's noisome little *brat*."

Oren's face twisted as his glare found Talilia once more. "And *you!*" he exclaimed. "Of all people! I thought you'd met your death years ago, *cousin*. Like Pachus did. He killed himself before he could be taken captive. You wouldn't know, since you deserted him too."

"I didn't—" Talilia protested before she fell silent, her face written with misery.

Chilled water coursed through Elizabeth's veins. "You are one of Gadianton's followers, Oren? But you were a palace guard! You took a sacred oath! How could you?"

Oren's eye raked up and down Elizabeth, and she shuddered as if his gaze stripped her to the skin. "Gadianton's rewards were sweeter than the paltry wages of a *palace guard*."

Elizabeth gulped hard. She staggered back a step, keeping herself between Jonas and the five men who drew forward. She saw no mercy in their eyes. If she did nothing to stop them, Jonas would soon be dead, and her fate, along with Talilia's— Elizabeth shuddered, and nausea rose in her throat.

Yet in the same moment, a swell of determination seized her heart. No matter what they did to her, they would not hurt Jonas!

Her teeth clenched, Elizabeth swept up a gnarled stick from the ground. Oren and his companions paused in their advance to trade expressions of mocking amusement.

"Oh, no," one snorted. "A woman and a stick. We may not survive, my friends."

"Stay away from us," Elizabeth commanded, clutching the branch in both hands.

Oren's grin twisted into a look of impatience. He nudged the arm of the man who had spoken. "Giddian, get her."

"Gladly." The man sneered and started forward.

"Talilia, take Jonas down the tunnel!" Elizabeth cried as her heart leaped in terror.

Talilia's skirts rustled, and Jonas's trembling hands pulled away from Elizabeth. She did not dare to turn, though she hoped desperately that Talilia had fled into the tunnel with the little boy.

Elizabeth swung the branch, her heart jumping in her throat as the stick struck and ripped across Giddian's bare neck. He yelped and staggered back, stumbling into his companions.

A foul epithet escaped Oren's lips, and he sprang toward her. Turning on him, she lashed the branch toward his scarred face. But Oren dodged the blow and lifted a hand in the same moment, catching the stick in midair.

Oren ripped the branch away, tearing her palms as he wrenched it from her grasp. He flung it aside, his lips curled in a predatory grin.

Even with the loss of the tree branch, Elizabeth clenched her teeth, refusing to be cowed. Her hands balled into fists. She swung out at Oren's sneering face, but he slapped her arm aside and lunged forward. He barreled into her, throwing her to the earth.

The bewilderingly sweet scent of grass filled Elizabeth's nostrils as her back slammed into the earth, Oren's solid weight crushing her.

His hot breath washed her face, and terror shot through her as Elizabeth met the single gleam of his eye where his face hovered above her own. His glare burned into her, ravenous and wild, like a rabid jaguar ready to tear into its helpless prey.

But when a sharp crack sounded above her, once, then again, Oren's wild expression mutated into a look of angry pain. Uttering a curse, Oren rolled off her, freeing Elizabeth of his crushing weight. He clutched his side where two angry gashes slashed across his ribs, blood oozing from the torn skin. He glared with contempt at Talilia, who had backed against the wall of stone, brandishing the same stick Oren had torn from Elizabeth's hands, swinging it at any of his companions who ventured too close.

Drawing in a sharp breath, Elizabeth scrambled to her feet only to feel an arm whip around her waist like the coil of a snake.

A metallic rasp sliced the air, and then something cold and sharp pricked the flesh beneath her chin. "You're not going anywhere, lovely one." Oren's voice felt hot and fierce near her ear. Then louder, he called, "Drop it, cousin, or I'll cut her throat!"

At Oren's threat, a gasp tore from Talilia's lips. She wilted, and two of the men lunged forward, snatching her arms. Giddian yanked the gnarled branch from Talilia's hand and broke it across his knee.

"Talilia, you should have run!" Elizabeth cried. "Where is Jonas?"

"She's right! You should have run, *Lylith*!" Oren spat. His arm almost crushed her breath from her. The painful tip of the cold metal pressed into her skin. "It would have been just like you, after you and your father, Pachus, deserted us, your own *kindred*!"

Between her captors, Talilia squeezed her eyes shut.

"Enough of this, Oren." Blood ran down Giddian's neck where Elizabeth had struck him, as if his throat had been slashed. He jerked his head toward Talilia. "She sent the boy down the tunnel." He flung the broken stick aside and jerked an obsidian knife from his belt as he strode toward the low fissure in the rock and peered inside. "But he'll not get far."

"No!" Elizabeth pleaded, her cry echoed by Talilia.

"Let the little demon go!" Oren barked as Giddian bent to enter the cavern.

Giddian, already half in the tunnel, turned back. "If we don't kill the brat, he'll return to the palace and tell them we're here."

Oren laughed, the sound harsh and void of humor. "Of course he will."

Giddian emerged and turned to face Oren, his expression one of glowering frustration. "Have you gone mad? Gadianton will slay us all if we fail."

"Don't panic, Giddian," Oren pressed his jaw against Elizabeth's hair and drew in a deep breath before he exhaled, his breath hot against her scalp. Nausea boiled in her stomach. "These two could be of use to us. Especially this one."

Giddian's mouth twisted in frustration. "Do you mean to *let* them follow us?"

"*He* will follow us. That's what matters." Oren's voice slithered over Elizabeth's skin like the touch of a serpent. "And once we have him, then we kill him, and any with him."

Giddian persisted, "How can we be certain that Joshua will come after her?"

"Come now, Giddian," Oren said. "A blind, half-witted beggar could see that the son of Antipus worships the very ground she treads upon. If he knows she's in danger, we won't need to go into Zarahemla. As surely as the sun rises, he will come to us."

Elizabeth's heart gave a wrenching thud at these words.

"Joshua?" she hissed. "You've come back to—"

"To kill him."Oren offered a guttural chuckle. "And cut out the traitorous spy's heart."

At this, all coherent thought vanished as fire poured into her veins. She snapped her elbow into Oren's already tender ribs, heedless of the knife against her throat.

Tearing herself from his hold, she turned on him. "You'll never—"

She caught a glimpse of his mangled face, etched with fury before Oren's fist smashed into the side of her head. Stars exploded before her vision, and then blackness, cold and silent, closed over her mind.

Chapter 25

Joshua's limbs felt as if great weights clung to them. He longed to find a quiet corner and sit, undisturbed, at least for a moment. But he had Zeram beside him, and a duty to fulfill, so he fought his exhaustion as he strode toward the palace through the morning bustle of the plaza.

Tomorrow was the Sabbath, and in preparation, the market stirred with greater fervor than it did during the week. All around the two soldiers, the plaza hummed with life and sound. Here and there, snatches of conversation about Gadianton and his escape reached Joshua's ears, and his heart grew heavy. He cast a glance toward the younger man, but Zeram's eyes remained fixed ahead, his gaze lifting toward the palace. Joshua could not tell his emotions.

Tightening his fist around the bow in his hand, Joshua turned forward as well, following Zeram's gaze toward the crest of the palace steps. Helaman stood beneath a standard where the Title of Liberty fluttered in a gentle breeze. A young soldier steadied the pole behind the chief judge while two soldiers flanked Helaman.

As Joshua reached the base of the steps, he drew off his helmet and tucked it under his arm.

"Are you all right, sir?"

He looked at Zeram, who had removed his helmet as well, the younger man's yellow hair damp with sweat.

"I…" Joshua's throat tightened. "Let's get this over with." He began to climb, aware that his armor, aside from the stains of sweat, remained unmarred. His sword rested in its sheath, and his quiver of arrows lay full across his back.

The veranda where Helaman stood came to Joshua's eye level. For a moment, Joshua contemplated the chief judge's leather-clad feet and hesitated, a childish fear bidding him to turn and run. He fought it back, thankful for Zeram's presence at his side, and climbed the last steps. He strode toward Helaman and stopped.

"Your Eminence." He slapped his chest in a salute. At his shoulder, Zeram did the same.

Helaman stepped forward, his eyes fixed on Joshua. He looked as exhausted as Joshua felt as he returned the salute. "Your other men?"

"Some are still on duty," Joshua said. "The others I dismissed at the west gate, though Zeram insisted on staying with me. I, however, am solely responsible for our...for our failure, sir."

"No," Zeram cut in. "Sir, Captain Joshua did everything that—"

"As captain, I did not achieve my objective. I failed to capture Gadianton. I alone should receive any appropriate reprimand." Joshua's tone silenced Zeram.

A moment passed, but it seemed an eternity to Joshua before a smile touched Helaman's mouth.

"Failure?" Helaman asked. "Reprimand?" He shook his head. "I think not."

"Your Eminence..." Joshua's brows knitted. "We—*I* failed to apprehend Gadianton or any of his followers. I did not achieve what you wished of me."

"Come with me." Helaman turned toward the doors as the guards drew them open. "Give me a full report."

Drawing a deep breath, Joshua followed Helaman and Zeram through the wide doors and into the shade of the inner corridor. "There is nothing else to say, sir," he said. "We lost them."

Helaman turned to him.

"Scouts are still searching, but..." Joshua swallowed hard. "I fear Gadianton and his men have vanished into the vastness that is Hermounts."

Helaman nodded, grim. "And sending men into that trackless jungle would be suicide."

Joshua's heart felt like lead. "I fear so, sir."

"You have sent word to Gideon and the other cities?"

"Yes, sir. Runners have been dispatched along all trade routes. Your son Nephi is on the road to Melek even now. All the villages and cities within our lands will be wary of Gadianton and his people within a day or two."

Helaman smiled and nodded. "Well done, Captain."

"I wish it were so," Joshua said. "But my duty was to capture Gadianton."

"Joshua." Helaman's voice held a thread of humor in it, his expression one of both sympathy and gentle rebuke. "Our adversaries may have escaped, but none can say that you did not do all that was in your power. And for now, our people are safe. For that, I and all our people owe you our thanks."

"But sir…" Joshua shook his head. "I fear we have not heard the last of Gadianton. It would have been better if we found him, even if it had led to a battle and lives lost."

"You're probably right." Helaman paused a moment, his face thoughtful as he mulled over Joshua's words. "But do not forget that God still rules in the heavens. No matter what the evil one and his followers do, good will ultimately triumph."

Joshua said nothing as he studied the gleam of conviction in Helaman's eyes. The grip of uncertainty on his own heart began to ease.

The soft tap of a woman's feet coming along the corridor from the palace garden found Joshua's ears and he turned, his heart leaping that he might see Elizabeth drawing near. Instead, Pazia's smile welcomed him, a look of apology upon her face as if she had sensed his hope.

Behind her, he saw the forms of two men coming, their features indistinct from the light spilling in through the archway into the garden.

Joshua recognized Tuloth, but not the other, a tall, sturdy man also of Lamanite descent. As Joshua studied the nearing stranger, the premonition that he somehow knew the man settled upon his mind. Beside him, Zeram shifted his weight.

As the men drew near, their voices came clearer, reverberating off the walls.

"I never guessed that *he* was her sire," Tuloth's voice said, weighted with regret. "Her soul is so gentle. I would never knowingly wound her."

"I know you would not, for I have noted your regard for her," the other returned in a Lamanite accent. Joshua's nerves jumped, something prickling the depths of his memory at the sound of the voice.

"Would that I could unsay my words," Tuloth said. "To reassure Talilia of my regard for her."

"It would mean much to her if you would," the other man replied.

"My dear." Pazia touched her husband's arm. "Master Amasa came earlier seeking Master Tuloth. He had hoped to see you as well, but you were in council."

"I'm glad he is here," Helaman said, "for this is a fortuitous meeting."

Joshua's eyes found those of the Lamanite, his aged features and strong form clear now that he and Tuloth had stopped but paces away.

Helaman offered his wife a pleased grin. "Joshua, this is Amasa of Amulon."

"But you are…" Zeram cut in, his voice rushed and excited. "Joshua, this is the man—"

"Who found me wounded," Joshua cut in, understanding flooding through him as he took a step toward the man. "After the battle. And treated my injuries, though I was a Nephite."

The man drew in a breath and nodded.

"You saved my life," Joshua said, a thousand thoughts racing through his mind. There was so much he could say to this man who had shown mercy to a nameless enemy.

"Thank you." The soft words reverberated off the stone walls.

To this, the Lamanite Amasa offered a faint, but genuine smile. "It was my honor."

"*Joshua!*"

A child's wild sob from the steps below the veranda shredded the peace of the moment like a serrated blade. Joshua's eyes jerked toward the outer doors still open to the market below. His heart tightened as Jonas, dirty, wild-eyed, clambered to the top of the steps.

"Here now, little Jonas." One of the guards stepped forward and leaned down, reaching for him, but Jonas pushed past the man's extended hand.

"No," he cried. "I have to find Joshua!" He staggered through the open doors, stumbled, and fell to his hands and knees.

"Jonas?" Joshua darted forward and scooped up the boy, noting the strain and fear upon the little boy's face. Dirt and rents covered his tunic as if he had been running and had fallen many more times than this. Raw, bleeding palms and a bloodied knee with dried blood caked down his shin attested to Joshua's surmise.

"Jonas?" Joshua demanded as the boy sobbed against his neck. "What's wrong?"

"Joshua," Jonas sobbed, gasping. "Y-you ha-have t-to save Elizabeth! And the-the other. Her friend!"

Ice seized Joshua's heart. "Jonas, what is wrong with Elizabeth?" he demanded.

"You ha-have to help them!" Jonas wailed. "You have t-to go save them!"

"Tell me." Joshua forced a calm he did not feel into his voice. "What has happened to you? What has happened to Elizabeth?"

He felt the others crowding near, but he kept his eyes fixed upon the child.

Jonas forced his words out between sobs. "Talilia t-told me I must run—"

"*Talilia?*" both Amasa and Tuloth echoed in voices tense with alarm.

"What has happened to her?" Tuloth demanded.

"I d-don't know! She told me to run into the tunnel. It was s-so dark. I fell down. But I k-kept running, and then I saw light again, and I got out."

Another sob racked the child as he wailed, "They k-killed Micha! And they—"

"*Micha?*" Joshua gasped as the others about him uttered exclamations of shock and dismay, but he did not look up, all his senses focused on Jonas.

"They took Elizabeth!" Jonas wailed. "And her friend. They took them both!"

"Who?" A spear of panic lanced through Joshua's heart. "Jonas, who took Elizabeth?"

"Bad men. F-five men." Jonas sobbed. "I heard them s-say *Gadianton*."

"Gadianton?" Joshua demanded.

Jonas nodded at that, and put his hands to his face.

"Jonas, come here," Pazia said, and Jonas did not protest as she stepped forward and scooped him out of Joshua's arms.

Joshua reeled on Helaman as Pazia turned away trying to comfort the sobbing boy. "Let me go after them. Five of Gadianton's followers near the tunnel by which they escaped. Jonas's words were clear enough. Their tracks would be fresh now."

Helaman's brows furrowed. He reached out and grasped Joshua's shoulder. "As much as this is personal to you, Joshua, you must *think*! You cannot run after them like a madman or they will slaughter you. We must gather a company of men to—"

"*That time cannot be taken!*" Joshua jerked his shoulder from beneath Helaman's hand, heedless of his insubordination in his rising fear. "What these curs have stolen away now—"

Joshua's chest rose and fell as he struggled to check his wild emotions, his eyes studying Helaman's stern expression.

"Please, sir," Joshua pleaded. "It may even be an advantage to go alone. They might not detect one man. I can travel faster and catch them before they join the larger body of Gadianton's people. Please, sir. Let me go after them!"

"Two men can hide no less easily than one."

Joshua's gaze shot to the old Lamanite who drew forward, his jaw taut, his eyes filled with fire.

"Talilia is my child," Amasa said, "and I will heed no man who tells me to stay behind when she is in danger." The man met Joshua's gaze. "Lend me a blade. I can be of use to you."

"And I as well, sir." Zeram's spoke now. "Elizabeth is like a sister to me, and I promised Pacumeni I would keep her safe as long as she needed me. I gave him an *oath*, Joshua. You were there." He turned to Helaman. "Please, Your Eminence, give us your leave."

Helaman's hand came up, brushing across his mouth. "Three against five—"

"Let me go too."

Tuloth stepped forward now. Joshua's heart swelled at the courage in the Ammonite's face.

"Tuloth." Helaman held out a hand in gentle protest. "You would not break your oath."

"I will keep my oath. To the death, if I must. But I will *not* stay here while Talilia is in danger." Tuloth turned to Helaman. "I was a tracker in my youth, Your Eminence. Let us go together, these with their blades, and I with my eyes. Even if I die— if I could help save Talilia…"

Helaman studied Tuloth's face a long moment, then turned to Joshua. "If these men are followers of Gadianton, they won't be taken easily. The danger you will face—"

"For Elizabeth's sake, I will take that risk." A deep breath swelled Joshua's chest. "I love her, sir."

Helaman studied Joshua's face, his expression still as stone before he turned to Pazia. Something seemed to pass between husband and wife before Helaman turned back to Joshua. "I cannot argue with such words." His hand touched the scabbard at his side as he loosed his own sword belt and offered it to Amasa, who accepted it with a terse nod of thanks. Helaman's glance moved from Amasa, to Tuloth and Zeram, and lastly to Joshua. "You four have my leave to do what you must. May God go with you all."

Joshua slapped his chest in a salute. With no further words, he turned, and with his three companions beside him, he darted through the open doors into the sunlight.

Chapter 26

The world appeared to be little more than a blur as Elizabeth came to her senses upon soft ground, thick trees rising all about her. The smell of earth and growing things found her nostrils. She stirred, but her hands could not draw apart. Stiff rope bound her wrists.

The events that had passed before Oren had struck her rushed back into her mind. She pushed herself up, ignoring the throbbing that fell like a hammer against her temple.

I must warn Joshua, her mind cried. She scrambled up, lunging toward the trees.

She had run no more than three paces before a tug on her bound hands whipped her around. Her feet flew out from under her, and the ground rushed up, jarring the breath from her as it struck her.

"The younger one's awake," a voice said through a mouthful of food.

Lifting her head, her eyes darted in the direction of the voice.

A fire fluttered in the center of the clearing, clawing hungry fingers toward the canopy. Around the writhing flames sat men gnawing at the bones of a recent kill. Oren sat nearest her on a rock, his eye fixed upon her. The tortured firelight flickered off his scarred features.

"Peace to you, *Lady* Elizabeth," he mocked. His teeth tore a chunk of roasted meat.

"Leave her alone, Oren," a woman's voice demanded, and Elizabeth turned to see Talilia huddled not many paces away, glaring at the men. Dirt caked her dress, and a bruise marred her cheek. Rope bound her hands as well. A plaited rope snaked across the ground from Talilia's wrists like a dog's tether, running under the rock where Oren sat.

Elizabeth glanced down to see a similar tether that trailed from her wrists disappearing beneath the same rock.

"Come," Talilia urged, scooting nearer. "Sit if you can."

Elizabeth obeyed as Talilia helped her to her knees.

"And do not envy them the meat they are eating." Talilia shuddered. "It is unclean."

Elizabeth shivered at the words. They were eating some poor animal the Law of Moses had forbidden. A small dog, perhaps. Or more likely a hapless monkey they had snared whose life had been created for friendship and playful chatter, not food. She looked away from the pile of stripped bones. She did not want to know.

"Where are we?"

Talilia shrugged in a helpless gesture. "Across the river and east of Zarahemla. Perhaps near Gideon. I'm not certain, for we have stayed in the thick parts of the forest. They are not in a great hurry."

"Because they want Joshua to follow us." Elizabeth's throat tightened.

"And he will." Oren's gaze slid over her body. "Not that I could blame him."

Elizabeth shuddered and recoiled, refusing to look at him.

"Oren!"

Elizabeth jerked as a figure leaped into the clearing.

Her wild hope that Joshua had come to rescue her crumbled as Giddian stumbled to a stop, his chest heaving.

"What is it?" Oren lurched to his feet. The others scrambled up.

"They're coming," Giddian gloated, his eyes wild as he pointed behind him. "*He* is coming, Oren. Just as you said he would." He gulped on a breath. "There are three with him. A boy who looks like he barely knows how to hold a sword, and two Lamanites. An old man, and that *healer.*" He spat the word. "Tuloth. The one who doesn't even fight!"

"Let's go meet them, then." Oren laughed, and Elizabeth's heart twisted at the eagerness in his tone.

With these words, the other men moved to the opposite side of the clearing, snatching up weapons, heavy clubs, and bows with quivers of arrows.

Oren tossed the bone he had been gnawing into the fire and shot a cold grin at Elizabeth. Keeping his one good eye upon her, he bent down near the stone that held the women's ropes in place, seized the woven tethers, and with a clean swipe, severed the ends.

"You, take my cousin," Oren ordered, tossing Talilia's rope into one man's hands and jerking on Elizabeth's wrists, forcing her to clamber to her feet. "I will take this pretty one."

"What are you going to do with us?" Talilia demanded. "Oren, at least let Elizabeth go!"

Oren ignored Talilia as his comrade jerked on her rope.

Talilia's gaze met Elizabeth's before the man pulled her into the thickness of the forest where she disappeared. The other three robbers followed after, vanishing into the undergrowth like ghosts.

Before Oren followed, he jerked Elizabeth to a stop. Twisting her tether around his hand, he pulled her closer, his eye filled with cold light. She winced and struggled to back away, though the rope would not let her.

"It is no wonder that Joshua wants you," he hissed, his breath washing her face. "Your beauty is bewitching. If we did not have this present trouble to contend with…"

One hand reached toward her as if to stroke her cheek, but Elizabeth twisted away, her bound hands shoving his arm away from her. "You're a traitor and a murderer, Oren. When Joshua reaches us—"

Oren's free hand seized her chin in a painful grip, and his one remaining eye grew hard. "When he reaches us, I will kill him, and cut his heart out as you watch."

With a humorless snort, he released her face and turned away. "Come. It is time to go meet your fearless champion."

Yanking her behind him, he turned in the direction his men had gone and strode after them, the shadows of the trees closing over their heads.

"Tuloth," Joshua gasped, his breath like fire in his throat as he ran behind the Ammonite along the wild animal trail that wended eastward through the thick forest. "How near?"

They had been running for what felt like an eternity, and sweat weighted and dampened his hair. Joshua's muscles burned from the strenuous punishment of their swift run, but he cared nothing for the weariness of his body. His every thought fixed upon Elizabeth and saving her from the beasts that had her.

What are they doing to her? Fear ricocheted around in his mind like an angry wasp that could not find release. The dread of what they had taken her for, what she was suffering at their hands, burned in the pit of his belly, fueling his anger and giving him strength he would not have had otherwise.

In front of him, a generous beam of sunlight washed across the trail, spilling through a wide break in the canopy above them. Before they reached the splash of sunlight, Tuloth's feet slowed to a stop, the others halting behind him. Zeram's head sagged as he pressed his hands against his knees, drawing in great gulps of air.

"Are we nearing them?" Joshua asked, breathing hard.

"They passed through here not long ago." Tuloth snatched up a slender branch that had fallen on the trail, torn from a tree beside the path. He studied the twisted wood before he tossed the branch away, his eyes scanning the earth as if some message had been written there. "They are not moving with much haste. We may be near."

Tuloth turned, and his gaze met Joshua's. "Your regard for Elizabeth is strong indeed."

Joshua heaved a breath. "I'd die for her."

"I would do the same for Talilia." Tuloth offered a nod toward Amasa. "I care not that she was once called Lylith. Nor do I care who sired her. She is Talilia to me." He turned away, his eyes reading the ground again.

"Wait a moment." Zeram straightened with effort, and Tuloth turned back. "This other lady was once called *Lylith*?"

Zeram shot Joshua a look of wonder, and Joshua strained to understand why the youth would seem so anxious, now.

"She was. Once," Amasa said.

Zeram looked as if he meant to say something before the old warrior lifted a hand.

"Hold." Amasa's eyes filled with alarm. Joshua turned to scan the profuse growth around them. For a moment, he could see nothing. Then a movement deep within the trees to his left caught his eye. A figure, indistinct in the green shadows, moved nearer, its movements imbalanced and irregular like the jerking gait of some corpse that had dragged itself from the grave.

Joshua whipped an arrow from the quiver at his back, nocked it to the bowstring, and raised his sights toward the figure, drawing the arrow to his cheek. "Who are you?" he demanded. "Speak!"

"Ho, son of Antipus!" the figure called. "Do you wish to risk hitting Elizabeth?"

A jolt of fear speared through Joshua, and he eased the tension on his string as the figure lurched from the shadows into the light. Joshua's blood grew hot. "*Oren*," he snarled.

"Peace to you, *sir*," Oren scoffed, one muscled arm about Elizabeth's slender waist as she stumbled in front of him. Her eyes pled with Joshua over Oren's thick hand clamped on her mouth. A strap of dirty leather bound her hands, and it took all the restraint within Joshua to keep from flying across the space between them and tearing Elizabeth out of Oren's grasp. Joshua's gaze fell to the knife at Oren's waist. He could do nothing. The knife would be unsheathed and Elizabeth dead in the moments it would take Joshua to reach them. And so he stood his ground, helpless, clenching his bow so tightly that his fingers grew numb.

"You were a palace guard, Oren! You served under Captain Micha! How could you murder him? How could you betray all you swore to protect?"

"With the same ease by which you killed Kishkumen and betrayed Gadianton's people, *spy*. Now, to what do we owe the honor of your coming?"

"You know why we've come. Give us Elizabeth and her companion. Where is the woman named Talilia?"

"*Talilia?*" Oren sneered. "I know no *Talilia*."

"Cur!" Tuloth shouted as he lunged forward a step, his hands clenching into fists. "What have you done to her?"

"Peace, Ammonite," Oren soothed as a wicked grin drew across his face. "My long-lost cousin, *Lylith*, daughter of the traitor Pachus, we do have." He glanced toward the shadows behind him. "Bring my cousin! A suitor has come to call on her."

Another figure emerged, tromping forward through the undergrowth as he wrenched his burden along with him. The man eyed Tuloth with rancor as he came, clutching Talilia against himself in the same manner that Oren held Elizabeth. Talilia's eyes fixed upon Tuloth over the man's hand, and tears glimmered in her eyes.

Joshua's heart prickled with anxiety—Jonas said he had seen five men. What of the other three?

"Are you and your vast host satisfied now, *Captain*?" Oren mocked.

"Let her go!" Zeram demanded, anxiety tightening his youthful voice."Let them both go!"

"They are not your chattel, Oren," Joshua said."The only women you get are the ones already foolish enough to follow Gadianton."

"You heard him," Oren said. "Release the daughter of Pachus."

With an angry grimace, the man released Talilia, shoving her hard in the back. She stumbled forward and nearly fell before Tuloth darted to her and caught her in his arms.

"Tuloth?" she asked as he raised her gently to her feet. "You came after me? But—"

"Your father told me everything, Talilia," Tuloth choked. "I am so very sorry."

Zeram stepped toward Tuloth and the woman as if he wanted to speak, his expression anxious and uncertain.

"Talilia," Amasa murmured stepping past Zeram.

"Father." She turned and tumbled against Amasa's chest like a lost child newly found.

Joshua's eyes darted back to the two robbers, his ears tuned to any hint of the other three. "And Elizabeth as well. Let her go." He stalked forward a step.

"I think not. I enjoy her company." Oren pressed his face against Elizabeth's hair. She shuddered and tried to pull away. "So soft to hold."

"Take your filthy hands off her!" Joshua roared, raw fury clawing his throat.

To this, a cold grin parted Oren's lips. His eye darted beyond Joshua's shoulder.

Elizabeth's own eyes grew wide with horror, and with a wild wrench of her head, she tore her mouth free. "Joshua, look ou—" she shrieked before Oren's hand clamped over her mouth again.

Joshua spun and saw the figure in the shadows, heard the twang of a bowstring, the hiss of an approaching arrow. He ducked, rolling to the side as the arrow buzzed past his head and struck the ground, sending up a spray of earth. Rolling in a single motion to one knee, Joshua drew his own bowstring to his cheek and released the arrow.

His arrow struck its target with a thump, and the man in the undergrowth toppled to the ground with a fading moan.

But Joshua's relief turned to dust as two more men leaped from the trees, weapons gripped in their hands, their teeth clenched in anger. The scrape of blades drawn echoed through the forest as Zeram and Amasa drew their weapons forth. The two warriors stood facing away from one another. Between them, Tuloth sheltered Talilia, murmuring soothing words as he struggled to untie the impossible knot binding her wrists.

Snatching for another arrow, Joshua aimed at one of the robbers closing in on his friends. His finger left the string just as a heavy force smashed into him from behind, crushing him to the ground, his mouth filling with moist, gritty earth. A shriek and a curse from the direction his arrow flew told him that his shot had not been entirely wasted. His attacker, one sharp knee digging into his back, wrenched the bow from his hands. His arrows clattered as they spilled from his quiver, scattering across the ground in all directions.

"Think you are so mighty now?" The man twisted Joshua's arm behind his back, then jerked his sword from its sheath and threw it away into the trees.

Lava coursed through Joshua's veins. Twisting against the pain and spitting earth from his lips, he rolled hard, toppling his attacker from his back and smashing his elbow into the man's ribs as he fell. Joshua heard a muffled snap and then a grunt of pain as the robber's grip released him. Joshua leaped to his feet, snatching his iron knife from his belt as he spun to face his downed attacker.

"Enough!" Oren shouted, and drew his hand from Elizabeth's mouth. A metallic rasp echoed through the trees, and Joshua jerked to a stop. Oren held his gleaming knife in a fist mottled with rage, the razor-edged point pressed against the tender flesh of Elizabeth's throat.

Joshua's attacker clambered up, clutching at his ribs, his teeth clenched in pain and fury. He glared at Joshua, but made no move toward him, backing away to Oren's side as Joshua's scattered arrows crackled beneath his feet like dry twigs.

"Joshua!" Elizabeth cried, her voice thick with tears. "You should not have come! They mean to kill you! They took me to lure you away—"

"Silence!" Oren pressed the knife more firmly against her skin, and Elizabeth winced as a single bead of blood appeared beneath the point of the knife, crimson against her slender throat.

Joshua's chest tightened in impotent fury as Oren's eye turned again to him.

"You fool," Oren sneered. "Do you think Gadianton's thirst for women is the only reason we took her? She was bait to draw *you* into our trap, son of Antipus."

"Me?" Joshua demanded. "Why me? I'm no one of any great—"

"You robbed us of our glory, *spy*!" Oren spat. "But for you, Helaman would be dead!"

Joshua's limbs stiffened. He risked a glance at the two robbers circling the others before he whipped back to Oren. His second arrow had pierced through the arm of one of the robbers, but only through a pinch of flesh, and the man had not lost his grip on his heavy club.

Oren's knife tip pressed deeper into Elizabeth's skin. The bead of blood became a trickle of crimson, trailing down the smooth flesh.

Joshua's heart wrenched. He swallowed hard, meeting Oren's eye.

"If it is me you wish to kill," he said, stepping forward, "let Elizabeth go." He spread his hands in a pleading gesture. "Let her return unharmed with my comrades to Zarahemla. I will stay, and you can do what you will with me."

Clutched in Oren's grasp, Elizabeth's face grew pale. "Joshua, no," she implored, her eyes pleading with his. How lovely they were, like jade, or emeralds, but brighter.

"Oren," Joshua pleaded," let her go, and I swear that I—"

"Enough!" Oren shoved her toward his companion beside him. "Hold her." Oren turned toward Joshua, brandishing his gleaming knife. A spot of blood stained the tip. Elizabeth's blood. Joshua's stomach churned with fury. "Make sure she watches *everything*."

"*No!*" Elizabeth wailed, wrenching at her captor's hold.

Turning to Joshua, Oren renewed his grip on the knife. "I'll finish Joshua myself. And you two," he ordered, jerking his head toward the others, "kill his friends."

Chapter 27

"No!" Despair plunged like a javelin into Elizabeth's heart as Oren gripped his knife, advancing on Joshua. The other two men circled Zeram and Amasa, their eyes guarded, searching. Joshua held nothing but the short knife in his hand, his stance ready for battle.

Beyond Joshua, Zeram gripped his sword with determination. Giddian, despite the arrow pierced through his arm, surged forward, raising his club.

Amasa darted to meet him, the metal of his sword ringing through the trees as it battered aside the weapon.

The other robber rushed toward Tuloth and Talilia, his weapon raised. But Zeram leaped in front of them, deflecting the man's sword.

The man reeled back, startled, but recovered quickly and lunged forward again. Zeram met the man's blows with desperate fury, exchanging ringing blows with the robber, the crash of weapons echoing through the trees.

At the furious sounds of battle, Joshua risked a fleeting glance over his shoulder, and Oren took that instant to charge toward him, his knife raised.

"Look out!" Elizabeth shrieked, and at her warning, Joshua jerked to the side as Oren flashed past, his knife a blur, the sound of tearing cloth filling her ears. Elizabeth sucked in an agonized breath as Joshua rolled to his feet, a ragged tear in the cloth across his chest. But she saw no blood. Oren wheeled around, his eye flashing as he threw himself at Joshua once more.

Joshua jerked back as Oren's knife slashed, just missing his face.

In that moment, a grunt escaped Zeram's foe, followed by a fading moan as the man crumpled. Beyond Joshua's shoulder, Zeram staggered back from his enemy, his face white as he lifted his blade and studied its crimson-stained tip, a look of sickened horror on his face.

A moment later, Amasa caught Giddian's wrist in his fist, twisting until the club dropped from the robber's hand. Amasa kicked it away, then shoved the man to the ground. Giddian looked up, fear and hatred on his face.

Amasa turned from his kneeling foe to the stricken youth. "Are you hurt, boy?"

With Amasa's eyes turned away, Giddian clambered backward on his hands and feet, then turned and scrambled up. Without a backward glance, he darted away, vanishing into the shadows of the trees.

"Giddian, you coward!" Oren roared. "Gadianton will set your head on a pike!" But only footsteps and the fading sound of undergrowth answered his threat.

"You," Oren shouted over his shoulder toward his one remaining comrade as he continued to advance upon Joshua. "She's too troublesome to keep. Snap her neck."

Behind her, the robber who held Elizabeth chuckled darkly and released one arm to grasp a fistful of her hair, wrenching her head back. Pain lanced down Elizabeth's spine as her eyes took in the green haze of the twining branches above her.

"No!" Joshua roared from behind her. A moment later, a sharp whistle sliced through the air, followed by a heavy thunk just above her head.

Something warm and wet spattered her hair and the side of her face as a gurgling grunt escaped her captor's throat. The pressure on her neck and spine eased, and the man's grip released her so suddenly that she stumbled and fell to the leaf-strewn ground.

Pushing herself up on trembling arms, Elizabeth turned. The robber lay beside her, his glassy eyes stared up at the canopy. The gleaming hilt of Joshua's knife protruded from the dead man's throat, blood pooling beneath it.

Elizabeth crushed her eyes shut, fighting nausea as she clambered to her feet. Lifting her face, she met Joshua's eyes across the distance between them. His hands, now weaponless, hung at his sides. *Elizabeth,* his lips moved.

"She'll never be yours, son of Antipus!"

Oren charged at her, his hand crashing across her cheek. Stars burst in her vision as she fell, her palms scraping over earth and leaves. One hand closed around a long slender shaft of wood as Oren's arm seized her around the waist and ripped her off the ground, flinging her over his shoulder.

"Elizabeth!" she heard Joshua shout, his voice fading as Oren plunged into the thickness of the jungle, thrusting Elizabeth into a muffled world of shadows. Oren's feet pounded as he ran, his shoulder digging into her stomach with each leap.

Elizabeth's head throbbed, and she fought to remain conscious as Oren lurched on, plunging farther into the murky gloom. Little light penetrated the shadows here, for Oren followed no defined path, and the growth overhead and about them grew thick and tangled. Branches scratched her arms and her face, tearing at her hair.

The world became a blur of confusion as she hung from Oren's shoulder like a felled deer. Elizabeth could not guess in what direction Oren carried her nor how far they had gone as her captor continued to run deeper and deeper into the forest.

She felt her hold on reality beginning to slip, but then Oren staggered to a stop, puffing and cursing. After glancing behind him, he flung her down upon the ground like a sack of grain. The fall was rough, but the spongy ground cushioned her, and Elizabeth landed winded, but unscathed. Shaking her head to clear it, her eyes fell to her bound hands and the object she had snatched from the ground. Seeing what she held, her heart jumped. She tucked the broken arrow closer and began sawing the sharp obsidian tip against the strap about her wrists.

"Cursed woman," Oren gasped, his chest heaving. "You are too much trouble to keep. If Gadianton wants a heart, I'll give the idiot a heart. As long as he thinks it's Joshua's…"

Elizabeth struggled to keep the movement of her hands hidden as she looked over her shoulder into Oren's single cold eye. His knife gleamed in his fist.

"Your lover will find you soon," Oren sneered, still struggling to regain his breath, "or what will be left of you." His knife glittered in the half-darkness of the forest as he clenched her hair in his free hand and lifted his knife high into the air.

But before he could swing the blade down into her body, the strap around her wrists snapped. Elizabeth twisted, lashing at him with the broken shaft of the arrow. The razor-sharp head sliced across the flesh of Oren's forearm.

Oren shrieked and staggered back as he clutched at the bleeding gash. Snatching her chance, Elizabeth scrambled to her feet and plunged away through the trees, praying that she ran in the direction from which she had come.

"Joshua!" she screamed, hoping her voice carried through the thick trees.

Behind her, an inhuman howl of rage rolled after her, and the crashing sound of Oren's pursuit followed. Elizabeth vaulted over moss-covered logs, pushing aside tangled curtains of vines and leaves. Her feet flew and branches slapped her face, snatching at her hair. Her lungs burned, but still she ran on, the crashing and cursing behind her drawing nearer.

"Joshua!" A root caught her foot. She stumbled and fell. The broken arrow flew from her hands and skittered away, lost in the gloom. After a moment of frantic, fruitless searching, Elizabeth scrambled up, not knowing where she ran, knowing only that Oren pursued her, mere paces behind. She could hear his harsh breath, the slap of his feet upon the ground. And then he leaped from behind, catching her wrist in his iron grip. He spun her to face him, his one eye livid with rage. She could see murder in its dark depths. His hand lifted, the gleam of his knife in his fist—

"*Elizabeth!*"

Joshua's voice reverberated through the trees as his silhouette, followed by another, leaped over a fallen tree and into her vision.

Oren's face jerked up, and he shoved her to the ground. Elizabeth's head struck against the side of a log and lights exploded before her eyes as Oren lunged toward the two shadows, shrieking curses.

Elizabeth struggled to push herself up, dizzy, her vision blurry as Oren's blade flashed in the waning light, followed by a sharp thump as the knife struck the indistinct shadow.

"No!" she screamed as the stricken man toppled to the ground. Her heart turned to ashes within her. Oren had killed Joshua!

Oren turned then, his eye flashing a look of deepest loathing at her before he plunged away, the crackle of undergrowth fading into the gloom.

No one pursued him, and Elizabeth's eyes did not follow him, her gaze fixed upon the prone figure on the ground. The hilt of a knife rose from his shuddering chest as the shadow of his companion dropped to his knees beside him.

Elizabeth clambered over the ground on her hands and knees, her vision clearing as she neared her rescuers.

Joshua, unscathed, knelt at the side of the old Lamanite, fumbling in his pack for a roll of bandaging. Blood soaked the cloth of Amasa's tunic.

"Tuloth!" Joshua shouted, his voice echoing through the trees. "We have wounded!"

His face twisted with guilt as he met Elizabeth's eyes. "This is my fault," he said, his voice coming through his teeth. "Oren was coming at me. Amasa threw himself between us. It should have been *me*."

"Hush, lad," the old man gasped, waving Joshua into silence. "Better me than you."

The man managed a weak smile as his eyes found Elizabeth. "You are unhurt, child?"

"Thanks to you," she said as she reached out and touched the man's damp brow.

Joshua began to bind the wound around the knife still embedded in the old warrior's body, desperately trying to staunch the blood. Lifting his voice, he shouted once again, "Tuloth!"

"I know the pain of watching my beloved die." The Lamanite sighed as Joshua's cry echoed away into the trees. "I could not let either of you endure such agony."

Elizabeth swallowed hard at these words and glanced at Joshua, whose eyes met hers before they returned to the old Lamanite.

"While there is breath in me," the old Lamanite gasped, "I must ask your forgiveness."

Joshua shook his head. "Amasa, you have done no—"

"I have done *much*." The old Lamanite drew in a weak breath. "I mocked your god, and spurned my own kin when they became His followers so many years ago. I made my own mother and daughter believe I was dead. I came against your people in an unjust war, and slew many honorable men. I have not even told you my true name."

Elizabeth's lips parted at his words and in that moment, a warm surety swept over her like an ocean wave. She clasped the old man's hand and squeezed it. He turned his face to meet her eyes.

"Your name is Shemnon," she whispered.

The Lamanite's head tilted and he studied her. "How did you know?"

Beside her, Joshua stiffened, though he did not speak, nor cease his work staunching the wound.

Elizabeth's heart hammered within her. "Your wife was Keza?" she continued, breathless. "And Delia was your mother?"

Shemnon's eyes widened all the more. "What is this? How do you know these names?"

"My mother thought you died long ago," she whispered. "She said you died of fevers in Tulum."

"Your mother?" A sharp breath caught in Shemnon's throat, and he studied Elizabeth's face with tender intensity. "What was your mother's name, child?"

Elizabeth drew in a broken breath. "Hana."

Shemnon blinked, his face unreadable for a long moment as if what she had told him was impossible to comprehend. Then his chest swelled. "You are my grandchild?" he whispered in his native tongue.

Elizabeth nodded as her vision blurred with tears. "The only one, I fear."

"It is no matter. You are my daughter's child."Shemnon lifted a hand. His fingertips touched her face, trembling as they caressed her cheek.

"I should have known. From our first meeting, something whispered to me, but I could not hear its voice." He smiled. "You have your mother's eyes."

Elizabeth lifted Shemnon's hand and held it against her cheek, struggling to smile through the tears that filled her eyes and spilled down her face.

Zeram, then Tuloth with Talilia's hand in his, rushed into the clearing and stopped. The faces of the men grew grave, but Talilia's face filled with agony.

"Father!" She fell to her knees across from Elizabeth and caught up his other hand.

"Tuloth, what must we do?" Joshua asked as the healer dropped at Talilia's side and bent to examine the wound.

Zeram knelt a short space away as he looked on in subdued silence, his brows knit.

"This wound is grievous," Tuloth's voice broke. "There's nothing I can do—"

"Then we must take him back," Joshua said.

"He will not make it back to Zarahemla. You'll only cause him unnecessary discomfort."

"To Gideon, then, if it's nearer." Joshua moved to scoop Shemnon up in his arms like a child before the wounded man's hand shot out and gripped Joshua's arm.

"No," Shemnon insisted. "Do not trouble yourself."

Joshua's brow furrowed, and he shook his head. "Sir, I must take you to the nearest city where they have the means to treat you! I care nothing for the difficulty."

"The most skilled physicians cannot save me."

"I cannot let another good man die for me!" Joshua's eyes filled with pain. "Not again!"

"It is not your choice, boy."

"I cannot believe that!" Joshua moved to pick him up again, but Shemnon's hand gripped his arm, forcing him back.

"You saved me!" Joshua wrenched his arm away. "Why can I not save you?"

"You cannot control all things. I have seen such wounds in battle, young one." Shemnon's breath came with effort. "No matter your efforts, even were I surrounded by physicians, with all the means available to them, I would not live past this day."

Joshua shot a tortured look at Tuloth, whose expression confirmed Shemnon's words.

Shemnon turned gentle eyes upon Talilia, reaching up a hand to touch her cheek. Then he turned to Elizabeth, offering her the same gentle look.

"Let me spend my last few minutes in peace. With my children."

Joshua shook his head, his eyes filling with tears, but he did as the man bid him and sat back on his heels, his head sagging as if he were weary beyond endurance.

"Talilia," Shemnon breathed, "my bright candle. This is Elizabeth, your kinswoman. Child of the daughter I lost. Child of...Hana."

Elizabeth lifted her eyes to Talilia's and managed a trembling smile.

"My one sorrow, Talilia, is that I do not know if the child to whom you gave life still lives. How I wish that—"

"But I'm right here."

In the stillness of the shadowed clearing, Elizabeth's tear-filled eyes found the youth where he knelt a space away. Zeram's eyes fixed now upon Talilia.

Talilia turned and blinked at him through her tears. "Zeram?" she asked, speaking the word as if testing it upon her tongue.

"But you said your mother's name was Miriam," Shemnon said.

"I did." Zeram's voice trembled. "My mother *is* Miriam, and my father is Jacob. They adopted me." He eased nearer to the small group and reached out, taking Talilia's hand. "But I never forgot you."

New tears gleamed in Talilia's eyes, and Shemnon smiled, reaching to grasp their joined hands before his grip weakened. Talilia caught Shemnon's hand before it fell away.

"Your god has blessed me beyond my merits," Shemnon said. "Would that I had known him as you have, but something in me whispers that I need not be afraid."

He drew another rattling breath and turned his eyes now upon Tuloth, now upon Joshua. "Watch over my daughters."

"I will," Joshua and Tuloth echoed one another.

"Then I am content."

Elizabeth's eyes fixed on Shemnon's face. As the weight of Joshua's hand came to rest upon her shoulder, she reached up and grasped it in her own. She touched a hand to Shemnon's weathered cheek. He smiled and reached for her hand, clasping it.

"My mother never forgot you, Grandfather," she murmured. "All her life, she loved you."

"Will she be there?" Shemnon asked. "Will my mother, my little son—" A rattling sigh escaped him. "Will my beloved be there? Will your god let me see them?"

"He is your god as well, Grandfather," Elizabeth whispered, tears spilling from her eyes. "And He will be there, along with all our dear ones. Every one."

Shemnon let his head fall back. He lifted his gaze again to the small patch of blue sky that pierced through the canopy above him, the light reflecting in his eyes. A faint smile came to his lips. "Keza," he murmured aloud. And then his breath stilled.

Yet even as his eyes dimmed, his face took on an aura of peace. Elizabeth, studying the tranquility there, knew he had found what he had sought.

Talilia began to weep. Tuloth gathered her near, her sobs muffled against his shoulder. But Elizabeth remained still, gazing down upon Shemnon's face.

"Elizabeth," Joshua murmured. She felt his breath against her hair and she turned to him, letting him gather her into his arms. She tucked her head against Joshua's chest, comforted by his warmth, by the strength of his arms as they encircled her, and the steady beating of his heart. Safe in the shelter of his embrace, she let the tears come at last.

Oren cursed beneath his breath, cradling his bleeding arm as he stumbled through the shadows and crowding trees.

He had been so close to killing Joshua, but the foolish old man had leaped between them and taken the blade instead. Oren stumbled over a root, cursing before he righted himself. Gadianton's orders had been clear. Return with the heart of Joshua son of Antipus, or die.

What could he do now? To return to Gadianton empty-handed would be suicide.

With his head down, Oren barely noticed the thinning undergrowth, but at a familiar voice, he looked up and staggered to a halt. Giddian sat across the small clearing, his legs folded beneath him as if he had been waiting. "Where is the heart?" Giddian demanded.

Oren scowled. "You abandoned me, Giddian. Yet you ask me if I got his heart?"

Giddian clambered to his feet. The arrow had been pulled out of his arm, and now a fragment of dirty cloth wrapped his wound.

"We cannot return without one or we both die." Giddian's eyes burned like malevolent bits of coal. His hand grasped the knife at his belt and jerked it free.

Throat dry, Oren snatched for his own knife before he remembered he had abandoned it when he fled from Elizabeth's rescuers.

"This is the story I will tell Gadianton," Giddian hissed. "We found the cursed son of Antipus and his men and ambushed them. They fought like dragons, but we fought harder. In the end, we killed them all, but not before my brave comrades were slain. Among them, Oren son of Kanan. I alone lived to carry our bloody prize back to Gadianton."

An icy fear gripped Oren, and he stumbled backward as Giddian stalked toward him.

A flock of birds resting in the branches of the trees above the small clearing startled at a scream, wild with terror that echoed through the jungle below them. Cawing their alarm to one another, they took to flight, beating their wings up and away, across the waving green sea of the treetops. Below them, the scream echoed away into the trees, dying into silence.

Chapter 28

The brilliant sunset that once washed the sky had faded to soft dusk over the open roof of the portico where Elizabeth stood beside a pillar, a hand pressed against the firm stone.

The shadows of trees and ferns stirred as a wind flowed through the palace garden, brushing at her dress and through her hair that fell unbound about her shoulders.

Elizabeth swallowed at the lump in her throat as she studied the evening star where it gleamed in the night sky. Good, faithful Micha had been buried earlier in the day with full military honors. And later, little more than an hour past, she had bidden farewell to her grandfather.

Shemnon's burial had been sorrowful, but sweet also. He was at peace, and with those he loved. Still, she missed him.

A soft footfall sounded behind her, and she turned her head. Her breath caught as Joshua appeared beneath the archway, the strong angles of his face lit by the torches from within.

"Joshua." She stepped away from the pillar and turned to him as he left the doorway, striding toward her through the twilight with a grace that stirred her blood.

"Elizabeth," he greeted, drawing to a stop a pace away. "Pazia said I would find you here. She is with Talilia now, speaking of Shemnon."

Elizabeth dropped her eyes. "That is good." Her voice softened. "I have been thinking of him."

Joshua drew back a fraction. "If you wished to be alone with your thoughts…"

He began to turn, but Elizabeth reached out, touching his hand. "No," she murmured, lifting her eyes. "Please stay, Joshua."

Joshua turned back, meeting her gaze. Elizabeth's breath caught at the undisguised hope in his eyes. "If you want me to," he said.

"I do."

Her heart throbbed furiously as Joshua turned his hand, his lean fingers weaving through hers. He moved nearer and stopped a breath away, his warm shadow hovering above her. Elizabeth drank in the scent of him.

"In truth, I had been hoping you would come," she said.

"Then I'll stay. And I am glad, for I wished to speak with you."

Elizabeth studied the tenderness of his gaze. "What of?"

"Pacumeni asked an oath of me in the hours before he fell in battle. One he wished me to fulfill if he died and I lived. Something he wished me to tell you."

Joshua lifted his free hand, and his fingertips touched her cheek. "I have not yet fulfilled that oath. But I intend to before another moment passes."

Elizabeth drew in a breath as she studied his familiar gaze. This was Joshua, whom she had known and trusted since her childhood, but now, she saw him anew. Not only as her faithful friend, but also as the man with whom she wanted to share the whole of her world.

He leaned near, his breath soft against her face. "I love you, Elizabeth."

The words sang through her soul like the brightness of the sun breaking through the clouds after a storm. But in the same moment, a shard of pain pierced her heart.

"You've loved me for years."

"Yes," he admitted.

"Oh, Joshua." Tears filled her eyes, and one escaped, trailing down her cheek. "How I must have hurt you."

"You didn't." Joshua's thumb brushed her cheek, smoothing away the tear. His other hand released hers and found her waist. "Not deeply. For your happiness has always mattered to me more than anything else."

Elizabeth looked up, searching his eyes. She drew a step closer and lifted her hands, resting them against his chest, her fingers pressing against the corded muscles beneath the soft cloth.

"And I have always wished the same for you," she murmured.

His hand slid around her waist as he eased nearer to her. The press of his lean fingers against her back and the warmth of his body through the cloth of her tunic sent quivering trails of delight through her.

His brow came to rest against her own. She had looked into his eyes many times since childhood, but never before had his eyes been so clear as they were in these evening shadows. "There is no better man in all this world than you, my dear one." She released a soft sigh. "And you deserve to know that my heart no longer belongs to the past."

Joshua's chest swelled with a deep breath, and his eyes gleamed in the dark. The hand against her cheek trembled a little as his thumb caressed her lower lip. Elizabeth's blood tingled with pleasure at the touch.

"I have come to love you, Joshua." Her voice fell to a whisper. "With *all* my heart."

"Elizabeth…" Against her lower back, his hand tightened, and his face bent toward hers.

Her heart fluttered as her eyelids fell closed and her lips parted. Joshua's breath caressed her face. Then, with the gentleness of a feather, Joshua's mouth brushed hers, not unlike the tender, unexpected kiss they had shared on the shores of Bountiful.

Joshua withdrew a fraction and she looked up at him, his eyes gleaming in the shadows between them. Elizabeth released a breath, Joshua's heart quickening beneath the thin cloth of his shirt. The throbbing of her own heart mingled with his as she sought his eyes.

"Elizabeth," he pleaded, his voice husky. "Will you have me as your husband?"

"Yes, Joshua," she said. "Forever." And now, unlike that first, brief kiss beside the sea, Elizabeth tilted her face toward his again.

In a moment, Joshua's mouth claimed hers once more, stronger and more fervent now, exploring her lips with a tender power that sent trails of longing through her body. Surrendering to the yearning that pulsed through her, Elizabeth slid her arms up his chest and around his neck, responding eagerly to the implorations of his mouth, longing for him to know how deeply she loved, and wanted him.

To her delight, Joshua's own caresses grew all the more ardent; his arms pulled her to him, crushing her body against his own as he plied her parted lips with deepening hunger.

After long, blissful moments in his arms, Joshua's strength eased, and at last his mouth released hers. She slid her arms from around his neck, her palms coming to rest against his chest as it rose and fell with his rapid breathing. His heart pounded against her fingers. Their breaths mingled as his forehead came to rest against hers.

"Joshua," she gasped, breathless.

"I love you, Elizabeth," he whispered.

"And I love you."

His hands cupped her face as his eyes sought hers through the shadows between them.

Love is stronger than evil, Pacumeni's prophetic words resounded through the corridors of her memory. *And love that is true, that is founded on love for God, can overcome anything…*

"Pacumeni once said that love could overcome anything," Joshua murmured, his words echoing her very thoughts. "I could not see then how true his words would prove."

"But they have," she said. "In wonderful ways."

A breeze washed over them, stirring the leaves of the garden into joyful whispers.

Far away, a soft melody like the notes of a flute floated on the wind, faint, but filled with joy.

Elizabeth and Joshua drew apart, and she lifted her eyes to his as the soft notes faded upon the wind.

"We have his blessing," she murmured.

A breath swelled Joshua's chest, and his arms went around her again, drawing her into a tender embrace. His jaw came to rest against her hair, and Elizabeth lay her head against his chest, listening to the murmur of his heart, content in the newness and wonder of their love.

Chapter 29

A deep purple sunset hung low in the west, and the first bright stars glinted in the sky. The rhythmic hiss of the sea whispered beyond tall, flickering torches set in a wide circle around a stretch of sand. Talilia stood at the edge of the circle of light, the trees of the forest stark shadows against the fading sunset.

She turned to study the newly wedded couple who stood together a short distance away, their faces alight with such happiness that Talilia's heart ached.

Elizabeth looked radiant, her white gown soft and light, flattering her slender form, the loose tresses of her hair catching in the wind that washed over the silver sand in gentle whispers. It was no surprise that her new husband looked upon her with such adoration.

A band of musicians on one side of the circle of light played a bright tune that carried over the talk and laughter as the crowd moved about, some toward the tables laden with food, others toward the center where couples danced. A few moved toward Elizabeth and Joshua to offer their blessings, but Talilia turned away and stepped beyond the light toward the shadowy trees.

Several paces away, a narrow sandy path, silver in the dim light, disappeared into the forest. It would lead her back to the city of Bountiful, and Talilia wondered if she should follow it back to the city, and to the small room she had secured for the few days she was here for the wedding.

Yet something compelled her to remain a few moments longer and drink in the happy sight. Elizabeth and Joshua spoke now with Lady Pazia and her husband, Helaman. Beside them stood little Jonas, one hand clinging to Helaman's, his bright eyes upon Elizabeth.

Pazia moved against Helaman's side, looping her arm through his as she spoke. Helaman turned to gaze down at his wife, his adoration for her evident in his face.

Talilia let her eyes trail across the crowd until they alighted on one figure standing amongst a small cluster of other youths. Her throat tightened.

Zeram's face, still so much like the little boy she remembered, smiled as his hands clapped in time to the music, his eyes following the dancers in the center of the lighted circle.

Behind him, Jacob and Miriam, his parents, stood arm in arm, talking with two other couples, Thobor and Esther, Talilia remembered from Zeram's earlier introduction, and his uncle and aunt, young Jacob and Rachel.

The other women wore their hair in elegant braids twined against their heads, but Miriam's dark hair hung in a long braid down her back, glimmering in the torchlight. She was as lovely as she had been when Talilia had known her so long ago. No doubt she had been a wonderful mother to Zeram.

Zeram seemed content to do no more than watch the dance, standing with the other young men, until a maiden scurried up to him and caught him by the hands, urging him to dance with her. Zeram's eyes showed surprise at first, but then his face broke into a grin and he followed her, soon lost with her amongst the dancers.

Miriam touched her husband's arm, pointing out their son as he whirled away. Jacob turned his head and said something which made Miriam smile up into his eyes, her face alight with affection. What would it be like to know such an enduring love as these other women did with their husbands?

Talilia studied the sand beneath her feet for a long moment before her eyes trailed back toward the spot where Elizabeth and Joshua had been standing. But the pair had vanished. Her lips parted in wonder before she spotted them hand in hand, hurrying away through the shadows beyond the torchlight before the two of them disappeared down the silver path.

The soft crunch of footsteps sounded behind her. A moment later, a hand covered her shoulder.

Talilia drew in a breath as the warmth of Tuloth's closeness seeped into her back.

"Here you are," he murmured. "I wondered where you had gone. Are you well?"

She turned, lifting her gaze to his. His dark eyes reflected the torchlight. "I suppose I needed a moment alone to think. And to remember."

Tuloth drew in a deep breath and glanced about him at the darkening world, the white-tipped waves washing the shore, and the rim of the moon that rose over the distant edge of the sea, spreading its silver tresses across the water.

He wore a new linen tunic, and his dark hair fell about his face. He looked wondrously handsome. Talilia's heart gave a painful throb before she glanced away.

"This seems a good place for both," he agreed. "What were you thinking about?"

"Zeram," she said. "And what a fine man he is becoming."

Tuloth glanced over his shoulder toward Zeram, where he and the young woman danced among the other couples beneath the torchlight.

"He is," Tuloth agreed before he turned back to her.

"I'm also uncertain," she continued, her throat growing dry, "if I should return to Zarahemla, now that my father is gone." Her gaze fell. "A midwife's skills are needed anywhere there are women. Perhaps I might find employment in Melek or Aaron, or—"

"There are many women still in Zarahemla," He said, his voice soft but earnest.

Talilia met his gaze. "You wish me to return to Zarahemla?"

"I wish you to be happy, wherever you are."

Talilia's cheeks grew warm. "I wish happiness for you as well, Tuloth."

Tuloth shifted his weight in the sand, and she could feel the touch of his gaze upon her face, as gentle as a caress.

The moon rose further, bathing the shores and forests in a silver glow.

The music and cheerful voices within the circle of torches mingled with the gentle hiss of the surf before Talilia spoke again. "It is a beautiful night."

"Yes." Tuloth stepped nearer, his voice softening. "But not so beautiful as you."

"Tuloth…" She lifted a hand, but as Tuloth caught it in his own, her words fell silent.

She studied their clasped hands, his large and strong, hers small and slender, her fairer skin against his dark.

"And when I speak of beauty, I speak of your soul as well as your face and form."

Tuloth stepped nearer to her, and though he did not touch her save for their clasped hands, Talilia could feel the warmth of his nearness.

"I must confess, you are utterly captivating to me, Talilia," he murmured.

Talilia's heart melted within her. "You know I was once Lylith, daughter of Pachus."

"To me, you are and always will be Talilia, daughter of Shemnon. But before you were any man's daughter, you were God's."

Talilia lifted her gaze, drinking in the reflection of the torchlight in his dark eyes, deep as the night sky.

"But I'm not a… I cannot change the past."

"Nor can I. But I am trying now to do what is right, and I know that you are too."

Insistence entered Tuloth's voice. "With these very hands, I once *killed* men, Talilia."

He released her hand and turned his palms upward as if he held something in them for her inspection. "Good men who were defending their families and freedoms from the tyranny of Amalickiah and Ammoron. I did not know how wretchedly mistaken I was. When the Nephites captured me, they showed me mercy rather than the cruelty our overlords said we would find, and I began to realize how wrong I had been. After my conversion, I dedicated my life to God, and determined to do all I could to repay my mistakes. Even so, I know that I need God's mercy to do what I cannot. Do you believe you are beyond God's mercy? Do you believe your father Shemnon to be?"

Talilia shook her head. "Never has a better man lived than him."

"And there is no better woman than you, Talilia. Your worth is infinite. And every day, I pray that you will one day come to see your great worth as I do."

"You pray for me?"

Tuloth's smile warmed her to her core. "I've prayed for you since the day we met."

"I am not sure how to pray."

"I can teach you. If you wish."

"Will you?" she pleaded. "Will you teach me everything you know about your god?"

A deep breath escaped Tuloth's chest. "Nothing in the world would please me more."

Solemn excitement trembled along her limbs as his fingers gently touched her jaw, tilting her face upward.

For the briefest moment, Tuloth's lips hovered a fraction above hers, their breaths mingling before he closed the space between them and pressed his mouth against her own.

Talilia's breath caught in her lungs as Tuloth's fingers brushed down her throat to her shoulders, drawing her gently to him. She had never been kissed like this before, with such tenderness, such controlled power as Tuloth possessed. She felt sweet and clean in his embrace, cherished, and adored. She sighed when the kiss ended.

Tuloth smiled as he drew back, searching her eyes.

"But for now, will you come dance with me?" He offered her his hand. "There is much happiness in this world, if we seek for it."

"I will." Talilia slipped her hand into his and he drew her with him, down the shores of Bountiful, back toward the music and laughter and light.

Epilogue

In the silence of the night, Elizabeth opened her eyes and drew in a long, contented breath, tasting the sweet tang of the sea. Moonlight filled the room with a silver glow as it spilled through the curtain that veiled the window of the bedchamber where she lay in Joshua's arms, her head cradled against his shoulder.

Careful not to wake her new husband, she drew herself from the warmth of his embrace and sat up.

Without his strong arms about her, Elizabeth shivered in the cool air that brushed her skin. Reaching down, she gathered her robe from off the floor and drew its silken folds around her as she rose from the bed they shared. She gazed about the muted shadows of their room before she turned her eyes back to their bed, and to Joshua. She paused, studying the strong lines of his form etched in moonlight where he lay, lost in peaceful sleep. Joshua. Her husband. In both soul and body. He was so beautiful.

Elizabeth's heart grew full within her as she contemplated their future, anticipating the delicacies and joys of weaving two separate lives into one, the children who would come to them, and the delights and sorrows they would share as they passed through life together.

Elizabeth padded in her bare feet to the curtain, where she parted the thin cloth and gazed up at the full moon. Listening to the silence of the night, she could hear the faint beat of the surf against the shore beyond the city walls.

"Elizabeth?"

Joshua's voice reached out to her as his quiet tread came from behind. His strong arms circled her waist. She let the curtain fall back into place, filling the room again with shadow. His hand rose and smoothed aside the loose tresses of her hair. He bent his head and pressed a soft kiss to her throat.

"Joshua," she murmured. "I didn't mean to waken you."

"I'm glad you did," he returned, his voice warm. He rested his cheek against her hair. "My dreams of you are sweet, but nothing compared to the reality of you."

Elizabeth turned within the circle of his arms. She lifted her eyes, loving the way the muted moonlight played over the strong angles of his face.

"What are you thinking of?" he asked.

"Of you," she said. Joshua smiled. "And of our children who are to be." With a sigh, Elizabeth leaned her head against Joshua's chest. He pulled her closer and rested his jaw against her hair. Her arms slid around his warm torso. "And of the future. And all it will bring. The joys and the sorrows. We cannot know all that will come."

A breath swelled his chest. "We cannot." Joshua shifted his weight, drawing her more firmly against himself. At the movement, the muscles of his back rippled beneath her fingers, and Elizabeth's blood grew warm, her heartbeat quickening.

"But whatever happens," he said, "God still rules in the heavens."

"And some things will always be certain."

"Like my love for you." His voice grew husky. "My *wife*."

"And my love for you. My husband."

Drawing back, Joshua sought her eyes through the shadows between them. He touched her chin tenderly, his thumb caressing her lower lip before he bent his head, claiming her mouth in a gentle, searching kiss.

Far away beyond the curtain of their bedchamber the sea continued its eternal whispers as waves washed against the shores of Bountiful.

About the Author

Photo by Janet Grant

Loralee Evans has enjoyed reading and writing stories since she was a child. She grew up on the Wasatch Front, graduated from Bingham High, and attended Southern Utah University with an athletic scholarship. She served an LDS mission in Sapporo, Japan, and later graduated from SUU. She is the author of several books including *The Birthright* and *Felicity~ A Sparrow's Tale*.

Read more about her books on her website:
www.loraleeevans.com

Or visit her blog:
Loraleeevansauthor.blogspot.com

You can also follow her on twitter: **@EvansLoralee**

www.ingramcontent.com/pod-product-compliance
Lightning Source LLC
Chambersburg PA
CBHW060311260626
47160CB00007B/2566